MW01225762

SHOOT THROUGH

J.M. Green is a crime writer based in Melbourne's western suburbs. Her debut novel, *Good Money*, the first hardboiled-crime novel featuring Stella Hardy, was shortlisted for a 2016 Ned Kelly Award, the Sisters in Crime's Davitt Award for best debut, as well as the 2014 Victorian Premier's Literary Award for an Unpublished Manuscript. She divides her time between writing in her backyard studio and working as a librarian. *Shoot Through* is the third in the Stella Hardy series, following *Too Easy*.

SHOOT THROUGH

J.M. GREEN

SCRIBE
Melbourne • London

Scribe Publications
18–20 Edward St, Brunswick, Victoria 3056, Australia
2 John St, Clerkenwell, London, WC1N 2ES, United Kingdom

First published by Scribe 2019

Printed and bound in Australia by Griffin Press, part of Ovato

Scribe Publications is committed to the sustainable use of natural
resources and the use of paper products made responsibly from
those resources.

9781925713848 (Australian edition)
9781925693676 (e-book)

A catalogue record for this book is available from the National
Library of Australia.

scribepublications.com.au

For Heidi
A dear friend

And for Derryn
A beautiful human being

PROLOGUE

HAVE YOU ever been on the run from the police *and* a mercenary assassin? No? Just me, then. Just me, standing here, with the wind in my hair, my life in tatters, and no hope of a good *bún chả giò chay* for hundreds of kilometres in any direction.

How did I get into this pickle? For a while, I believed that the whole rotten business started with the death of Joe Phelan. But when I think about it, the trouble really started a week before, when my sister, Kylie, turned up at my flat, pounding on the door and brandishing a wad of documents.

It was early — well, early for a Sunday morning — when Kylie woke me with her hammering. I was bleary-eyed and still half-asleep as she paced around my kitchen in clean, pressed moleskins, a check cowgirl shirt with pearl press-studs, and brand-new R.M. Williams riding boots. She seemed to be speaking in riddles, and I strained to make sense of the words. Phrases like *virtuous circle* and *moral hazard* made me wonder if she had joined a cult, but then she said something about *tax minimisation* and *trust funds*, and I thought she'd joined the Liberal Party. Very quickly, she lost her patience, took my blank look as a personal affront, and became enraged. She spun on her Cuban heels, walked over, and snapped her fingers in my face.

'Getting any of this, Stella?'

'Not really.'

'But I explained all this at Christmas!'

'You did?'

In a huff, she dropped the pile of paper on my table. I noted the dozen or so *sign here* stickers protruding from the side. 'Sign these. Then go to wherever Ben is and make him sign them, too. Make sure he does it properly. When that's done, return them to me.'

The door slammed, and she was gone.

'You're welcome,' I said to my empty flat.

The whole encounter was completely baffling. With great effort, I thought back to Christmas two months earlier, held at the Hardy family farm in the dusty Victorian town of Woolburn. In the delirium of the forty-degree heat, the tepid beer, and the turkey roasting since nine in the morning, I'd nodded along woozily as Kylie had droned on and on about her plan to take over the farm from my mother and Ted.

My mother, Delia, and my stepfather, the very Catholic retired real-estate agent, Ted, had been thinking for some time of selling up and retiring from farming. They'd even had a buyer — Shane Farquhar, my high-school tormentor, who was desperate to buy the land so that his adjacent farm would double in size. Kylie and her jack-of-no-trades husband, Tyler, had tried and failed at many get-rich-quick endeavours. But suddenly of late, cattle farming was all they could talk about. They had argued with Delia that the farm should stay in the family, although they couldn't afford to buy it.

Ted had loved the idea and had created a *discretionary trust*, a tax minimisation angle that really fluffed up his moustache. He would install Kylie and Tyler as managers and pay them a wage. But that was not how Kylie had envisioned things. She despised Ted's version of the plan because it meant she wasn't technically the owner of the farm. Consequently, she'd turned into a raging paranoid monster, terrified that Ben and I would attempt to unseat her.

As I read through the papers, this all came back to me and things started to make sense. It appeared that my sister had had legal documents drawn up in which Ben and I swore that we would never *ever* attempt such a coup.

Somehow, in the boozy, sweltering haze of that Christmas day, I'd missed the part about this apparently vital administrative step. But I knew all too well why Kylie had made it my mission to see it completed.

Hardy family dysfunction was complex. I was willing to visit our brother, Ben, in prison, whereas Kylie was not. Kylie could spend entire days with our mother, whereas I lasted about twenty minutes.

So, after signing Kylie's papers myself without pang or hesitation, I was now left to face an inconvenient trip to the country prison where Benjamin Hardy was incarcerated. This was my punishment for being too slow-witted to understand I was being played. And too passive to react once the penny dropped. And for generally being too damn accommodating.

I had no inkling yet of the unholy mess that was to begin with that visit, but as I contemplated the long drive ahead, it was my fervent hope that, at some point in the near future, it would be possible to have these faults surgically removed from my personality.

1

THE ENGINE struggled to climb the long inclines. The Mazda was capable, but becoming irritated. I knew the feeling. I passed Ballarat and continued on to higher altitudes. It was Sunday morning, a week after Kylie's visit, and I'd left Ascot Vale before nine while nearly all of Melbourne was sensibly snoozing or just stirring — only farmers in utes and the occasional truck to contend with on the highway.

A mildly ingratiating voice told me the exit was coming. I changed lane accordingly.

I'd had to cancel a weekend with Brophy to make this trip, and I wasn't happy about it. Peter Brophy was a spunk, who happened to be my boyfriend. We'd been together for about four years now, and I never got tired of saying that: my *boyfriend*. Sure, we had some issues. When we'd met, at an exhibition of his paintings in his Footscray studio, he had been on methadone for many years. Before that, he'd been an intravenous drug user, with all the lifestyle complications that go with that. Now he was a clean but impoverished artist, with little prospect of a regular income. Actually, that last part didn't bother me. I admired his commitment to his art. And besides, I had a regular income. So we were sitting pretty.

Our only real problem lately had been finding time to be together. We'd been talking about a getaway for a while: staying in a rural B & B, eating, drinking, lounging around. Something to put the mango chutney back on our relationship samosa, which, to my distress, was going a bit cold of late. We'd found a suitable date, but Kylie had found a way to snatch it away. So Brophy and I had now rescheduled our date to the Labour Day long weekend. He had been his usual very accommodating self, but I seethed. I cursed my sister, my brother, and the whole Hardy family for good measure.

When Brophy had told Marigold, his pre-teenage daughter, that I was going to a prison, she'd been curious to know more. Prisons were magical places, invisible to regular folk, and she'd wondered aloud if they really did exist. I told her they certainly did exist, but that I thought her observation was wise beyond her years. The system worked best when good citizens lived in blissful ignorance of prisons and what went on in them.

Personally, I'd seen the inside of a few. I'd taken clients to visit family members in immigration detention. And there were a couple of memorable times I'd joined Phuong Nguyen at Barwon Prison when she questioned a witness. Phuong was my long-time best friend and also happened to be a police officer. She wasn't any old cop. She'd reached the rank of detective senior sergeant, and she liked to remind me of that.

So, I was not blissfully ignorant, nor a good citizen for that matter, but this was my first visit to this particular minimum-security prison farm — the Sir Athol Goldwater Prison. Ben was eighteen months into a two-year stretch there, and yet, somehow, I hadn't got round to making the three-hour drive to pop in to see him. These privately run places were supposed to be the last word in well-managed institutions. But I was sceptical.

According to the website, the Sir Athol Goldwater Prison housed roughly three hundred inmates, whose crimes were mostly of a non-violent nature, though there were some child sex offenders. There was a list of visitor rules, including a cruel proclamation that no visitors were allowed in any Victorian prison on Christmas Day. Rocking up unannounced on any other day was not advisable, and I had booked the visit in advance. I was a properly registered visitor and had ID of all kinds at the ready.

It was just before noon when I turned onto a road barely better than a dirt track. The bitumen covered a central section just wide enough for the Mazda. Another car was approaching, going in the opposite direction, and we both moved to the edges, tyres flinging up stones and dust. Once the other car had passed, I returned to paved road and checked the basket on the seat beside me. At the request of the prisoner, it contained Finest Balsamic Vinegar of Modena, wasabi-coated peanuts, Verjuice, kalamata olives, Egyptian dukkah, and a 'decent' spatula. It was more like an executive Christmas hamper than a food parcel for a convicted criminal. My delinquent brother was not letting prison get in the way of his gourmet aspirations.

Beside the basket sat a manila folder containing Kylie's papers for Ben to sign.

Here the road was flanked on either side by high fences, behind which a herd of cud-chewing cattle peacefully observed the Mazda pass. They must be part of the three thousand Angus stock I'd read about on the prison website. It was a going concern, the Sir Athol Goldwater Prison, and cattle were fetching a good price. Prisoners received training in agricultural work, the locals had employment — everyone was happy. Except me, but I was rarely happy.

The road ended at the entrance to the prison. It was a proper, security-conscious facility, with a series of gates and guards checking IDs. This impressed upon those visitors who may have found the grazing cattle charming not to mistake this place for a regular farm.

I parked in the visitor car park, making sure I left my mobile in the car. I went through the sign-in, the metal detector, the bag search, and the usual palaver. The checking of registration took a good twenty minutes. The sun was still climbing out of the valleys, but was already intense, and the day was starting to heat up. Other families had already arrived and were setting up food on picnic tables for an early lunch. The electric barbecues were built into a brick housing. A jack was cleaning one of the hotplates.

A crowd of men in green t-shirts and shorts were milling about near the visitor area. Ben was not among them, and I was starting to worry. We had discussed my visit on the phone; he should have been waiting. Knowing Ben, he'd done something stupid, on a dare or bet, been caught, and had his privileges revoked. Naturally, he had forgotten to inform me.

My entire day wasted when you factored in the travel. I was furious. And I was not the only one left waiting for a prisoner who failed to show up.

An older woman — short, intelligent brown eyes, grey hair in a clip — was leaning on a walking stick. She was with a younger woman, mid-forties, possibly her daughter. The younger one seemed familiar, but I couldn't place her. She was wearing dark jeans and a blazer and had a plastic lemon on a strap over her shoulder — some kind of novelty handbag. The two women shared a strong family resemblance and the same defiant bearing. Their inscrutable expressions were likewise identical. The prison officers seemed to be wary of them both and studiously avoided eye contact.

I caught the daughter's eye and rolled my own, to convey my frustration at our ordeal. Also, I hoped she would remember me, because it was annoying me that I couldn't recall how I knew her. But she looked through me, and I looked away. After a while, the older woman called to a prison officer.

'I'm sick of this. Where's Joe?' she demanded.

Good on her, I thought. I looked to the daughter: she had the tiniest hint of a smirk, causing a fragment of memory to surface. A work function — no, wait — a training day. She was a youth worker. She clocked me, and this time we acknowledged each other without speaking. This place wasn't conducive to social niceties.

The prison officer — a woman, early fifties, maybe older, with perfect eyebrows and acrylic nails — gave a weary sigh.

'Joe's finishing a job in the metal shed, Mrs Phelan. He won't be long.'

'He's expecting us,' Mrs Phelan said. 'We have things to discuss.

Get him down here, now. This is our time, and I don't want to spend it being fobbed off by some painted fart of a jack.'

The officer put a placating hand up. 'I need you to calm down. Take a breath.'

This instruction had the opposite effect. 'Patronising me? Jumped-up door bitch.'

The officer's other hand went to her utility belt, ready to employ some pre-emptive capsicum spray. Mrs Phelan scowled and backed off. I got the impression she was not accustomed to backing down. The prison officer turned to me. I glimpsed the name tag: *Nell Tuffnell, Operations Manager.*

'Name?'

'Stella Hardy.'

She checked her list. 'Hardy, Benjamin. I saw him in the greenhouse this morning. He's around somewhere.'

This vague account of prisoners' whereabouts was not reassuring. Even for a lax prison farm.

She addressed all of us now. 'Wait here. I'm sending two officers to fetch them up. I would appreciate your patience.'

'Oh, *do* fetch them up,' Mrs Phelan echoed. I was a little intimidated by her.

We waited for another ten minutes — the limit of my patience. Mrs Phelan and her daughter fell into a whispered debate.

Ben was never going to show, I decided. Bugger this for a joke. I pulled out my car keys. And, of course, that was when Ben came ambling along in his green tracksuit, a big smirk on his face, holding a tray covered in a tea towel.

'Glad you could come,' he said, like this was a normal family lunch.

I followed him over to a picnic table.

'Of course I came, Ben. I do what I say I'm going to do. I show up. On time. Where the hell have you been?'

He seemed sincerely wounded. 'I was getting everything ready.'

He put the tray on the table, then noticed the basket I was holding. 'What's that?'

'The stuff you wanted.' I handed him the shopping bag.

'Brilliant.' He leaned in to give me a hug, which I allowed.

'I'll fire up the barbie. Been marinating tofu — I know you like it.'

I began to thaw a little. 'Is it that mix of yours with the ginger?'

'No, this one's new. You'll love it.' He touched an ignition button, and gas erupted under the cooking surface. 'I've been experimenting with lemon myrtle.'

He lifted the tea towel. Tofu on skewers with zucchini, onions, capsicum, and — oh dear — pineapple pieces. He put them on the hotplate. There was bread and butter and a large bowl of salad greens. I set out cutlery and plates while Ben put salad servers in the bowl and started shaking a jar of dressing.

'It's all from the garden. We sell the excess at a farmers market once a month.'

I was proud of how proud he was. 'Even the coriander? That's very cool, Ben.'

'Joe grows all the herbs. Sells them in pots — you can buy one today if you want.'

I figured I may as well get the documents signed and out of the way. 'Ben, we need to talk about the farm — this family trust set-up. Kylie's —'

Ben cut me off. 'Can we just enjoy our lunch? Let's discuss all that later.'

'Sure.' I watched him work a pair of tongs, turning the skewers. 'Is everything okay?'

He shook his head, looking troubled. 'I'm worried about my girlfriend.'

'Since when did you have a girlfriend?'

'She's struggling on the outside without me.'

'I'm sure she'll manage.'

'Nah. She's broke, and the landlord wants her out.'

'She'll find something.'

'She's not working. Her situation is pretty desperate ...' He grimaced. 'Stella, please. I wouldn't ask if it wasn't important.'

'Tell her to get in touch with the relevant agencies. I work in migrant services, haven't worked in housing for years.'

'I said she can stay with you.'

'You *what*?'

He glanced around, then leaned closer to me. 'She's pregnant,' he whispered.

I took a moment to absorb his words. I did a quick mental calculation. 'Not to you, obviously,' I said. 'It's your — what? — second year here, and ...'

The look on his face told me otherwise. *This is what happens when you go soft on crime*, I thought. Here, prisoners were not locked in cells at night, they shared unit-style accommodation and could, if they chose, walk away in the night. In general, they didn't. Daily head counts just in case. God help me, I still had to ask.

'But *how*?'

He grinned. 'When two people give each other a special hug —'

'I swear, jacks or not, I will fucking deck you.'

'She came for a visit. We went for a walk.'

'Quite an energetic walk.'

'Yes,' he said sheepishly. The stupid grin returned. 'Not shooting blanks, then.'

Was I supposed to cheer this stupidity? Taking credit for biology? 'Shut up, idiot.'

'Shhh.' He looked around. 'We have to keep it quiet.'

I dropped my voice to a hiss. 'Just get to the point, Ben. What do you want?'

'I want you to take her up to the farm. You have to, Stella. I promised her you would.'

'Delia will have a fit!'

'No, she won't. She'll be pleased. Loretta's a country girl. I reckon they'll hit it off.'

'Loretta. Is that her name?'

'Loretta Patsy Dolly Swindon. Her mum was into country music.'

Was? That didn't sound heartening; it was the precise opposite of heartening.

'Look, Ben. I feel for the poor girl, having your baby and all, but if you think Mum's going to welcome this Loretta person, you are out of your mind.'

'That's why you have to handle Mum carefully. She'll be mad at first, but once you convince her how great Loretta is, she'll be down with it.'

What was I, the family go-between? 'Why don't *you* talk to Mum?'

He shook his head. 'They monitor my calls.'

'How convenient.'

'Tell her that Loretta needs to hang there till the baby's due. I'll take care of her and the baby when I get out.'

He wasn't fit to take care of anyone, let alone a baby.

'I told Loretta how to contact you,' Ben continued. 'She'll come in a couple of days to stay with you, then you can drive her up to Woolburn. Hope you've been taking good care of my Mazda.'

'Oh yeah? When am I doing this?'

'In two weeks. It's a long weekend, so you've got time to stay over a couple of nights while she settles in.'

The Labour Day long weekend. Cancel my weekend with Brophy yet again? No dice. Nothing doing. 'I'm sorry, Ben, but —'

I was interrupted by an extremely loud *whoop whoop whoop* coming from the PA. Prison officers ran around shouting at everyone to get ready for a head count. The prison was in lockdown, they said, and no one was to leave.

'Someone's probably done a runner,' Ben said before rushing to his unit for the count.

That was my first thought, too, until I heard an ambulance siren.

12

My second thought was, *Damn, forced to abandon my tofu skewers!* Sometimes life was so unfair. We visitors were corralled into a dining hall and told to wait until the all-clear. No apology, no explanation. You deserved none if you were visiting a prisoner — you were inferior by affiliation.

Time dragged. Some visitors conducted hushed conversations in small groups. Some paced. I stood at the window and watched the movements of the staff. After what seemed like hours, some police arrived. Strange they didn't use their siren. *Forensics* was written across their jackets. Meanwhile, some of the prison officers stood together in a nearby assembly area, smoking, with consternation in their faces.

I paused in my vigil and took a turn about the room. The tense atmosphere was excruciating. When I went back to my post at the window, I let out a gasp. Two ambos had come into view, wheeling a patient on a trolley. The rest of the visitors in the hall rushed over to see what was happening. The ambos showed no signs of urgency as they pushed the trolley towards the open rear doors of the ambulance. The patient was motionless under a sheet that was pulled up over the face.

The jack called Tuffnell was suddenly among us. 'Would the family of Joe Phelan please step into the next room.'

Mrs Phelan stepped forward with her stick and, helped by her daughter, made her way through the group. Tuffnell followed them into the other room and shut the door behind her. I drifted forwards and pressed an ear at the hinge.

'I regret to say that Joe experienced a lethal head trauma. The officer who found him called the ambulance and immediately began to administer first aid.'

Mrs Phelan was confused. 'You mean he's dead?'

'I am deeply sorry to have to tell you this, Mrs Phelan. But he was pronounced deceased moments ago by the ambulance crew.'

'If he's dead, just fucking say so.'

'He is dead, madam.'

'How?'

'There will be a full inquiry. But it appears he was using a power tool when something went wrong. A head injury is all we can say.'

'I'll tell you what went wrong,' she said. 'It's this bloody place. It's a joke.'

Tuffnell coughed. 'All the details will come out in the inquiry. But at this stage, it looks like a terrible accident.'

'Like hell.'

'Accidents are not unheard of in the metalwork area.'

Tuffnell offered her condolences, and Mrs Phelan continued to abuse the daylights out of her.

We were allowed to leave, but only to go straight out to the carpark. No goodbyes. I was fine with that. Back in the car, I turned on my phone and checked the time. I'd wasted an entire day waiting around in a prison. I had failed to get Ben to sign Kylie's stupid papers, the very reason I'd gone there in the first place. And I now had another stupid family errand to add to my growing list.

2

IT WAS late when I arrived at the modest apartment building that was my home. Pine View was a sixties block of one-bedroom flats with white concrete balustrades and a foyer that smelled of oily chips. I climbed the stairs to my top-floor flat. Once upstairs, I threw Kylie's papers on the kitchen table and muttered a curse. In so doing, I had summoned the devil: Kylie's name immediately came up on my ringing mobile.

'Has he signed?'

'Listen, Kylie, about that. There was an incident and the place went into lockdown.'

Breathing on the other end.

I continued. 'I had to leave before he —'

'Go back.'

'It's really a long way —'

'Please, Stella. I need this. I never ask you for anything.' That was true. 'And it's closer for you.' That wasn't true.

'I had a look on the map. It's actually about half way.'

'I can't leave the farm. The Dexters are just getting settled in.' The Irish cattle breed Kylie and Tyler were gambling their future on. 'Anyway, he gets on better with you. Try again this week.'

'I have work.'

'Thanks, you're a sweetheart. Bye.'

I dropped the phone on the couch. The situation called for serious self-care. I went into the bedroom, dragged an old suitcase out from under my bed, and flipped the latches. There, in neatly stacked thousand-dollar bundles, was my stash.

The money had been hidden under the floorboards of a house used by bikies for growing cannabis. It was the profit of their evil trade in drugs, human trafficking, and whatever else they turned their hands to. My pulse raced at the memory of sneaking it out of the house. And that hadn't even been the first time I'd helped myself to the hard cash of hardened criminals.

Several years before, I'd stolen money from the flat of two junkies. They were my clients, living in a high-rise housing commission flat, and had called me late one night in a state of panic. When I got there, they were both dead. Near their bodies were bundles of cash in plastic shopping bags. Call it a brain snap — I don't know how else to explain it — but I'd taken the bags, containing a total of fifty thousand dollars. It was a stupid thing to do, and for years afterwards I'd lived in terror of being found out. After that incident I'd said to myself, *never again.*

Then I did it again. Only the second time, I took much, much more. My suitcase currently contained over four hundred thousand dollars.

In my heart, I knew it was tarnished. Not the money, my soul. My precious immortal soul. I'd intended to give the money to my sister to help her stupid plan to buy the farm. But Ted had come up with his tax minimisation scheme, and she hadn't needed it.

What was I supposed do with all this cash? Put it back? Hardly.

In the course of my community work, and my sideline in ... let's call it *problem-solving*, I'd been threatened, assaulted, abducted, and almost killed. The money, to my mind, was a form of righteous compensation.

I called it the *fund*, and it lived under my bed. Not exactly secure, but apart from Brophy no one came in here, so it was safe enough. From time to time, I'd sneak out a couple of hundred bucks for the occasional treat. Until a better idea came along, an impoverished artist like my beloved Brophy and a low-wage community worker

16

like me could occasionally splurge on an extravagance.

Tonight's treat would be a couple of bottles of wine and far too much Indian takeaway.

I showered and changed. I needed to be fresh, and cleansed of prison dirt, real and psychological. I went to the Narcissistic Slacker — Brophy's studio, art gallery, and domicile above a shop in Footscray — to give him the bad news about the weekend.

He must have heard me on the landing. The industrial metal door to the studio was sliding open before I reached the top step. He seemed worn out and a little thin.

'Are you alright?'

He coughed, standing aside to usher me in. 'Just a cold. How was the trip to the agrarian slammer?'

'Bad. For several reasons.'

'Hit me.'

'For one thing,' I said, 'Labour Day weekend isn't going to work out. I'm going to Woolburn. Family business.'

There was real disappointment in his sigh. 'What's he done now?'

He'd managed coitus in a secure correctional facility with security cameras and guards everywhere. Some in Australia would say that made him a bloody legend. They did not use protection, and now poor foolish Loretta was going to be part of the great Hardy Family Fiasco. When I got to the part about taking Loretta to stay with my mother, he was laughing. I supposed it *was* kind of funny. To an outsider.

Later that evening, Brophy swirled a soapy sponge over a plate and slotted it in the rack. 'What's the prison like?'

'Nice enough. Places to disappear for a little outdoor recreation.'

'That's really upset you, hasn't it?'

'My idiot brother fathering a child? In so many ways, yes.'

'You don't know what kind of father he'd be.'

Tea towel ready, I lifted the plate. 'Yeah, I do. The kind who leaves his kids in the car while he scores.'

He made a noise, and slotted another plate into the rack.

Criticism of parenting was a sensitive area for Brophy. I moved us back onto safer pastures. 'And then there's the girl, the mother, the victim — whatever — Loretta. He's never mentioned her before, never hinted that she existed. Now I'm driving her to Woolburn.'

'Maybe this is a good thing. For Ben, I mean.'

'Five hours there, five back. Introduce her to my mother. In the same breath, I ask if Loretta can move in for a while.'

'Parenthood might be good for Ben. If he's serious about it.'

'He's serious about kimchi ice-cream and turmeric smoothies and stir-fried milk.'

Brophy's cough sounded disapproving. He looked in the cupboard under the sink and withdrew a mangled old steel-wool pad.

I watched him scour a saucepan that we'd used to reheat the curry, and worried that I'd turned a loving relationship into a receptacle for all my grievances. That wasn't optimal.

'Personally, I blame the private contractor for letting it happen,' I said.

He scratched at something stuck to the pan. 'Private contractors? How is a prison a profitable business?'

'I don't know, but it's a very lackadaisical operation. A prisoner died while I was there.'

He paused his scrubbing and looked at me.

'The whole place went into lockdown. Visit over. We were all shunted out of there.'

'How?'

'A power-tool accident, apparently.'

Brophy's mobile buzzed in the next room, and he went out.

It was upsetting to see him so despondent. I was desperately thinking of a way to cheer him up, when a sudden crazy idea struck me.

'Come with me!' I shouted. 'We'll have our weekend away in beautiful, romantic Woolburn.'

He returned with the still-ringing phone in his hand. 'That is a brilliant idea.'

'Aren't you going to answer it?'

'It's Mandy. I'll let it go to voicemail.' The buzzing stopped and immediately restarted.

It was none of my business, but sometimes I thought Brophy was a little immature when it came to Mandy. His ex was the mother of his daughter, but he acted as if she were a stranger. Personally, her existence didn't bother me, and I hoped he wasn't dismissive towards her for my benefit. But these things were never easy; it wasn't for me to judge.

'At last!' he was saying with apparent delight. 'An invitation to the mythical Woolburn. I'll bring the easel and some paints and the —'

The phone stopped and immediately started to buzz again.

'Must be important.'

We locked eyes. He sighed as he swiped. 'Mandy, what's up?'

I turned away and wiped the tea towel over the saucepan.

'You do this every time, change things any time it suits you.'

I placed the pan in the cupboard.

'No. Sorry. I've made plans.'

I wiped the sink.

'Fine. But this is the last damn time.'

He slapped at the phone, thrust it in his pocket, and glared about him.

'So …'

'So, Marigold will be joining us on our romantic weekend in Woolburn.'

I was home watching the news. Why at home? Because Brophy and I had had a fight. It was mainly my fault. In my defence, the prospect of time spent at my family's house in Woolburn always made me tense. I was overwrought and said something mean, Brophy snapped back. And here I was, home alone.

I poured myself another glass of wine and turned on the television. The familiar and flabby face of Marcus Pugh, Minister for Justice, was on the late news.

Marcus and I went back a long way and had a hate-hate relationship. Over the years, he'd cut funding to all the support agencies in his area. We in the sector called him Mucous Pukus. He sleazed his way in to photo ops, took credit for everything, and was a generally unpleasant arse.

He was shrugging off questions about a prisoner who had died while in the custody of the private prison operator, BS12.

'No,' Pugh wheezed, 'in relation to the aforementioned death, liability or other blame cannot be apportioned to the contractor without a proper investigation. However, initial reports are that it was the result of a terrible accident.'

The prisoner, a journalist explained, was Joe Phelan. A beloved son and brother, he had a sad story of petty crime and juvie, ending in a prison farm on a fairly minor charge of credit card fraud. I turned off the TV and went to read in bed. I'd had quite enough of Marcus Pugh.

3

I ENTERED Buffy's — an establishment named in honour of the awe-inspiring vampire slayer — for my daily caffeination and found the proprietor, Lucas, fellow nerd and zombie enthusiast, in a trance.

'What's this?'

'A new brewing technique.' The lovable nerd leaned over a funnel attached to a hose connected to a contraption that looked like a child's chemistry set. 'The cold-to-hot-to-warm method. Delivers a more robust flavour.'

'Your flavours are quite robust enough. Give me your conventional swill or give me nothing.'

He blinked. 'What?'

'The usual, please. And the paper.' I handed over my reusable insulated coffee sustain-a-mug that Marigold made me use. At twelve, that child had a more clear-eyed awareness of the planet's mortality than the average citizen.

Cup in hand, I paid and left, looking forward to the peaceful ritual of reading the paper on the tram.

But the tram was late, and it was packed, and spreading out news-sheet was impossible. I stood, holding a strap, my nose in proximity to an underarm. Thus cocooned, I was left to my thoughts. One thought being that whenever this Loretta made contact, I'd need to lay the ground rules for Hardy farm behaviour. Never ask for help, never appear weak, never show sentiment or feelings of any kind. Never leave towels on the floor. A two-minute shower was permitted, but frowned on, three minutes was seriously indulgent, four was grounds for banishment. Always have your own money (never put your hand out unless you want a smack). Always, *always* offer to do the dishes (but never offer to cook). And, for harmony's sake, I'd recommend she refer to herself as Ben's fiancée around Delia and Ted. If she followed those rules, she might last a couple of days.

I made it to the office half an hour late, which was about my normal amount of lateness for a typical work day at WORMS, the Western and Outer Region Migrant Service. I logged on and checked my email. I was minding my own business, doing actual work, and despite everything, I was starting to feel pretty good. The whole office was on the up, lately. Our new boss, Fatima, was a boss. She had the energy of a kelpie, the business acumen of Bill Gates, and the political chops of P.J. Keating. In short, I was a little in awe of her. Under her stewardship, we'd gained more funding, employed new people, and lifted our productivity. That meant more migrants were getting the services they were entitled to, and our minnow of an agency was kicking bottoms and taking names. We had a place at important tables. We mattered. The ALP had approached Fatima for a sweet seat in the federal senate. She had declined. See? Totally awesome.

Around mid-morning, every WORMS staff member migrated to the foyer. I followed to see what the fuss was. Shaninder, a fellow long-suffering colleague, had brought in child number three, a fat cherub with a gurgle that made my ovaries tingle. We passed the infant around, had a selfie, and were then ordered back to work by Fatima. She said this with a smile, while holding the baby.

'Except you, Stella. See me in my office.'

I went through the usual negative possibilities: I was getting the sack, getting retrenched, getting more work. Or the happy possibilities: I was getting a raise, getting an award for services to the community, getting an assistant.

'Stella,' Fatima began, 'I'm right in saying that WORMS has partnered with the justice department to work on a number of projects in the past?'

I sat up straight. 'Yes,' I said, with conviction.

'I assume that went well.'

Well was too strong a word. But I felt an urge to impress her and to come across as competent. 'It was great, incredibly great.'

'Good. Because the department has expressed an interest in working with our agency again.'

I stared at her.

'On a new project,' she continued.

I said nothing, kept my face blank, waiting.

'We've been asked to nominate a person to join a prison inspection group. The delegation will inspect all the private prisons.' She smiled. 'You're going to be our nominee.'

I returned her smile, but mine was fake. 'Great.'

'We're lucky to partner with the department on this one.'

'Lucky. Yep.'

'There are opportunities to lobby, and to influence policy around support for non-English speaking people.'

'Lobby how?'

'You'll be working closely with the minister's office.'

I groaned and slid off my chair to the floor. Marcus Pugh, Minister for Justice. I was sick to the back arse of Pugh, with his conscience-free will to power and his ideological shifts to advantage. 'When they do it, it's bad. When we do it, it's necessary.' *Politically expedient* was the new *principled*.

'Stella?'

'Yes?' I started to roll around on the floor.

'You okay?'

'Back exercises.'

'Oh, right.' Fatima hesitated, no doubt wondering if I was in my right mind. She continued, 'I'll send the details through. Let me know if you have any questions.'

I staggered to my feet and smoothed down my clothes. 'No worries, Fatima. I'm on it.'

'He asked for you, personally,' she said.

'Me. Personally. That is ... so great.'

Back at my desk, I received an email from Fatima saying that she'd just heard from Pugh, who wanted an informal meeting ASAP. I was ready to let forth a stream of expletives. Then it occurred to me that Pugh might authorise a visit to the Sir Athol Goldwater Prison this week on urgent justice department business. I could take the papers to Ben, then, rather than on the way to Woolburn. That would save me a detour and a lot of time. I replied to Fatima with enthusiasm, and I sent an email to Pugh's office suggesting a time tomorrow. They replied with a place, and we were on. I added the appointment into my computer calendar. What a morning. I was killing it. Time for coffee.

I was on my way to the staff room, when I tripped over a walking stick that seemed to be placed deliberately in my way. I turned and clocked an old woman sitting on one of the visitors' waiting chairs in the general area. She was wearing a big brown duffle coat, never mind that it was thirty degrees outside. Her grey hair was held back with a clip, and her brown eyes were fixed on me. A stare that could bore a hole right through you. Where had I seen her before?

'You Stella Hardy?'

I almost denied it.

'I've been waiting for ages for you, so sit down and listen up.'

I remained standing, my face tensed into that smile I used for insolent shop assistants. 'What can I do for you?'

'Phelan's my name. I saw you at the Athol Goldwater.'

Oh. Joe Phelan's mother. I sat. 'I'm so sorry about Joe.'

'Thank you.' She fiddled with a wooden toggle on the coat. 'My Meredith was with me. She recognised you.'

Meredith Phelan. Now I had the name, I remembered speaking to her at work functions. She was tough and plain-spoken. I liked her.

'How is Meredith?'

'Alright, under the circumstances. She works for some outfit that tries to keep youths out of trouble. Ironic, don't you reckon? One of me kids was in jail, and the other was trying to keep kids out of there.'

Irony was in there somewhere, I agreed, though of a deeply tragic kind. She looked at me with a softer gaze. Silence followed. I waited, hoping she'd get to the point.

'Meredith told me you help people. She said that, in the past, a couple of times now, you've gone outside the bounds of your work and really looked into, er, *things*. And you'd got results.'

I had. It was true. But I'd hoped no one had noticed. I looked around — everyone else was in their cubicles typing and murmuring. Mrs Phelan was the only person in the waiting area. 'And you want me to do what exactly?'

'They say Joe's death was an accident, but it weren't. I want some answers.'

'What does Meredith say?'

She screwed up her face. 'She won't help. She reckons I have to let them get on with the inquiry.'

'She's right.'

'No. Look, you've got a brother inside, you know how these things go. And you're on that prison delegation.'

'How did you—?'

'Meredith heard. She's been trying to get someone on the delegation herself. She said you're alright. And with your brother inside, and the prison delegation, you've got a bit of pull with the powers that be.'

'Um. That's not right, I'm afraid. I have zero pull.'

'I thought you'd say that. I was gonna keep at you. Keep ringing and coming in. But the thing is, I haven't got all day, so save us both the bother and just bloody help me out.' She leaned back in her chair, looking frustrated. 'People like me are never believed.'

People like her: code for the poor. I suppressed a sigh. Grief needs someone to blame. But I'd also seen for myself that the prison was dysfunctional, probably negligent. 'Mrs Phelan, why are you so sure it wasn't an accident? What do you think happened to Joe?'

She shrugged. 'Mate of Joe's, he knows.'

I gave her a look. 'Save us both the bother.'

She grunted out a tight laugh and gave a grudging nod. 'They're old friends and loyal. Did time together. And this bloke reckons Joe told him ... things.'

'What things?'

'Told him his life was in danger.'

'Mrs Phelan, that just sounds like a conspiracy theory.'

'Not if Percy Brash is saying it. Percy knows plenty. If he says there's more going on, I believe him. He's always been good to me, Percy has. Came over soon as he heard.'

A rumour monger. Probably planning to rob her. 'Any time someone dies in custody, there's a full inquiry,' I said.

She glanced around the room, eyes fierce, as if looking for support. 'The inquiry'll just tell us whatever they want us to think. A damn cover up.' She sucked on her bottom lip, fighting tears. A knot in my chest hardened. 'What if it was your brother? Would you believe he died in a stupid accident?'

I frowned. Best I didn't answer that.

'All I'm asking is for you to get back in Athol Goldwater and talk to the other prisoners.'

'Whatever they tell me will be scuttlebutt, with no basis in fact.'

'That's a start, then,' she said, getting to her feet. 'And I reckon Percy'll probably want a word with you, himself. He's good at *convincing* people.'

The threat was not very subtle. The nerve of her!

'I'll leave you to think it over.' She slapped me on the shoulder in a power move that galled me. I curbed the urge to shove her hand away.

'Sorry about Joe,' I said, and I meant it.

'Joseph was no angel. Me own fault, I suppose. I know what he was, but he didn't deserve to die like that, bumped off in prison.'

I thought about Brophy and how he'd raised his daughter, Marigold. She was a bit messed up. And what kind of future awaited the child of Ben and Loretta? Being a parent was a heck of a business.

'Was he a good boy when he was a kid? Just got in with the wrong crowd?'

She shook her head. '*He* was the wrong crowd.'

She turned and used her stick to shuffle out of the building. I watched her go, wondering what on earth had just happened. I had been intimidated by an old-age pensioner and somehow press-ganged into her service. And, it appeared, I was going to be paid an unwelcome 'visit' by one of her son's criminal friends. Many feelings overwhelmed me as I returned to my desk: impotent fury, defeat, a dash of resignation.

4

IN THE morning, I quickly heaved the suitcase out from under my bed. I dragged it down the stairs and shoved it in the boot of the Mazda. Rather than drive to work, I went to the arse-end of West Footscray. There, in a self-storage place I'd googled the previous night, I chose a package offering two years' access to what was really an oversized locker. I anointed a machine with my plastic card and picked up the key. The locker was a good fit for the case — a sign, I told myself, that the universe took a benign view of my doings — and I secured the lock. If some strange Loretta person was going to be staying with me and snooping around in my stuff, I could hardly leave the fund lying around.

With my sense of accomplishment set to 'high' and the storage key added to my bunch of house, car, and work keys, I strolled into WORMS at fifteen minutes past my usual time of 'running late'.

Around midmorning, an alert I'd set up on my computer told me I had a meeting to go to. I shifted my status from 'In' to 'Out' on the staff activity board and made a note: *Mtg with puke.*

The board was a Fatima initiative, allowing her to keep track of her staff's whereabouts. Mine, mainly. My previous boss had taken a laissez-faire attitude to my laissez-faire attitude to working hours. Not Fatima. She thought such things mattered, and I'd had to adjust my habits. So far, it wasn't working. I'd actually received a written warning from her, which I'd filed under 'F' for folly. My wings would not be clipped.

Besides, my methods got results. On occasion. In a profession that could be a fruitless battle against the tide of human nature and imperfection, and in the knowledge that people often didn't act in their own best interests (case in point: *moi*), any win should be regarded as a massive victory.

Marcus Pugh, minister for justice, and the state member of the Legislative Assembly for a safe seat in the leafy conservative east, waved at me as I entered Jar Jar Drinks, a café in Camberwell, at the appointed time. He was also glaring at me like I'd done something wrong.

'Nice to see you too, Pukus.'

'What?'

'Nothing. Look, if you don't like me,' I said, 'why did you want me to be on your team?'

'Hardy, just because you offend and disappoint me on a regular basis, doesn't mean that I don't need your particular skill set from time to time.'

'What skill set, exactly?'

He sighed in a formal register, a difficult feat. I imagined he must have practised it. 'Well, you know people, that's one thing. You have an ability to get into other people's business, that's another.' He paused, there was something more to say, but he didn't want to say it.

I grinned. 'And ...'

'And ... you seem not to care for your personal safety.'

I wasn't expecting that. I thought he'd say I was an intrepid seeker of the truth, willing to stand up to bullies, whether they be bikies or men of means and influence. That I was an excellent investigator, who attacked complex networks of corruption head-on. But I supposed, in a roundabout way, he was saying that I was brave, so I let it stand.

'Well, isn't this a nice little love-in. Should we hug?'

'Fuck off.'

'Be nice. You need my skill set.' I picked up a menu. Eggs Benedict in a jar, noodle salad in a jar, trifle in a jar.

Marcus Pugh waved at the waiter, who arrived bearing two glasses of water. 'Cappuccino and two of those friands. Hardy?'

'Black tea, please.'

The waiter nodded and departed.

I smiled pleasantly and waited.

Pugh fiddled with his napkin. He pulled out his phone and put it facedown on the table. He sipped some water. 'The inspection team will visit every Victorian prison and assess the way each operates — open access, nothing to be hidden. They will then report back to the department with recommendations.'

'Who else is on the team?'

'Topnotch people. Respected people. Retired lawyers, mates of mine. The right people for the job, you know.'

'Right.'

'Bloody prison activists have their blood pressure up. I've had to include social-justice propagandists, throw a little bone for the social-media jackals.'

'It must be so trying, appeasing so many interest groups.' Sympathy. I could fake it when necessary.

'You have no idea. Anyway, as I mentioned to your esteemed new boss, I'm nominating you to join the delegation.'

'Because of my skill set.'

'Yes. And because ...' He looked about the café. One other man, a few tables over, was reading the paper. The radio played. He leaned across the table. 'It will give you opportunities.'

'Right.'

'As you go about in your capacity as observer ... you might ... look into things.'

'Things?'

'Yes.'

'You know, I'm not qualified for this kind of thing. Prison certification, or whatever, it's a highly-specialised occupation. How am I going to assess it with no knowledge of what constitutes best practice?'

'Who cares? You're a bolshy do-gooder with a track record of stirring up trouble. You'll fit right in.'

'No one will suspect me of being your stooge.'

'Oh, for heaven's sake.' He mopped his sweaty forehead with the serviette.

'Relax. You can trust me. I'm on board. This is about the death of Joe Phelan, isn't it?'

He reared back, wobbling the table.

'It's on the news, Marcus. It's not a secret.'

He recovered himself. 'I know it's not a secret ...' He glared at me. A new thought fluttered his eyelashes. 'I need to know I can trust you. What I'm about to ask you ... Well, this is all highly confidential, of course.'

'Of course.'

He licked his lips. 'Alright. The fact is, there's been rumours about Athol Goldwater for some time. My office is concerned that some off-the-books enterprise — unauthorised, freelance, call it what you will, a side-line pecuniary activity — has been going on under the radar.'

'Unregulated free-market capitalism gone astray? Say it isn't so.'

'Hardy, you really are the most dire of human tragedies. Making a profit from activities other than those set out in the prison contract contravenes the terms of the contract.'

'Your department's job, I would have thought — oversight of the contractor.'

'Yes, yes. And we do. There is. We are. But that incident has added a layer of complexity to managing those concerns. Even though the matter, in and of itself, is a minor complication.'

'Yes, his mother thinks it's a minor complication, too.'

He ignored that. 'Your brother is in there, am I correct?'

'All going well, he gets out at the end of the year.'

He frowned. 'Dangerous, is he?'

'It's minimum security, Marcus.'

'Quite. And if you asked him to be discreet, would he be?'

The waiter brought over a cappuccino in a cup, and the fruity friands on a plate. And for me, apparently, a jar of hot water accompanied by a teabag, still in its paper envelope.

I unwrapped the teabag and jiggled it in the water. 'I don't know about being discreet, but Ben would be amenable. Especially if there was some kind of reward in it for him.'

Pugh grunted. No reward then.

'Come on, Marcus old boy. What are they up to at Athol Goldwater?'

I watched his sad fat face fall even further as he dunked a friand in his coffee.

Poor old Puke. It pained him to talk about such things. Privatisation was the gold standard of neo-liberal ideology. It was meant to rain benefits down on us all. And instead, well. Secret rain fell on some, while others, the taxpayers in the state of Victoria for instance, were left with appalling contractual obligations and not a drop of rain.

I used a serviette as a pot-holder, raised the scalding jar to my lips, and sipped.

'It's a silly little fiddle, actually. One of the employees. We don't know who.' He frowned and ate the second friand. 'If we go through our usual investigative channels, sooner or later, public will hear of it.'

'And there's an election coming.'

Pursed lips, dusted with sugar. 'Indeed. What about a discreet word with your brother?'

'Can't do hints, he's a nitwit.'

'Look, just ask him if he knows of any prison employee taking extravagant holidays, or turning up with a new car, splashing extra cash, that sort of thing.'

'Okey-dokey, how's Friday?' I'd checked my appointments, and

Friday was the earliest I could get away from work.

He stared at me. 'Well, that is excellent, Hardy. I must say I didn't expect you to be so cooperative.'

'I'm great at cooperating.' And at finding ways to do annoying family business under the guise of work.

His phone vibrated, and he snatched it up. 'Those fucking incompetent morons,' he muttered and started tapping out a message with a single index finger. It was painful to watch. No wonder the young despised the older generation.

'Have to go, Hardy. My office will be in touch before Friday with the paperwork. Think in terms of sudden windfall, living beyond one's means. You get my meaning.'

He flung down a twenty, lurched himself upright, ricocheted between the tables, and went out.

5

THE NEXT day at work, around midday, I was deep in concentration. Would I have the ramen soup from the new Japanese place on Flemington Road, or would I go for a salad roll from the deli? My desk phone abruptly interrupted this essential process.

'Stella Hardy?' A male voice. Not friendly.

'Who is this?'

'You sneaky bitch. You've got balls, I'll give you that.'

'I'm hanging up now —'

'I wouldn't do that if I were you.'

I lowered my voice. 'Who is this?'

'Percy Brash. Joe's mate.'

Ah, here he was. Mrs Phelan's associate. 'What do you want?'

'We've got things to talk about. There's a pub in Keilor, on the Old Calder — Coach and Horses. Meet me there at seven.'

A small voice in the back of my mind said *be careful*. But it was ridiculous. His superior tone, assuming my submission. I nearly laughed.

'No thanks,' I chirped. 'We don't have anything to discuss.'

'We have lots to talk about. What about all that money you have.'

A segment of consciousness broke free and stood outside my body, marvelling at how a simple sequence of words could disrupt my biological function to such an astonishing degree. Blood vessels flooded, other systems shut down. There was shaking and stuttering and violent confusion. Breathing was difficult, my skin prickled, and my tongue was dry. No words came from my gaping mouth.

'The Horses,' he said. 'Seven, and don't be late.' He hung up.

I looked around the office. Colleagues tapping on keyboards, others holding low-volume telephone conversations. A burst of laughter came from the staff room. I sent out a trembling hand to reach for my mug, but found only dregs of tea. A great wave of total freak-out was building up in me. Oh God, this was bad.

I had to calm down. I took a breath and another, slow deep breaths, in and out. That was better. Now, *think*.

How did he know about the money? Maybe he didn't. *All that money you have.* He could be referring to the contents of my wallet. He was a criminal after all. Maybe he was simply a common thief on a fishing expedition. It was an ambit claim. A gambit. An ambit gambit. Because, really, who even was this so-called Percy Brash? A mate of Joe's, who was helping Mrs Phelan in her time of need, and surely that meant he was, in fact, a decent chap. No, it didn't. Au contraire. He was a criminal. Joe was a criminal. Joe had been in jail.

For what crimes? I opened a browser and tapped in the address of a searchable case law website. Joseph Phelan had a recent conviction for credit card fraud. I relaxed again, remembering that's what they'd said in the news segment the other night. Fraud wasn't a violent crime. I read on. In sentencing Joe, the judge had noted his significant prior offences and whacked on another two years.

Priors. The website wanted payment for further information. I switched to a general internet search and was soon drowning in Joseph Phelans. It was a popular name. A search for his name plus *convicted* or *criminal* narrowed things down. Between juvie and the Athol Goldwater green tracksuit, he'd been a lesser light in a drug dealing gang involved in a terrifying killing spree in Melbourne. Somehow, he had survived that period of slaughter, when gang members were shot on the street in broad daylight. Nothing suggested that Joe himself had been violent. He had probably been a dealer. It appeared that after the gangland killers who were still alive had been put in jail, Joe had turned to stealing credit cards.

New thought: what if such people nursed old grudges against him?

Now I understood why Mrs Phelan suspected Joe's death was not an accident.

As for Percy Brash, his name was mentioned peripherally in online articles about those times. Gossipy criminal message boards named him as a killer who had survived that same period unscathed and un-jailed. There had been no evidence — no living witnesses — with which to convict him.

My next thought was how best to leave the country. An immediate, orderly evacuation to start a new life in, say, New Zealand. Call myself Nancy Something. Dye my hair, mow lawns for cash-in-hand. I was warming to the idea, until I remembered Brophy. He couldn't just pull up sticks and go live in another country with me. He had responsibilities. And I didn't want to go anywhere without him. Fuck it, I was going to have to deal with Percy.

Fatima tapped a knuckle on the frame of my cubicle, and I nearly had a heart attack.

'You have a visitor,' she said.

Percy Brash had come to break my arm. 'Oh my God! He's here? Already? Hide me.'

Fatima hesitated, looking at me with a mix of concern and wonder. 'It's a woman.'

'What *woman*?'

She touched my arm, spoke slowly and gently. 'It's alright. She seems okay. She said she's your sister-in-law.'

'I don't have a … Oh yeah, actually, I sort of do. Thanks.'

I went to the foyer. A small young woman was staring through the curtains at the street.

'Loretta?'

She spun around and grinned. But it was clear she had been crying. Her hair told a story of irregular trims and bad bleach jobs. A haircut was a luxury. Her belly protruded quite significantly. She came towards me with skinny outstretched arms. The ensuing hug was a brief breathless squash.

'Ben told me where you work. I thought I'd come to you. Save you the trouble.'

I looked down at the bursting tartan suitcases strapped to a small trolley. Plastic shopping bags hanging off it. She had at least two sloppy joes on. Her dirty feet were in black thongs repaired with gaffer.

'Where did you sleep last night?'

'This church in Footscray. It's cool. The priest knows. He comes around in the morning with a cuppa tea before he kicks us out.'

'Us?'

'Me and Nigel. Me dog.'

'Where is Nigel now?'

'Tied up outside. The lady told me I had to leave him outside. Some rule about dogs.' She had an air of defiance, as though that rule, indeed all rules, were a personal afront.

'What kind of dog is Nigel?' *Please be a small dog, please be a small dog.*

'Alaskan Malamute.'

I sat down.

'They're from Siberia.'

'Not Alaska?'

She frowned. 'Or from there.'

'I can't have an Alaskan Malamute in my flat. There's rules there as well.'

'Can't go back to the church.'

'No? What about under a bridge, or maybe a bus stop, just until the weekend?'

She blinked. 'What bridge?'

Oh, for the love of nachos. 'Okay, Loretta. You *and* Nigel can stay with me. Now, perhaps you both can hang out in the park while I do some work. Come back at five.'

Her eyes welled. 'Thank you *so* much, Stella,' she whispered.

I slid a box of tissues towards her. 'No need for tears.' It was my mother talking, the tough CWA type, not a sensitive bone in her body.

'It's hormones. Since I got preg, I bawl at the slightest thing. Saw this old bloke in the supermarket, he seemed so alone, I sobbed my heart out.' She sniffled and wiped her eyes. 'Then he starts to rant about the prices and the manager had to deal with him.' She paused. 'Cool distraction, though!' She lifted her jumper. 'I brought food!'

What I had thought was six months of unborn child was twenty packets of two-minute noodles that tumbled to the floor.

A proper house guest, this one. The jumper raised, the noodles gone, the belly did indeed protrude. This was a relief, because I wouldn't have put it past Ben to concoct some bogus offspring for his own dumb purposes. The sight of the large bump on such a tiny frame was alarming. 'How far along are you?'

Her grin lit up like a million-watt bulb that could be seen from space. 'Don't show much, do I? Seven, nearly eight.'

God help me. I stared at the charming little outie belly button on top of the bump. My vision blurred. I forced myself to snap out of it. What the hell, it was nearly lunchtime. 'You must be starving. Feel like some two-minute noodles?'

She grinned like she'd won the lottery. 'Love some.'

'I'll put the kettle on.'

When she'd slurped the last strand on her third pack of chicken-flavoured noodles, we went outside and found Nigel, tied with a Western Bulldogs scarf to the bike rack. Oh boy, was that dog huge. Size of a horse. I noted the boredom in his stare, but the tail wagged. His white bits were grey, and he was huddled against the wind. Odd for a cold-weather dog to look so forlorn. Loretta set down a bowl of noodles for him, and he went to work.

Both girl and dog were much improved after a hot meal. Nigel's tail whisked the air, and Loretta had colour in her cheeks.

'Here you are!' Fatima said, either astonished or annoyed, maybe both — it was hard to tell. She told me to join the rest of the staff inside for a presentation. I gave Loretta ten dollars to buy proper dog food and said I had to get back to work.

'Rightio,' she said happily.

'I'll see you back here at knock-off time.'

She unknotted the scarf from the pole and pulled the dog and the trolley towards the shops.

'Loretta!' I called. 'Leave the trolley here.'

'Thanks. Sick of dragging that thing around everywhere. The looks some people give you when you're trying to get on the train.'

I joined my colleagues in the meeting room, fended off their well-meaning enquiries about Loretta, and for an hour we heard about the introduction of a new gifts policy. In the interests of probity and accountability we were told that all gifts must be declined and registered. Even if it was just a bag of lemons from a grateful client, it must be declined and registered. As the meeting finished up, Fatima took the opportunity to stress the importance of ethical, fair, and honest behaviour by WORMS employees at all times.

Fatima caught me on my way out. 'Have you read my email?'

'Email?'

'About giving a presentation on behalf of WORMS for the other agencies.'

'Sure,' I said, though I hadn't. I'd read it later, some time, probably.

I walked away still shocked that a bag of lemons could be considered a form of bribery.

Back at my desk, I sent a text to Brophy inviting him to dinner. I was curious to see what he would make of Loretta and Nigel. He responded straightaway with a string of emoticons: yes, happy, love. Aww. I emoji-ed heart and kissing-face. Sickening, weren't we?

Right, time to do some work. I would read Fatima's email,

figure out what kind of speech she wanted me to give. But not right now. I was still shaky after the call from Percy, and I needed some light distraction. I googled 'Alaskan Malamute'. A breed favoured by nomadic reindeer herders. A friendly breed, they made terrible watchdogs.

A watchdog, now *that* was an idea. But with my luck, any dog I purchased would bite me, instead.

Before I knew it, my day was done. I logged off just as Loretta walked into my office carrying shopping bags of dog food.

'We have to walk,' I said. 'They'll never let us on the tram with Nigel.'

Just then, Fatima came out of the building and locked the front door. 'Need a lift?'

I told you. An exceptional woman.

Nigel, Loretta, and I piled into Fatima's station wagon. Fatima didn't ask a single question about the girl, the dog, or the suitcases, to my eternal relief and gratitude.

I gave her directions to my flat. 'It's the one with the giant pine tree,' I said, out of habit. I always spelled the name of my street and always mentioned the tree. Roxburgh Street, Ascot Vale, had only one building with a thirty-metre-tall Norfolk Pine in the front yard. That made giving directions to taxi drivers, Ubers, pizza delivery people easy.

It also made it easy for my enemies to find me. And over the years, I'd had a few of those.

After we said our thanks to Fatima, we started up the path to my building, the dog straining against the non-AFL approved acrylic.

'We should get Nigel a proper dog lead and maybe dog shampoo and a brush,' I said.

Loretta responded with tears of gratitude, and I found it very moving. Though it might become annoying at some point, if she kept it up all week.

In the foyer of my building, Nigel lifted a leg and sprayed urine on the bottom row of letterboxes. I didn't mind that too much, but my cranky-pants neighbour, Brown Cardigan, would no doubt write a letter to the body corporate.

The three of us staggered up the three flights, and once inside my flat, Loretta walked straight into my bedroom. I went in after her.

'It's only a one-bedroom flat, I'm afraid,' I said.

Loretta turned to me, seemingly nonplussed, or acting that way. 'So?'

'This is my bedroom. Where I sleep. I thought that you and Nigel could have the couch. It's very comfortable.'

Her gazed was blank as she absent-mindedly patted her tummy.

'You know what? Take my bed. I insist.'

In the kitchen, Nigel had pulled the half-eaten falafel out of my bin. He shook his head and spread onion, lettuce, and garlic sauce all over the kitchen floor.

'Bad dog!' Me at my most commanding, pointing a finger at him.

He showed his teeth, emitting a low growl. Perhaps an Alaskan Malamute was not as friendly as I had been led to believe.

'*Very* bad dog!'

He backed down, tail drooping, head bowed. I dragged him by the back of his neck to the corner.

'Sit!'

He looked at me.

I shoved his back end down. It stayed down. Alright then. This was more like it. I cleaned up the mess in the kitchen, then knocked on my bedroom door.

'Come in.' Loretta was leaning back in my bed, thumbs darting over a phone screen.

'You busy?' I didn't really regard phone activity as legitimate. But then, I was old.

'Updating my status.'

'Is that wise? This pregnancy needs to be kept quiet until Ben gets out of prison.'

'I never mention the baby.' She seemed indignant, as though I'd questioned her intelligence. 'I said Dakota should have won *The Bachelor*. What's up?'

'I'm driving to the supermarket for the dog things. Need anything else?'

'Nah. Maybe some liquorice? And sherbet if they have any?'

'You want lollies?'

'Yeah. I have cravings.'

'Cravings are a myth.'

She shrugged.

As I drove down Roxburgh Street, a man on the radio was muttering in a pleasantly hypnotic drone: *two slips and a gully, mid-on, mid-off, deep extra cover.* Deep extra cover, indeed. For the second time that day, I seriously thought about doing a runner.

6

I PARKED the Mazda next to a four-cab monster in the nearly full car park of the Coach and Horses Hotel and locked the door.

Construction workers and tradies had been marinating in the front bar since downing tools around mid-afternoon. They'd been joined by white-collar drones at five; add in sundry semi-permanent residents, and the pub was almost at capacity. My anxiety levels were already high, and with this rowdy crowd, I had the added difficulty of picking out a man I knew only by his threatening tone of voice.

I looked out for men on their own. A chap at the quiet-ish end of the bar had a glass to his lips, but his pale eyes darted around the room. Our eyes locked, and I freaked: Brash. He had a gut that enjoyed two family-sized pizzas before dinner. Despite his bulk, he leaned back, straining the bar stool, and drained the glass. Head the colour of a scalded crustacean. White hair, a chunky gold chain at the neck, an alarming dint in his forehead, and a piece of ear missing. His neutral mannerisms gave no hint of intent. He might fillet you or help you carry the shopping. He nodded to the stool beside him.

I walked over and offered a hand, a work habit, automatic civility to commence proceedings. This amused him, as though I'd tried to shake hands with a scorpion. He raised two fat fingers, and a woman behind the bar immediately tilted a clean glass under the tap.

'You don't seem the type,' he said, without looking at me.

I swallowed, trying to draw moisture into my mouth. 'What type?'

'"What type," she says.' He shook his head. 'That act might work with your average ignoramus, but not me. I know what you are.'

I almost laughed. I wished *I* knew what I was. 'How can you possibly know —'

'We've got mutual friends.'

'I doubt it.'

His face stretched into a smirk. 'Clacker ring a bell?'

'No. No bells.'

He showed his bottom teeth, and his growing irritation. 'Clacker AKA Darren. Think carefully before you answer.'

My stupid brain couldn't cope with the stress. Neurones misfired, thoughts bounced about ineffectually like a game of pong. For the life of me, I could not dredge up a 'Clacker'. My glance shifted to the door.

'Focus, Stella. Remember: I know where you live, where you work. I know your car.'

'But I don't know what you're talking about,' I said, horrified at how scared I sounded.

Two beers arrived on the bar. Percy passed one to me. I picked it up and drank some froth. He took a seasoned drinker's guzzle of his. When he set it down, I detected a hint of impatience. 'Darren Clyde Pickering. Died in a suspicious house fire while on bail.'

'Oh, *that* Clacker.' A lowlife murderer I'd known. He'd killed a teenager on the orders of Gaetano Cesarelli to cover his other crimes: kidnapping, torture, murder, conspiracy. 'We weren't friends. I hated Clacker.'

A grin. 'Good girl.' He scratched the spikes of white stubble on his chin. 'That's where the Venn circles overlap.'

Venn? Was he a gangster, too? Wait a fucking minute. 'You worked for Cesarelli?'

He closed his eyes. 'Good times, I must say. Still, does no good to dwell on the past. Joe and me were the last ones standing. And now it's just me.' He sniffed.

'My condolences about Joe,' I said, and I meant it. Losing a friend hurts like hell.

'Thank you.' He seemed genuinely touched.

I drank some beer, relishing the bitterness.

He sat more upright, a back-to-business signal. 'Mrs Phelan needs your help.'

'I know. And I said I'd help her.'

'We need to know exactly what happened.'

'You're not listening. I said I'd help, and I will. I've already made some enquiries.' A pathetic, but necessary lie. 'I don't see why you need to —'

'No, *you're* not listening.'

I looked down the bar. The staff were pulling beers, tapping credit cards, mixing cocktails. 'I need the bathroom.' I rose.

'Sit down.'

'You can't order me around,' I said, sitting.

He leaned towards me. 'I know. About. The money.'

I gulped in vain like a landed guppy. Air, where did all the fucking air go?

'What money?' I wheezed. I wasn't being disingenuous. Though perhaps a better question was 'Which money?' It was fair to say the financial side of my life was complicated.

'Ten years ago now. A couple of dealers OD'd in their commission flat before handing over the earnings. Cesarelli assumed the cops pocketed it. But I went down there and had a sniff around. My contact said you were seen entering their flat *before* the cops arrived.'

Brash let that sink in.

So, I'd finally been sprung. I drank some beer, remembering how I'd lived in fear and guilt, worrying I'd been seen, that one day someone would accuse me. But time passed, and nothing had happened. Then Cesarelli was murdered, and, like a fool, I'd begun to relax.

He finished his beer and tapped a coin on the bar. The woman came over. 'Perce?'

'Another. And one for me slow mate here.' He slapped my back. 'Drink up, Stella.'

45

The woman left.

'Either you're extremely stupid or you've got more balls than most cunts,' he said.

Extremely stupid was the correct answer, but I couldn't speak.

'Relax, will you? I never told Cesarelli, and he's long past caring.'

'Why didn't you?'

'To be honest, I didn't believe it. A social worker wouldn't do something so fucking reckless. But the truth is, that little stash was nothing. I mean, sure, gangsters don't like getting ripped off, and Cesarelli seethed for a while. But the ice market was crazy. Very fucking busy. Fucking shit-ton of money coming in. So I filed it,' he pointed to his bulbous beetroot head, 'here.'

I nodded. This was easily the creepiest conversation I'd ever had. One of them. Top ten.

'Then Joe gets popped in jail. I bring Mrs Phelan flowers. She goes, there's a Stella Hardy I need you to talk to. Her brother was in the Arsehole Bogwater with Joe. She's got access and she's got form. An A-grade sticky beak she is, gets to the bottom of things. I go, rightio, I can persuade. Then it hit me. Stella-fucking-Hardy. The light-fingered do-gooder.'

Lucky for me, the fund was sitting in a storage unit, cash at the ready for just these sorts of emergencies. 'When do you want the money?'

'*Wrong.* I'm not interested in that pissing little pile.' He announced this with a sly, knowing smile, and then sipped his beer. 'Some things are worth more than money, Hardy.'

'Such as?'

He raised his eyebrows, as though I'd amazed him. 'Your *life*, dummy.'

I released an involuntary high-pitched titter. Why did I always laugh when I was frightened?

'You think that's funny?'

'Oh God, no. It's just. I don't know … the banality of it. A gang-land hit.'

Brash shook his head. 'Nah. Too clichéd. I've been reading about the Mexican cartels. Now those blokes know how to get rid of some-one. I'm thinking lye, I'm thinking caustic solutions, I'm thinking you reduced to mush and bone fragments.'

'Okay. No need to get crazy. You want me to look into the prison thing? Ask around? I can do that.'

'No. I want the name of Joe's murderer.' He lowered his voice. 'So I know who to kill.'

That celebratory dancing going on inside me was my survival instinct. *How easy is that? Give him a name and you get to keep living.* I found myself nodding.

'*Whom* to kill,' I said, grinning.

His head cracked in half, and he roared like a machine gun. 'We have ourselves a deal.' His over-sized paw came at me, palm at a harmless angle.

I grabbed a part of it and moved it up and down. 'Yes, we do.'

'Give us your number.'

I wrote it down.

'Should take you ...' he thought for a moment. 'I reckon a week. Two at the most.'

'*What*? Are you kidding? I need more time than that.'

'Saturday week, Hardy,' he said. He cracked a horrible grin. 'Tick. Tock. Tick-tock.' He patted me on the head in time with the words. I was mortified. '*Whom*,' he said, and started laughing again. Then he sauntered out of the pub, still roaring with laughter.

I have no memory of leaving the Coach and Horses, or how I drove back to Ascot Vale. In a daze, I entered my local bottle shop. The shopkeeper was happy to see me.

'Mate, how's things?'

Beery gas escaped me. 'Nothing, I mean, who? Certainly, um, good.'

'Got a great special on wine casks this week.'

'You know me too well.'

He laughed.

'I mean it. You are way too familiar with my habits.'

He laughed all the more, but I was serious. I'd have to start buying my wine casks elsewhere. Sure, I was capable of blowing fifty bucks on a fancy French champagne for dinner with Brophy, but my standard partiality was a bag of plonk in a handy cardboard box. And now this busybody was judging me. Rankled, I made a show of pretending to know the finer points of viticulture. 'I'm looking for a varietal of the California region. Have any?'

He laughed again. 'Try that aisle, the reds.'

I caught his eye-roll as I turned away. The bottles seemed to be arranged without any thought as to their type, quality, or value for money. I crouched to study the label on a dusty bottle on the bottom shelf. Who was I kidding?

I dumped my usual cask on the counter. He was serving another customer, who was something of an oddity in this urban setting — a farmer gone to seed. Late sixties, poor attempt at a shave, dusty jeans, flannelette shirt. A circle in his thinning hair where the hat always sat. A knobbly hand took the change, and he limped out of the shop.

'Salt of the earth,' the bottle-shop man said, with an admiring nod at the door.

'Anachronism,' I countered.

'Real Australia,' he retorted.

'Dinosaur redneck.'

'Tough, hard-working, primary producer.'

'Socially regressive, subsidised, National Party voter.'

'Enjoy your *cask*.'

'Thank you, I *will*.'

That went well. Now for the supermarket.

The doors parted with a whisper, and I wrestled a trolley away from its pack. Shielded from my fellow citizens by a dark cloud of

fuck-off vapour, I ploughed the aisles, pulling random items down —
no thought, no plan. Fabric softener. Oh boy, was I ever in trouble.
Jar of pickles. Nah, just give Percy Brash a name. Dental floss. Any
name, like, some enemy of mine. Dozen eggs. No, bad Stella. Frozen
cheesecake. My epitaph, my memoir: *Made a mess of things, lol soz.*
One hundred Earl Grey tea bags. Come on, concentrate, what did I
actually need? A proper dog lead and a frozen pizza. I eschewed the
available self-serve check-out and waited for an age in line for a live
human to scan and bag the stuff and rote-wish me a nice day.

It was a clear evening when I drove up Roxburgh Street, one
of those bottlers, straight out of a postcard. If you want a postcard
from Ascot Vale. And who wouldn't? Home to million-dollar
semi-detached dwellings, with the occasional gangland hit in broad
daylight on the main drag, just to get the blood moving. The orange
sky turned to pink before my eyes. Cask, pizza, heavenly sunset —
everything was going to be okay.

I thought of the imminent baby. A blend of Ben and Loretta, poor
thing. I wondered what kind of child Brophy and I might produce.
A sensitive artist, like her father? Or a crook with a chip on her
shoulder, like me?

On the street, Nigel was pulling Loretta along by her scarf. I
wound the window down as far as it would go and yelled through
the crack. 'I've got dinner and some food for Nigel.'

'Great. See you later.'

Later? What was she doing? I drove into the garage and glanced
back. She'd crossed the street and was talking to someone … It was
the hayseed from the bottle shop. The man held up a hand, and the
dog immediately plonked his arse down. I watched in increasing
amazement as they stood back in the shadows and began passing a
whiskey bottle back and forth, deep in furtive discussion.

I ran up to my flat, two steps at a time, whacked on the oven, and
ripped the plastic from a pizza. Dinner sorted, I ran into my bedroom
for a quick rummage through Loretta's stuff before she returned. I

found my clothes strewn all over the floor, drawers open, and items spilling out over the sides and across the bed like a scene from *The Exorcist*. So, it all looked pretty normal.

Except ... wait, did I leave Kylie's legal papers on the floor in my room? I tried to remember. Why would I? I had no interest in it. But I was sure I'd left them in a stack on the kitchen table. And now the stack had moved to the floor of my bedroom, in a disorderly jumble. I gathered them up, knocked them into order, and put the stack in a folder in the kitchen.

Boy, did Loretta have a lot of questions to answer. And since she still had not returned, I took the opportunity to return to my original plan of rifling through her belongings.

The first suitcase held a few of those loose-knit jumpers, a pair of jeans, socks and a pair of worn-down runners. The other case contained some t-shirts, a battered book on pregnancy, and a plastic A4 document case with 'EBV — Angus in the Wimmera' written on a stick-on label on the front.

In farmer lingo, 'EBV' stood for 'Estimated Breeding Value', a method of calculating possible cattle-breeding outcomes. I opened the case and sifted through the papers. Documents about production traits in language I had not heard since childhood. There was stuff about fertility, calving ease, milking ability. Other documents were on selection decisions for better performance. I closed the clips and put the case back. The shopping bags held toiletries and a wallet with a driver's licence. Her name really was Loretta. Knock me down with a brick. Loretta Swindon was twenty. Ben was mid-forties. A man who had been in and out of prison most of his adult life. Some of Loretta's life choices were terrible.

Mine, on the other hand, were top-shelf. Notwithstanding the thieving and the gangsters and the deal to find the identity of a prisoner's killer.

The strong urge to flee flared in me again. *How much would I get for my flat?*, I wondered. And what might that buy me in, say,

Wellington. Or Tierra del Fuego. Or Nairobi. I was shaken from my reverie at eight, when Brophy hit my buzzer.

I held the door open. 'Jesus, look at you. Skin and bone. Given up eating for Lent?'

'Still fighting off the virus.' He wiped his nose on his sleeve. 'Can't shake it.'

Time stopped for a lingering smooch, no stupid virus would keep us apart. The smell of burning pizza, however, did.

It was black on the edges, but still edible. Loretta hadn't come back with Nigel. We ate half the pizza and put some aside for her. I rang the number, and it went straight to voicemail.

'She's on the phone. She must be alright.'

Brophy ran a hand under my t-shirt.

Later, I fired up my laptop, and we settled in on the sofa for a binge of *Midnight Sun*, a cop show set in northern Sweden.

'*Midsomer* with snow,' Brophy pronounced two episodes in. 'Half the town will die before they solve this one.'

Every time the streaming faltered, I topped up our glasses. After three episodes, and many glasses of wine, Loretta still had not returned. When some poor Swede got fed to a pack of wolves, I started to worry about her.

It was nearly midnight, and Brophy had to leave for work. He'd started a new job at the fruit and vegetable wholesale market. The crazy hours suited his lifestyle. At five in the morning, he'd go home and paint for hours. He picked up his keys, and, at last, the door unlocked. Nigel came bounding in, followed by Loretta. She seemed wired, and her beady eyes sized up Brophy suspiciously.

'Brophy, this is Loretta, and Nigel the wolfhound.'

'Alaskan Malamute,' she said and went into my bedroom and shut the door.

Brophy gave me a sympathetic look and left for the market.

I went into my room and flicked the light. 'Listen. I don't know what your game is —'

She was spread out on the bed, weeping like a child.

'Are you okay?'

'Just hormones,' she said, sobbing. 'Don't worry.'

I paused, weighing up whether or not to sit down and hold her hand. My feelings towards that unhappy creature were as mixed as a good martini. She was clearly dodgy, but then, so was I. She was tough and clever and independent. Ben was unworthy of her.

I turned off the light and shut the door. Nigel stood in the middle of the lounge room, hesitant, waiting for instructions. When I slumped onto the couch he wagged his tail uncertainly, panting, watching me. I got up, found a blanket and made a bed for him in the corner of the sitting room. The dog circled the bed a few times and flopped down exhausted.

'You're welcome,' I said.

He closed his eyes.

7

BIRDS MADE a racket around five in the morning. I sat up bleary-eyed. It had been a rough night on the couch. Nigel passed the time scratching incessantly, also snoring and whimpering in his sleep. I, conversely, had whimpered in my sleeplessness. I tossed about rehashing every stupid decision I'd ever made, particularly those I'd made in the last twenty-four hours.

And now I had the problem of needing to get into my bedroom to get ready for work. Luckily, just as I was wondering how to rouse her, Loretta appeared in the kitchen, apparently eager to breakfast on flat Coca-Cola.

'Sleep okay?'

'Yep,' she said.

'Everything alright, pregnancy-wise?'

She tapped her belly. 'Yep.'

'Anything you should tell me?' *Like what you're up to and who that old dude was …*

'Nope. Nuh-uh.'

'No? Okay. I bought you something. Well, for Nigel actually.'

'Oh my God.' Hands clapped to both cheeks in stunned delight. '*What?*'

'A dog lead. Nothing flash.'

She flew at me in one spry motion. 'Thank you!' She strangled me in a tight hug, then she flew to the dog. 'Nigel! Let's go try it out!'

The dog responded to this ruckus by leaping from the blankets and racing about the room, his tail a blur of motion.

I showered, dressed, and shoved some toast in my mouth. Loretta and Nigel returned as I was heading out. I waved a cheery goodbye and told her to call if she needed anything.

When I rocked up at WORMS with my coffee and hangover, I was shocked to discover Fatima had done some rearranging. Gone were the partitions between desks that offered some semblance of privacy. Everyone was exposed to everyone else, voices carried, screens were clearly visible. The insidious open-plan disease had infected our sector, and entire afternoons spent trawling the internet would be more difficult to achieve. New *workspaces*, Fatima called them. Our work practices would be more accountable, she said, looking at me. I tried to be enthusiastic, but no words came, instead a strange sort of whistle escaped me, like a punctured pool toy.

Seated in my new workspace, I cracked my knuckles and logged on. Then I typed 'MEREDITH PHELAN' into a directory of community workers. No hits. I typed 'PHELAN' and scored. Merri Phelan, senior advocacy officer for the adolescent prisoner advocacy organisation Adolescent Bondage a Ubiquitous State Error. ABUSE exposed the appalling mismanagement in the youth justice system: the overcrowding; the placing of children in adult facilities where they were terrorised. ABUSE worked against the weight of political expediency. They lobbied governments and provided early intervention programs.

I rang her number and was connected to her voicemail. I left my number and asked her to call.

My attention now turned to WORMS tasks. An email popped up from Fatima with the subject *RESENDING! URGENT!* and marked with red flags. No question: I needed to attend to it, and yet I battled a weird inertia. With a mighty burst of resolve, I pushed the curser over 'open' and was about to click, when some new clients arrived. I ran out to greet them and spent the morning walking them through the information they needed to embark on the long road to citizenship.

Just as they left, a courier delivered a large envelope from the Department of Justice, addressed to me. I tipped its contents onto my desk. There was a lanyard attached to a personalised *ALL ACCESS* pass and some documents. One was a letter from Puke, advising the general manager of Athol Goldwater Prison that representative Stella Hardy would be making a preliminary inspection of the facility on Friday at nine.

There was a wordy statement about the mission in there, too. The joint prison-assessment team was to inspect the facilities, review policies and procedures, and write up its findings vis-à-vis best practice, safety, security, and value for money. Since when was a simple bureaucratic chore a *mission*?

The phone on my desk rang.

'Stella, Merri Phelan. What can I do for you?'

She did not sound like someone racked with grief.

'Your mother dropped by the office yesterday,' I began. 'She was very determined to see me.'

'Mum came to see you? What for?'

'She's convinced the department won't investigate Joe's death properly.'

A sigh. 'She's looking for someone to blame,' Merri said. 'It won't bring Joe back. I told her that when she asked me to look into it.'

'She said you recommended me.'

'Oh for the love of — I never said any such thing. All I said was I knew you. I recognised you when we were waiting for Joe that day at the prison.'

'You told her I help people?'

A pause. 'I might have said that ... but only to mean you're someone I respect. I didn't think she'd run off and enlist you.'

'Well, I'm enlisted now.'

'Stella! What did you say?'

I hesitated, trying to think. I wanted to get to Percy Brash and the coercion, but I didn't want to explain what he had on me. 'I'm on Pugh's prison assessment team,' I said. 'So I told her I'd talk to some people, ask a few questions. It's no trouble. Really.'

'Talk to who?'

'My brother, Ben, mainly. She's convinced he'd know what goes on in Athol Goldwater.'

'That is good of you. I worry; she's on her own. I do what I can, but work is crazy ...'

'She has some support. An old friend of Joe's, apparently — a bloke called Percy. Know him?'

'Ugh, that guy. He's a bully and a creep. I told her not to believe a word he says.'

'He takes her shopping.'

'What? I don't know what she's playing at. Brash is bad. I hope he doesn't upset her.'

'Upset her?'

'Oh, Joe liked to rave about conspiracy theories. "The system's rigged, the company's corrupt, there's a giant scam going on." The usual drivel. It really riled her up.'

'That's what Pugh said — off the record, of course. He asked me to look out for it.'

'That's right, Stella, you're on his bloody *inspection* team, aren't you? You know, he hasn't allowed a single member of a justice advocacy group to be involved? Not one.'

'It doesn't surprise me.' The conversation needed steering back on track. 'Tell me about Joe's conspiracy theories.'

'Just wild accusations. Crazy stuff. I can just imagine Brash is saying similar things about Joe's death. Poor Mum believes it all and gets really distressed.'

'I wouldn't worry, your mum's pretty fierce. I'm sure she can handle herself.'

Merri laughed. 'She sure can. When the Coroner's office phoned and said they'd like her to come in to give her an update, she goes, "Good! That way, you can look me in the eye when you bullshit me."'

I forced insouciance into my voice. 'Oh, really? When's that?'

'I'm taking her this afternoon. I don't want to, to be honest. Besides I'm flat out here.'

'I'm free this afternoon, I could take her.'

'I hate to put you out, Stella.'

'No problem. I like your mum.'

'I owe you. I'll set it up and call you back,' she said and hung up.

It was hard to reconcile that the same man who takes his friend's mother shopping was also a bully and a creep who would happily turn me into mush and bone fragments unless I gave him the name of Joe's killer. Tick-tock, indeed, I barely knew where to start. I prayed the coroner would have some clues.

I looked at the unread Fatima email. Then decided I needed coffee. I faffed around in the staffroom for half an hour with the new coffee machine, but couldn't get it to work. I returned, defeated, to my desk with a mug of instant. *Come on*, I told myself, *do some work*.

Or I could see what the media had made of Joe's death. I looked around the open-plan office. Most people were out or busy. I did a quick google search and found a perfunctory piece that laid out the facts.

Corrections Victoria has issued a short statement relating to the death in custody of Joseph Phelan.

'The prisoner was left momentarily unsupervised in a work shed. He was later found by staff lying on the floor and appeared to be injured. The prisoner refused officers' requests to stand. An ambulance was called with medical attention immediately provided. Police attended the site and are investigating. The prisoner was confirmed to be deceased. His body was subsequently removed,' a spokesman said.

'As with all deaths in custody, the matter will be referred to the coroner, who will formally determine the cause of death.'

Phelan was sentenced in 2012 after being found guilty of fraud. He was due to be released in February 2017.

I closed the browser and at that exact moment, Merri called back. Mrs Phelan would be waiting outside the Coroner's office at three-thirty. I wrote *visiting a client* on the staff activity board and ran to catch a tram.

8

'PRELIMINARY POST-MORTEM examination indicates that the deceased suffered trauma to the left frontal lobe, due to the entry of an eighty-five-millimetre projectile, which penetrated the anterior fossa, where it became lodged in tissue.'

'In English?' Mrs Phelan demanded, leaning with both hands on her walking stick.

'A nail in the head.' The man held a thumb and finger wide apart. 'This big.'

I felt cold and looked away. My gaze roamed the bland room, beige carpet, cold blue walls. A place soaked in shock and grief. Beside the man was a woman in a dark-coloured pants suit, hair in a bun, a clipboard holding a wad of papers under her arm. Now she stepped forward. 'The prisoner had been using a nail gun, one that can fire nails that long,' she said.

Mrs Phelan glared at her.

'Brain trauma is the cause of death,' said the woman. She lifted the clipboard and began checking the documents. 'But the inquest will explore the events leading up to Joe's death. Was the custodial environment, in regard to his ability to freely access the nail gun, up to departmental standards? Was there adequate supervision in that area of the prison on the afternoon of the deceased's death?' She let the papers fan back into place on the clipboard and looked up at us. 'And finally, was the response to the deceased's death in line with requirements?'

I glanced at Mrs Phelan. Her small body trembled with fury.

'Suicide. Is that it?' she said. 'I'll never believe that.'

The woman shook her head. 'It's too early to say, but preliminary enquiries would suggest that death was the result of improper use of equipment. The department had purchased the nail gun twelve months earlier,' she continued, glancing again at the papers. 'The nail gun was specifically *for use with timber-to-timber fixing or materials of similar or lesser density*,' she read. Now she gave Mrs Phelan a look of deep regret. 'Joe was working with *steel* at the time of the incident.'

'Who are you, again?' I asked.

'Dileshwar,' the man said. 'Forensic pathologist.'

'No, I mean her.' I pointed to the woman.

A long silence followed. The woman tucked a stray hair back in its bun. 'As an indication of how seriously the department takes this investigation, I have been appointed to assist and report directly to —'

'Oh, shut up,' Mrs Phelan said. 'No one cares about your career ambitions.' She looked at Dileshwar. 'Any cameras in there?'

'I don't know.'

'No viable footage of the incident exists,' the woman said.

Mrs Phelan sniffed. 'Course not.'

'We have the contractor's report,' the woman said, and she again read aloud from one of the papers. 'An employee of BS12 observed Joe alone in Athol Goldwater Prison Shed 6 or AGP Shed 6 working on a sheet of metal balanced across two trestle supports, using the nail gun. She asked Joe if everything was alright. He said it was. She then left him. On her return, Joe was observed lying on the floor. The officer rushed in, prepared to perform CPR, thinking that the prisoner had perhaps suffered a heart attack. The officer found the deceased with a length of nail protruding from the side of the head. Emergency services were called immediately, and the prison was put on lock down.'

'So you're saying Joe was like this,' I mimed firing a nail gun down onto an invisible table, 'and the nail ricocheted off the metal,' I traced the trajectory with a finger in the air, 'travelled in a one-hundred-and-eighty-degree arc, and hit him here?' I touched my temple.

'He was probably leaning over the table.' The woman bent at the waist and turned her face so her nose pointed to the wall and her ear was directed at the floor. With her painted fingernail, she traced the nail's path so it ricocheted off the invisible table and went directly into her head. She straightened up. 'Rest assured the nail gun has been removed, the shed is closed, and full review of relevant safety equipment is underway.'

'What equipment?' I said.

'Safety glasses will be made available for all prisoners.'

'Glasses?' I tapped to my temple.

'Full face helmets, in fact,' she said.

Mrs Phelan and I exchanged a glance. She'd had enough of this poppycock, and so had I — except for one last question. 'Which BS12 officer spoke to Joe before the incident?'

The woman shrugged. 'I don't have that information.'

Mrs Phelan and I walked past the grey gallery building towards St Kilda Road as the skies opened. She sped up, working her stick like a cross-country skier, so I had to trot to keep up. The rain intensified. I unclipped the umbrella strap, hit the trigger, and it shot open.

'You get it now, don't you? It wasn't no accident. A classic hit more like it.'

She had a point, but I gave her a weak, non-committal shrug. I didn't want to hear about 'classic' hits. It reminded me that I was a hostage to her and that gangster Brash.

'Percy's a colourful character,' I said holding the umbrella over her.

She waved it away. 'Colourful's one of them euphemisms.'

'Well, yes.'

'All I know is, he's loyal. I trust him.'

Loyal to whom?, I thought. She answered as if I'd said it out loud. 'It's money, Joe, and then me — in that order.'

Money first. At least she understood that. And I understood that, despite what he'd said, he'd come for my money before too long.

'Like him?' she asked.

'Not really. You didn't need to get him involved.'

She laughed and patted my shoulder.

The rain came all the harder, tepid and dirty. We rounded the corner and marched towards the city. Cars drove too fast, showering passers-by. Under the shelter of a tram stop, I collapsed my umbrella. A tram rolled up, spraying brown muck over our feet.

'You right to get home by yourself?'

She rolled her eyes. 'Not a bloody invalid.'

'Okay, well, soon as I get something, I'll give you a call.'

She winced, irritated. 'No. Percy will get in touch with you.'

She climbed up and waved her stick at me as the tram moved off. I walked over the icky Yarra River, around the corner at Flinders Street Station, and down to Elizabeth Street to catch my own tram.

For the sake of my longevity, I needed something useful to tell when Brash called. At least today's excursion had given me something to work with: sheet metalwork in Shed 6, a chat with a BS12 employee, then, unsupervised, no cameras, a nail gun to the head. A classic hit was putting it mildly. A loud metallic clack startled me as the Ascot Vale tram switched tracks, trundled slowly forward, and halted at its city terminus. Best I check out Shed 6 for myself.

Loretta was watching TV when I returned, with Nigel sitting on the sofa beside her. She was absent-mindedly pulling out clumps of his summer fur and letting them fall to the floor. I dropped my handbag on the kitchen table, disturbing a pile of moulted dog hair. Drifts of fuzz covered every centimetre of floor space in the flat.

'Winter coat coming on.'

'What?' she said, staring at some reality television home-improvement dross.

'Mind sweeping up his fluff for me?'

'What fluff?'

I sighed. 'What do you feel like for dinner?'

'Anything.'

'Okay, great. What about fish and chips?'

'It gives me gas.'

'What about Thai?'

'Sure, if you like it. I won't have much, it's too spicy.'

'Chinese?'

'No.'

'Pizza again?'

'Sure, anything. I'm easy.'

Half an hour later, two cheese pizzas appeared, and in a matter of minutes, disappeared. Loretta was eating for two. And I ... I liked eating. Besides, pizza-cheese was an essential part of every diet. I dashed downstairs with the boxes and some empty wine bottles to the communal recycle bin at the back of the flats. By the time I was back, I'd made up my mind to confront Loretta about the past and her whereabouts.

'What church were you sleeping in again?'

'Um. I forget.' She was smooth, I'd give her that.

'Who was that old man I saw you talking to yesterday?'

'Me grandad,' she said without hesitation.

'Does he know you slept in a church?'

'Oh no. It would upset him.'

I bet. 'Does he live around here?'

'He hates town. Only come down to see me, make sure I'm alright.'

'Next time your grandfather is in town, I'd like to meet him.'

She shook her head. 'You've done so much, having me here, giving up your bed. I couldn't ask you to have Grandad as well.'

After an exaggerated yawn, she went off to bed. I set my alarm and stretched out on the sofa. Nigel walked in a circle on his bed, settled down, and started to snore.

Loretta and Nigel were testing my family obligations to the limit. I thought about Meredith Phelan. How her mother was a borderline sociopath who loved Percy Brash, and how he intimidated people for her. And how Merri seemed like such a different person to her mother, yet still supported her. She was pretty excellent really. And I started to wonder if maybe I could do better. I *would* endure Loretta and Nigel. And Ben. And I'd be more tolerant of Kylie. And my mother, Delia. And her church-going, real-estate-selling, nob of a husband, Ted.

Maybe not Ted.

And maybe not Kylie, either.

9

A **TIRED-LOOKING** guard checked my ID and waved me through the gates. He pointed out an empty parking space. Not empty. The jack who'd taken charge of things last weekend was standing there, waiting. I stared at her name badge: *Tuffnell*. That's right.

'You're late,' she said.

'It's just on nine.'

'That's the meeting time. Visitors must allow fifteen minutes for processing.'

'No one told me.'

'Just hurry up and get out of the car. I'll conduct the search myself.'

I followed Tuffnell to the visitor waiting room. She tipped the contents of my bag onto a table and began sorting through every single item with disdain. Her long nails like tweezers, picking things up and letting them fall. She pulled out the lining of my sunglasses case, looking for a hidden compartment. The process was galling and embarrassing.

And to think the day had started with such promise. The pink morning sky had made me want to sing. And I was looking my best in a floral silk blouse and cream linen pants. My feet were comfy in a pair of soft cotton socks and cream leather mules. I'd lifted my sartorial game lately, having hit the fund. I'd even lashed out on designer sunglasses, polarised for extra glare reduction. I'd had my old pair for years. It was a weird universal law that you never lose or sit on the sunglasses you don't care for.

I'd even remembered to bring all the things I needed: Kylie's papers, the guidelines for the inspection, and the departmental ID. So that was a win. I had an old clipboard from a conference I'd attended, and I'd attached all the Department of Justice paperwork to it, with Kylie's papers at the back.

Tuffnell pried open the clipboard, took all the paper out, and flapped the pages around. Then she scrutinised my lanyard, noted the photo, and scowled at me. I smiled and put it on.

'Come on,' she said. 'I'll take you to Ranik.'

Alan Ranik, according to my notes, was the general manager of Athol Goldwater. I gathered the papers, reattached them to the clipboard, slung my handbag over my shoulder, and marched after Tuffnell and the resonating clap of her boots spanking the lino. We came to a carpeted area for administration offices, and the clacking came to an end. She knocked at a door at the end of the corridor, and then opened it and went in. I followed. She had a silent interaction with a young man sitting behind a desk, and then turned and left without a word. The man waved me through to a second room.

Behind the door, a small man with blond hair in a timeless page-boy cut, reminiscent of a Beatles wig, stood bouncing on his toes in the middle of a large office. Most of the office block had a prefab, temporary feel, but this room was decorated for permanence. The walls featured two large abstract paintings, some framed qualifications, and a bookshelf stocked with leather-bound books. A brown chesterfield said *old money*. The white MDF desk said *Ikea*.

'Mrs Hardy, welcome. Pleasant journey?' Traces of England in the rounded vowels and polite manner. We shook hands.

'It's Stella.' The hair — I couldn't help but stare. It seemed to be unironic.

'Alan. Let's get started, shall we?' he said. 'Time to make up.'

'Let's.'

'I only have an hour and a half, I'm afraid. Then I'm meeting some department people. Should be plenty of time, and I'm happy to support it. Quite a good initiative, inspection teams.'

He spoke as we walked, giving me a breakdown of the leadership team. 'The operations manager handles the high-level, day-to-day operational needs of the prison.' I trotted behind him, not giving two hoots about the leadership team. '... responsible for managing a team of custodial and non-custodial officers delivering a range of correctional services.' Bored, so terribly bored. '... and our OM is highly experienced, twenty years in the UK.'

'Are the staff here employed by BS12 or Corrections Victoria?'

'BS12. I'm on a contract. But most staff are full-time employees, covered by an enterprise agreement. I can get that out of the files, if you like?'

'No thanks. Can I meet him, the OM?'

'He's on leave. I'm acting OM until his return. Basically, the role ensures that policies and procedures are followed by liaising with internal and external stakeholders ...' I didn't care. '... to ensure that offender-management issues and requirements are being met ...' Bored to the point of physical pain. '... and the services to the various areas within the prison, reviewing practice, and procedures relating to prison ...' Where was a cliff to jump off when you needed one? '... and court custody activities, and develop and implement policies and procedures ...' None of this was relevant to my brief. Maybe that was the idea, to drown me in guff. '... contributing to continuous improvement initiatives.' He drew breath.

'What about the regular prison staff? Like the woman who brought me here?'

'Who? Oh, Nell? She's not regular. She's the principal practitioner.'

'The PP.'

'Yes!' He regarded me with new interest. 'It's a key position, reports to me directly.'

'But what is her role?'

'Manages escalation behaviours ...' *blah blah* '... through line management by the RD and myself.'

'RD?'

'Regional Director. It's in your notes. We helped write them. The PP works with the OM and staff from CV.'

'Corrections Victoria?'

'Yes. One big happy family: Adult Parole Board, Victoria Police, the Major Offenders Unit, Sex Offender Management Branch, Parole Central Oversight Unit.'

'What about your average jack, I mean, screw, I mean, officer-guard-person?'

'They ensure the smooth running of day-to-day operations.'

'Overseen by the PP.'

'The PP *and* the OM,' Ranik said.

'Okay.' I clicked my pen and wrote, *Nell Tuffnell* followed by three question marks.

When Ranik announced we would now begin a tour of the prison, I wanted to weep with joy. We walked to a maintenance garage, marked *AGP Shed 1*, where a fleet of prison vehicles waited. He clicked a fob, and a gleaming Land Rover with BS12 branding beeped.

We drove along a narrow paved road linking the prison buildings, passing signs requiring all prison vehicles to drive at walking pace. At a fork, we took a path that led away from the main compound with the accommodation units and work areas, and continued through open paddocks for about five kilometres.

'First stop, the agri-tech hub, up and running now for about three years. The future is tech. Even the hub building is hi-tech: steel prefab construction, lightweight, yet withstands cyclones and earthquakes. We're at the forefront of agri-tech.'

'Fascinating.' I stifled a yawn. 'Prisoners work here?'

'Some. The ones with aptitude. Learn valuable skills here.'

As we rounded a hill, a structure that was more warehouse than farm shed came into view. A massive, ugly skeleton of steel beams and struts supported sheet-metal walls. It was even bigger and nastier than the self-storage place where I'd stashed *the fund*. AGP Shed 2 was three storeys high, with multiple aerials and a large satellite dish on top, and a series of separate roller-door entries down one side. A dark-haired man in a check shirt and moleskins stood in the doorway, a mobile to his ear.

'That's Enrique Nunzio. He runs the tech side of things. Topnotch BS12 man.'

I wrote, *Enrique Nunzio.*

Ranik parked in the makeshift parking area beside another BS12 vehicle. A muddy path led to the shed. I glanced at my spotless cream mules and sighed. I should have known better.

'Out you get,' he said, impatiently.

I took up my clipboard and tiptoed gingerly behind him.

The man on the mobile greeted Ranik with an apologetic expression, and gestured to the phone.

'Ah,' said Ranik. 'We may have to get by without Enrique today.'

He waved me inside AGP Shed 2. The place was reminiscent of an agricultural show, replete with pleasantly familiar aromas: fertiliser, hay, manure, animal urine, bovine breath. But something was off; it was stark and sterile. Soft moos and grunts came from closed pens. I walked down the central aisle, security cameras positioned above me every five metres or so. A giant fan at either end of the shed circulated air. Halfway down was a series of small pens. I stood at a stall and slid open a viewing window. A fat black cow was contentedly chewing, there was fresh hay on the floor and water in the trough.

'Here,' Ranik said. 'Have a look in the lab.'

He led me to the rear of the building and pulled open a glass door. Carpet, new furniture, several desks, all with multiple monitors. Large plastic tubs full of stock eartags were stacked on the floor. A map of Australia, with stock locations shaded in, took up one wall.

'Enrique is an expert in animal nutrition, grazing management, and pasture production. Had a very successful ranch in Argentina. With us, he's initiated a GIS mapping program.'

'What's GIS?'

'Geographic Information Systems. The project remotely monitors and analyses cattle. Through a deal between BS12 and a consortium of agri-businesses, Athol Goldwater Prison is one of a number of testing grounds. Bleeding-edge stuff. The data can be sent to an app on a smartphone. Imagine farmers assessing pasture performance from the comfort of their Jason recliner! It will revolutionise farming. Even the small pastoral holdings will benefit.'

I thought of my father. And every farmer I ever knew in Woolburn. They liked being outside, using their eyes and ears and hands. They inspected feed with their callused fingers and broke chunks of soil open to feel the dirt for signs of moisture. Were he alive today, my father would have thought sitting in our kitchen using an iPhone was a form of torture.

'These technologies reduce costs, time, and labour, with the added benefit of improving animal welfare.'

'Animal welfare? How?'

'Earlier detection of disease or injury.'

'Sounds like you don't need farmers at all.'

'Oh no, not at all.' He laughed. 'Not yet, anyway.'

I watched him pick up an eartag. It was like no tag I'd ever seen, more like a Fitbit for cows. There were an array of models. Beside the tags, there was a stack of objects that looked like plastic collars — large, cumbersome things. I picked one up. It was heavy.

'What do these do?'

'Ah, that's even more ground-breaking. It's a GPS locator.'

I waited.

'If cattle stray where they're not supposed to, a mild electric shock is administered. Expensive fences will soon be obsolete.'

'It's a shock collar.'

'I think of it as a mobile electric fence. The future of herd management. Neat, huh? Now I'll show you how we attach the tags. The cattle are in the pens ready to go.'

He took off at a trot. I hung back and opened a drawer: stationery, a couple of USBs. Another drawer contained a pile of invoices. I took some pictures on my phone, and as I was closing the drawer, bumped a keyboard. A monitor woke up. An open email appeared on the screen from 'Al Coleman': *Enrique darling, we're all set and ready to go here ...*

I snapped a photo of that, too.

'Stella? You coming?' called Ranik.

I went out and found him gazing at that one black cow. She really was a delight, with her glossy coat and lovely big wet nose.

'Listen, Alan,' I said. 'These innovations really are marvellous, but I do need to inspect more buildings. Tick off the accommodation blocks for one, and then there's AGP Shed 6.'

Ranik's shoulders slumped a little. We'd moved from his favourite topic to his least favourite. 'Of course. Let's go.'

10

RANIK DROVE back to the prison, turned off the main path, and headed towards a cluster of small weatherboard dwellings. 'You'll want to start at Callistemon.'

'I will?'

'The unit your brother is housed in.'

'Ah. They told you.' Was that an attempt to unbalance me? I studied him for signs of smugness. He beamed, as though having relatives in jail was just terrific. I decided he was an idiot, too stupid to intentionally undermine anyone. 'Good idea, let's start there.'

I checked Kylie's papers in the clipboard. Ideally, Ben would sign them without Ranik noticing. It was possible Ranik wouldn't care. But I wanted to keep it on the down-low. Otherwise, it would be apparent that this whole inspection initiative was not merely a cynical pantomime; it was also a shameless exercise in self-interest. And it was anyway, since it started with Pugh's hunt for a moonlighting jack. I groaned inwardly, remembering that that, too, was on my list of clandestine chores for today. The principal one: dredging up a name for Percy Brash.

'Benjamin Hardy,' Ranik said wistfully. 'If only all the inmates were as compliant. We support his rehabilitation by supplying him with top-quality ingredients. He's such a talent.'

A compliant talent? Ben? Ranik parked, and we got out and walked towards the houses. Ranik pointed to one of them. 'That's Callistemon. They're not dangerous in there, but do still be careful.'

'Right.'

He suddenly stopped. 'That prisoner's death was a tragic accident, you know.' He gave me a beseeching look.

I shrugged. 'Right.'

He turned away. 'We've cooperated with the investigations. Given access to everyone.'

'Who's everyone?'

'The department, the police, CV, the coroner, Workcover, you name it. We've put on extra staff, stretched our resources. Every assistance, every step of the way. Whatever rumours you've heard to the contrary, we have nothing to hide.'

Ranik trotted up the steps to the unit's front door. From the outside, the unit was bare and institutional-looking. A plaque featuring a red bottlebrush was attached to the front door, the only aesthetic trace. No bars on the windows, only a deadlock to suggest that the people living here were being held against their will.

Inside, Callistemon seemed much larger and was, in fact, a hub of four units, each with six bedrooms, a communal area for reading and watching TV, and a kitchen. The place was clean and neat, if a bit sterile. Ben was in the kitchen with every kitchen utensil, every pot, every burner in use.

'Stella, Alan, come in,' he said warmly. 'You're just in time.'

Ranik lifted his nose to the air in exaggerated wonder. 'What is that marvellous aroma?'

'Chimichurri. An Argentinian special sauce. Perfect for barbecued meat.'

'It's ten in the morning,' I said. 'Bit early for a barbie.'

'Never!' Ranik said. 'Love a morning barbecue.'

Ben whistled, and five men in green t-shirts and shorts shuffled into the kitchen. They were dressed for a day in the garden or wherever. As Ranik said, they were harmless. Paedophiles, former cops, the people who'd be bashed on their first day in remand. Prison etiquette demanded it. Here, they were relatively safe. They were not violent and not well connected. Some of them were definitely unnerving, but not the kind to shiv you in the shower.

Ranik stood among them as though they were all the best of friends.

'What do you call this, then, Ben?' one of the inmates asked, to a murmur of laughs.

'Rissoles,' some wag answered.

'It's a *crunch bowl*, love,' Ben said.

I'd never seen him so happy. The men appeared to like him.

'Little late for breakfast, isn't it?' I asked. 'You're farmers. And prisoners. Prisoner-farmers. You should be up with the chooks.'

They all looked at me with scorn. 'We've *had* breakfast,' one said. 'Four hours ago.'

'Bircher muesli with locally sourced fruits,' Ben said.

'Then what's this?'

'It's brunch, Stella. A brunch crunch bowl. Jesus, we're not animals.'

He arranged some fried chicken and crispy chorizo on a bed of mixed ancient rice grains in seven bowls — announcing each item as he went — and poured in the chimichurri.

'You cooked the chicken this morning?' I said, incredulous.

'He's been up since five making all of this,' one of the men said.

Ben passed a bowl to each one. 'Taste the cloves? Not too much, I held back this time.'

Ranik's phone rang, and he went out to the front veranda to take the call.

To my amazement, Ben pulled me by the arm and hurried me out of the kitchen and into the communal sitting room.

'Ben,' I hissed, 'what do you know about Joe Phelan's death? And possible corruption in the prison?'

'Never mind that, how's Loretta?' he hissed back.

'Early.'

'What? The baby?'

'Relax, the baby's fine. As far as I can tell. I mean, she turned up a bit earlier than I expected,' I said, and hurriedly flipped the pages on the clipboard.

He seemed so relieved that I paused. This was a side to my brother I didn't know existed. I had to shake myself to focus. 'Here. Sign these.' I handed him the pen.

He clicked the pen. 'What am I signing?'

I exhaled. 'Kylie's contract. Stating that you and I will not attempt to retake control of the farm.'

'Well, maybe I do want the farm. I'm learning a lot about cattle here. Animal husbandry.'

'Idiot, you don't even know about human husbandry. Stop being difficult.'

'I'm not. I'm thinking about what I'll do when I get out of here. I need a plan.'

'Please, Ben. Loretta has my bed, and the dog's staying, too. Please do me one favour.'

'Dog?'

'Nigel, the fucking dog.'

A cloud of confusion came over his chimichurri-stained face. How close were Loretta and Ben, if he didn't know she had a dog? He clicked the pen a few times, just to annoy me.

'You're so bossy,' he said.

'I know.'

He laughed. 'Like I'd ever want to live in Woolburn again.'

And, sweet merciful Lord, he signed.

'Thank you.' I could have wept with relief. I checked on Ranik. He had just ended the call and was walking back to the unit. When I turned back Ben was scribbling on the paperwork.

'What the hell are you doing?'

'Initialling each page. Make it legal.' He gave me the clipboard and pen. 'Your *worship*.'

I didn't have time to argue. 'Ranik's coming.' We rushed back to the kitchen. 'Quickly, tell me about Joe Phelan's death,' I whispered.

'What's the word among the inmates?'

'Check the coriander pots outside Swainsona,' he muttered.

I had so many questions, but Ranik walked in and picked up a piece of chicken. 'We're behind schedule, I'm afraid. Have to cut this short,' he said. 'Just time for one more site to inspect. Any preference?'

'AGP Shed 6.'

The compound lacked shade, presumably by design, so that lines of sight were unimpeded. But the sun seared the earth's surface from a clear blue sky. Ranik ate the chicken while driving the five hundred metres to Athol Goldwater Prison Shed 6. He stopped the car as a group of men returning from outdoor work, dripping and beetroot-faced, walked passed.

AGP Shed 6 was still off-limits, and a guard was standing by. Ranik gave a curt nod, and I flashed the lanyard. Ranik twisted a key in the padlock, and the roller door retracted above us.

It was cooler inside than I'd expected. But the metal shell rang as it expanded, and no doubt it would be sweltering in here by afternoon. A skylight let in a blinding square of daylight. The concrete floor was swept and tidy, no stain of blood remained. Tools lined the walls, in order of size, and a long workbench was clear of clutter. It was the shed of an obsessive. A handyman's dream. My father would have swooned.

Ranik hit the lights and lowered the door. I walked around, not finding much of interest. Numerous people had been over the place, photographed the scene, taken all evidence, he explained in a nervous stream.

'… and the nail gun is with the coroner,' he said and drew breath.

'What happened to the component parts of the project Joe was working on?'

'Steel. It was recycled.'

'Not kept as evidence?'

He coughed. 'No.'

'What was Joe's project at the time?'

'A small repair job for a leaking roof. He'd been cutting a Colorbond sheet to size.'

'With a nail gun?'

'We theorise that he'd cut the sheet too short and was trying to join two pieces together.'

'Theorise?'

'Yes. The other explanation is that he was bored. Inmates take risks for a kick; our job half the time is to keep them from doing something silly.'

I thought about that. The sheets of steel might have settled the matter. I scanned the corners of the roof. 'Where are the cameras?'

Ranik pointed to a rafter. A camera was directed at the door. 'There's one over the bench as well. They're dormant until a sensor detects a moving object. State of the art, sees in the dark up to thirty metres with infrared night vision.'

'So the camera can move around, following people as they walk around the area?'

'No.'

'Any footage from that day at all?'

'I'm afraid not. My IT people tell me there was a problem with image capture — or was it file corruption? — some error at any rate. They're working on it. But we do know that only one person was in the shed at the time. Joe Phelan.'

The roller door went up again, and Nell Tuffnell was blocking the light.

'Look,' I said. 'It's the PP.'

'Yes, Nell?' Ranik said.

'Lacy's waiting for you,' she said.

He nodded. 'And that concludes the inspection.'

'Not quite. I'm going to inspect Joe's unit, then I'll call it a day.

Go to your meeting, I'll walk down. Which one is his?'

Ranik managed a smile. 'Swainsona. I'll take you.'

We rushed from the shed to the car. Tuffnell passed us and jumped in the back. Ranik drove in silence. Perhaps it was the heat but his high-spirits had evaporated. We drove by Callistemon. Ben was on the front steps smoking a cigarette. He waved as we passed. Swainsona was directly behind his unit, beside a kitchen garden. Ranik paused the car outside the unit for Tuffnell and I to unstick from the seats and get out. I took my clipboard and pen for show. Sweat dripped down my back. Once we were out, Ranik drove further down the road and parked on the verge.

The front plaque featured a Sturt's Desert Pea, and, beside the door, a plant was dying in a plastic pot. Once inside, I saw the building had a similar layout to Ben's.

'Is anyone in Joe's unit?'

'Not yet,' Tuffnell said.

She led the way to Joe's bedroom: a single bed, stripped; a built-in wardrobe, empty; and a desk with one empty drawer. The window had a view of a productive vegetable garden, with rows of tomato plants, some fruit still ripening in autumn. There were several varieties of lettuce, some strawberries, and other berries on stakes.

I returned my attention to the room, and kicked at the floor tiles with a toe.

'We tested each one, none were loose,' Tuffnell said. 'The linen's been changed, the mattress gone over. We checked the ceiling, the wall panels. We've pulled the place apart and found nothing.'

'What did you expect to find?'

Ranik arrived. 'Oh, it's routine in the event of an incident.'

I made a perfunctory knock on a wall, looked around. 'Okay. Thanks. Let's go.'

'Yes,' said Ranik. 'I'll get the car.'

Outside, Tuffnell and Ranik headed for the car. I hung back and crouched beside the dead plant. I drove my pen into the soil in several places and met no resistance. I stood, ready to admit defeat, when Ben came into view. He was making a cornering motion with his hand.

'Just having a quick look around the back, see the veggie patch,' I called out.

Ranik and Tuffnell exchanged a look. 'Fine. Come on.' And they started back towards me.

I ran around the side of the building. Along the wall, in the shade of eaves, was a row of black plastic twenty-five-centimetre pots, each one containing a lush green coriander plant.

'What's with all the coriander?' I used an outside voice, hoping Ben heard.

'Some of the prisoners sell surplus produce at the local farmers' market,' Tuffnell said.

'How good is this? Never get coriander this healthy when I try to grow it.'

Ranik's pageboy hair was damp, and he mopped his red face with a handkerchief.

Ben came trotting up to us. 'Guys! You have to taste this new recipe I'm working on.' He stopped, so that Ranik and Tuffnell had to turn towards him.

Straight away, I pushed my pen into each pot. Four, five, six pots, each received the pen easily. Ranik and Tuffnell were telling Ben to go back to his unit. I was down to the last pot, crouching over it to hide what I was doing. A solid object in the soil stopped the pen just below the surface. I glanced up.

Ben was arguing with Ranik, but Tuffnell turned around to check up on me. I picked a coriander leaf and made a show of smelling it. Ben shouted her name, and she turned back.

I quickly knocked the coriander pot over with my shoe. It spilled, plant and soil, onto the grass. I felt a corner of soft plastic in the soil, then a solid shape inside: a mobile phone inside a ziplock bag. I shoved it into my cotton sock, and the leg of my pants covered it.

Then I shoved the plant in the pot and started scooping dirt. I had it back in place as Tuffnell came over.

'Get in the car, Hardy. Mark Lacy's been in the OM's office for twenty bloody minutes.'

Ranik drove directly to the fleet-vehicle car park where we'd started. He got out and gave me a curt nod. 'Thank you for coming. I do hope you found the visit informative.'

'Sure did. Who's this bloke you're meeting now? Lacy?'

'Contract manager. Routine visit.'

Tuffnell walked me to the Mazda, which was now roasting in the sun in the public car park. A new white Camry with state government registration was parked beside it. She left me without a word and went back to the admin building. I jumped into my car, opened the folder and jotted down the name *Mark Lacy*.

11

I KEPT the needle on one hundred and ten, the window open, and the radio blaring a song I didn't know. Melbourne was in my sights. I was squinting because — of course — I'd left the designer sunglasses in Ranik's car. I glanced at the contraband mobile phone, still in the ziplock bag, lying on the front passenger seat.

About an hour outside Melbourne, I took an exit and entered a sleepy town with a pub, a petrol station, and a couple of sunbleached weatherboard houses. There was also a park with a fancy raised flowerbed, a cannon, and a drinking fountain. A sign thanked the local Rotarians for this charming community facility. Not a living soul stirred. Two cars outside the pub were the only signs of life. I pulled over and inspected the phone. Older-model android, a crack in the screen. I pressed the power-on button to no avail.

I walked to the servo and bought a bottle of water, an android charger that used the car's lighter port, and a discounted CD of Led Zeppelin hits. On my way out, I spotted a rack of sunglasses. I twirled the swinger, tried on a couple, and ended up buying a pair of wraparound speed-dealer Oakleys.

The Mazda lighter was missing. I plugged in the charger and waited to hear a ping of connection in Joe's phone. Nothing happened. No green lightning bolt or other sign of recharging. The lighter port in the Mazda was stuffed. And there was no point taking the charger back and getting one for a USB port; a car this old didn't have that kind of thing. The phone would have to wait. I put on the sunglasses and slotted the CD into the player.

With a seventies British scream and a frenzied guitar riff, I was set to go. No, I wasn't. Something buzzed. I turned the music off and checked my phone. Phuong had sent me a photo. A selfie in a hairdressing salon. Caption: *new do*. Long single strands of black silky hair clung to the plastic cape. Top quality hair, that. Over the years, I'd admired and even envied that which was now so recklessly discarded. Her smile was broad, as if this sharp pixie cut was the ultimate liberation, her spirit now free. And holy shit — how was it possible? — she was even more kick-arse. There'd been no warning, no *I'm thinking of cutting*, no *ugh my hair*. Just bam! Gone. I hurriedly responded with hearts and applause and champagne symbols. She answered with instructions to meet her at a new bar near her place, including a choice of directions, in case one was congested, and best parking prospects.

I responded with a thumbs up. Drinking was a brilliant idea. In fact, I wondered how I'd allowed my drinking to lapse so badly these past few days. Any sane person in my position would be shickered from morning till night.

Winds from the inferno of the central Australian desert had scorched the lower east of the country all day, and the heat had reached its zenith around three in the afternoon. Then, the wind direction shifted from north to south, and brought the chill of the Antarctic. This was summer weather. But these days, autumn was summer, up was down, and truth was lies.

By the time I hit Ascot Vale around five-ish, the air temperature was refreshingly benign, but my place was still an oven. I went through the flat, opening every window. Loretta was absent, and I assumed she had decided to take Nigel for a walk now the change had come.

In the safety of my secure domain, I took Joe's phone from its plastic bag. It was a thing of beauty. A sacred relic. With this object I might secure my very life. Surely, it would please Percy Brash. Surely, he would recognise its value. And, verily, he would let me be.

I plugged the phone into my own charger and connected it to a power outlet beside the couch. Then I hid the phone under a copy of *Gourmet Traveller*. I'd bought it on a whim, thinking Brophy and I might one day travel to some far-off place: stay in a posh converted Indian palace, or laze around a villa on an Aegean cliff, or island hop in the South Pacific — anything as long as it was an improvement on the holidays of my childhood. Those were caravanning horror stories that still gave me nightmares.

Next, I rang Kylie and left her a voicemail to the effect that I was the world's best sister and the papers were signed. She was welcome.

There was plenty of time before I was due to meet with Phuong. And, since Joe's phone would take some time to charge, I decided to check in at work. Besides, I had printing to do.

Fridays at WORMS were casual and relaxed. Sometimes, we knocked off early and had a few beers in the tea room before we went our separate ways. Other times, the place was cleared on the dot of five, with recently vacated desk chairs still spinning in the darkened office. Today, apart from Fatima in her office, I had the place to myself, and much googling to do, kicking off with Enrique Nunzio.

Media hits said the South American was a former cattle farmer with an interest in agri-tech. I trawled puff and guff about how he was headhunted by BS12 to work at Athol Goldwater, their flagship prison-farm-cum-tech-lab model. I saw nothing of note. Then, an old article on an incidence of biosecurity breach popped up. Nunzio's name was obliquely associated with a scam to import South American bovine blood products and relabel them as Australian, with the aim of on-selling the products at a huge profit. Even the CSIRO had been fooled. Nunzio denied all knowledge of it and had threatened to sue. Such threats were a sign of guilt, I baselessly concluded as I hit *print*. Here was a nice bone to throw to Marcus Pugh: Enrique Nunzio might be your scam-artist on the payroll. Had no one done a background check? It seemed pretty inept.

That gave me the idea to examine the administrative structures around the prison, and I started with Pugh. His press releases came up — *boring!* — with links to the departments and agencies under his command. I looked up key senior personnel and viewed the images: Justice Department secretary, a middle-aged white man; Police Commissioner, a middle-aged white man; members of the parole board, middle-aged white men. Better was the ratio of the Supreme Court of Victoria Justices, starting with the Chief Justice, who was an actual woman. And a smattering of women were on the Court of Appeal.

The organisational chart for Corrections Victoria showed the executive team: a family tree of homogenous Anglo male faces. Deputy Commission of Prisons, boring white dude. Contract manager, Mark Lacy, was also a boring white dude. In his photo, Lacy faced the camera with a confident smile, his red hair, thinning on top, combed back, his red moustache neatly trimmed. I remembered the name. He'd had a meeting with Ranik at Athol Goldwater today.

According to Lacy's profile, he oversaw delivery of every out-sourced prison service for Corrections Victoria: prisoner transport, youth detention, prisoner monitoring, home-detention systems, remand, and all private prison contracts. He was the image of a man without a care in the world. An old-school public servant with the confidence of a person who understood that if something was not accomplished today, there would always be tomorrow. If some aspect of contract management ran into difficulty, well, the government of the day, not the public servants, would pay the price. He looked like a man with all his ducks in a row.

After a quick search for numbers, I discovered that the system-wide costs of male prisons in Victoria was around eight-hundred million dollars. A big budget, and Lacy managed it all — awarded all the contracts. Try as I might, I couldn't find the cost of the BS12 contract.

I switched focus back to personnel, to Ranik. He'd had a long boring admin career and had been employed by BS12 at various sites since 2015.

Tuffnell: Nothing much. A cleanskin BS12 employee. Her Facebook page was a series of cringe-inducing self-portraits in resort-wear, beach-wear, swim-wear, eye-wear, head-pieces, statement pieces, and leisure-wear. Nell Tuffnell liked cruises and novelty over-sized cocktails. Nell like her nails long, in fun colours. She sometimes got too much sun.

I hit print on everything but Tuffnell's Facebook photos. While the printer was spitting out former trees, I took a new purple folder from the stationery cupboard and using a big fat texta wrote *Pugh/Prisons* on the front. If anyone questioned me for researching these people at work, in work time, using work things, I'd say it was part of my inspection-team duties.

I replaced the cap on the marker just as my phone buzzed with an incoming text.

Brash: *tick tock*

My heart lurched.

'How was the prison?'

'What?' I screamed.

Fatima sat beside me. 'Sorry to startle you.'

I pretended to laugh. 'Oh no! I'm fine, I mean, good. Prison was good.'

She didn't say anything. I looked down at my desk.

'Anything else to tell me?' she asked.

She had something in mind, but I was hopelessly oblivious. The work of WORMS had not been at the top of my priorities for days, possibly weeks. I shook my head.

'No?'

Would it be unprofessional, I wondered, to ask for a hint?

'How's the presentation coming?'

'Presentation?'

Her cheeks puffed, and she slowly pushed the air out. 'The one you're delivering next Thursday morning to the other agencies. We spoke about it. It's all in the email I sent you.'

I pretend-laughed again. 'Just kidding. Of *course* I remember.'

'It's not a joke. This is a whole new direction for us. I'm expanding the agency's work to include an inter-agency support role. It's an adjacent business that targets other agencies, provides mentoring, administrative advice, grant-writing assistance, cooperative planning, mutually harmonious projects, information sharing, and professional-development training. A favourable reception for your address is vital to its success.'

My mind was blown. I had no inkling of this new direction. When she left me, I dropped the *Pugh/Prisons* file into the bottom drawer of my desk, and I opened her email.

12

AS PER Phuong's instructions, I found the bar and scored an excellent parking spot in a side street. *Cui Bono?* was a vast brick-and-concrete drinking hall, serving a range of beers on tap, elaborate cocktails, and exotic share plates. Sure, they sounded delicious, but you'd need a second mortgage for half a spring roll and a sip of beer. If 'who benefits?' was the question, the answer was: the bar owners, their heirs and successors, *ad infinitum*, amen.

I swooshed my petrol station eyewear to the top of my head, and my eyes adjusted to the dark. The place teemed with covens of financially and emotionally independent professional women. I hoped they freaked out the old white guard, because they scared the hell out of me.

Phuong had secured first-rate terrain, a back-to-the-wall power position as advised by feng shui with clear lines of sight as per Sun Tzu. She wore a black stretch strapless dress; this afforded the mortals a view of her shoulders, décolletage, and slender neck. Her handbag, an over-sized raspberry, sat on the empty stool beside her. It was a collection of spherical segments in gorgeous red silk with a gold chain. I conquered the stool next to it. 'You spunk,' I said, eyeing her haircut.

'Less time in the morning.'

'Like you need a practical reason.'

Her bare shoulders shrugged lightly with an in-breath.

'Now,' I lifted the cocktail menu. 'Where's the booze?'

'I've ordered two martinis.'

'God bless you.' I dropped the list, placed the sunglasses in their case, and switched my phone to vibrate.

We remarked on the things of the day, the coming election, the heat, the latest madness from leaders in the UK and the US. Our locally made insanity was inferior, less flamboyant, just as egregious, myopic, lacking in courage, and delivered with the usual banality. Battles for seats, power, and money were all conducted with typical moral illiteracy.

This was grist for our mill, but I was aware that both of us were uneasy. The martinis were consumed. That helped. But Phuong, who was almost never on edge, continued to fidget.

'I've taken up rock climbing,' she said suddenly.

'Sounds dangerous.' But that was, of course, the point.

'No, it's fun. A good workout. I go to Rock With You, an indoor place in the city, but I'm going to scale a genuine rock soon.'

Today, a new challenge. Next week, she's broken the international record for backwards blind-folded rock-jogging. I said encouraging things, as always, though I sensed this information was merely base-camp for a much higher topic. One she seemed hesitant to mention. And her nervousness made me nervous.

She inhaled, paused, exhaled and said, 'Um.'

I waited.

She straightened her posture. 'That raid on that bikie house last year, remember? You and I and the crazy bikie woman with the AK-47, and then soggies arrived —'

'Of course I remember.'

'When she gave her statement ...' She paused again.

I sensed danger. We were straying close to the fund. I tipped my martini glass, missed my mouth, and spilled the precious alcohol down my front. 'She what?'

'Well, it seems ... That is to say, she said ...'

'Said what?' My mouth was becoming dry. I needed moisture. I poured some tap water into the cocktail glass. I took a sip of the water. This wouldn't do. I nonchalantly raised my arm to wave to a waiter for two more martinis. In the process, I smacked a passing woman in the face.

'Watch what you're doing,' she snarled.

'Sorry.'

Phuong ignored the exchange. 'So we didn't pay much attention. Then we had corroborating, that is, matching versions of … And now we're reasonably confident …'

'Jeez, Phuong, confident of what?'

'A very large sum of cash was stored at the site and is now unaccounted for.'

I tried to scoff, but only coughed. 'Based on the word of bikies? They're all liars.'

'Hmm.' She pulled an olive off the toothpick with her teeth and chewed. The pause was a tactic to make me talk. It nearly worked. I was nervous as hell. I could barely sip the water.

'It's funny because several sources say the same thing. They're so outraged, calling it theft and unethical and all that.'

'Probably one of the bikies took it.'

A petite shrug. 'Unlikely.'

'What do you think happened?'

She looked at me almost sadly. 'I have an idea.'

I could feel warmth on my face.

The woman I slapped was pointing me out to her friends, and they shrieked with laughter.

'An idea?' I muttered. 'You mean evidence. Fingerprints or something.'

'Not fingerprints. Other indicators: signs of a break-in at the house, and two witnesses reported seeing a woman at the house the day before the raid. Mid-forties, long dark hair.'

I nodded rapidly. 'A bikie moll.'

'Said she was a real-estate agent, that her name was Marion Cunningham.'

I laughed way too loudly.

'There's no registered estate agent in Victoria with that name.'

'Round up all the Happy Days fans!' I said.

Two fresh martinis appeared. I snatched mine up and drank half. Phuong stared at me. I felt a chill, colder than the vodka in my glass.

'We have a hair from the scene. That is a real breakthrough. It's gone to forensics for analysis.

'A hair? Big deal. Hairs are everywhere.'

'It was found in the secret underground location where the money was stashed.'

'Can I just ask something? Why do you guys even care? I mean, it's crime money, not the money of some upstanding citizen.'

Her gaze turned away, and I breathed with relief. I gnawed my olive and watched her for a change. I'd known her for twenty years, and she was as ageless as ever, with that unreadable Sphinx vibe. She turned back to me, her expression resolute.

'When can you provide a hair sample?'

'Me?'

'To rule you out.'

'Right. Oh, any time. Soon. I'm busy this week. And next week. Maybe the week after?'

I finished my drink, managed not to spill any. 'Well, it was great catching up, Phuong, but I have to go.'

She frowned. 'It's so early.'

'I know, but I have a house guest, and she's a real pain in the arse.' It was the most truthful thing I'd said all evening.

'Family?'

'Sort of,' I said, avoiding her gaze. She had terrifying powers of truth extraction. I had to leave before I made a full confession. How would that help? Phuong would have to arrest me, and, frankly, that would be really awkward. Honestly, I was doing *her* a favour.

90

'Loretta!' I yelled as I entered the flat. 'I need one of your hairs.'

No response. I checked the bedroom, the bathroom, the couch. The flat was empty. Perhaps she and Nigel had skipped town. I could live with that.

I kicked off my shoes, poured myself a white wine, and stared at the wall — the only wall that wasn't closing in on me. I felt under attack from all angles. Percy-bloody-Brash and his tick-tock text could get in the bloody bin. Phuong and the hair. I had to be careful with that. I understood now that taking the money had put my best friend in a difficult position. If she had any suspicions about me, then she'd raised the hair as forewarning — and that was *not* proper procedure. Procedure was a warrant and the hair in an evidence bag on the spot. She wasn't sure, but she suspected. And consequently, conflict now existed between her loyalty to her job and her loyalty to our friendship. Nice one, Hardy, you idiot.

I needed to work through every one of these complications methodically.

First, the hair. Surely fudging hair evidence wasn't difficult. Loretta had hair. If her DNA wasn't on a police database somewhere, the matter would be shelved. The bikies would stop crying. Phuong would move on. Everything would go back to normal. Sorted. Good.

Now the Brash dilemma. Could I solve the thing in a week? Maybe. I reached under the magazines for Joe Phelan's phone. It was charged and ready and, mercifully, Joe did not have a passcode. First impression: the phone was light-on app-wise. No games, no social media, only the bare necessities. The message inbox contained only three text messages, exchanged with a single unnamed contact. The first exchange was two months ago.

Phone (Joe): *lovage seed x 110 pks*
Response: *yes*

The second exchange was a month later.

Phone: *parsley x same?*
Response: *y*

And the third was three weeks ago.

Phone: *lovage and basil?*
Response: *orders cancelled. supply ceased.*

On the face of it, Joe had been ordering seeds. This he might have done through prison channels, since his herb business was sanctioned. Clearly, the herbs were a code for other goods. I used my phone to google the number, not expecting much. To my surprise, I got a match. An IT company called 'The Best Bits'.

I called the number, and it went to voicemail: 'Best Bits is currently unavailable. Leave your details and the nature of your IT snafu, and we'll be in touch.'

I ended the call without speaking. I was about to put my phone away, when I remembered the photos I'd taken at AGP Shed 2. The photo I'd optimistically snapped of the email from Al Coleman — *Enrique darling, we're all set and ready to go here* — was a whole lot of nothing.

I swiped through my photos from the AGP shed office and studied a series of invoices. They were billed to Corrections Victoria, marked *Attention of Enrique Nunzio*. Most were for boring farm supplies: feed, vet services, fuel. There was a bill for cattle haulage valued at fifty thousand dollars. And a bill from a company called BlackTack for consultancy for a hundred and fifty thousand dollars. That was expensive consulting. Actually, no. Consultants charged like wounded bulls.

I hated using my phone for research. Phones were great for a quick fact check — but for intense reading of long passages? Not when my eyes weren't getting any younger, and phone-neck was becoming an epidemic. A proper ergonomic desk with a proper computer monitor was preferable. Unfortunately, I couldn't wait until I was at the office. Consequently, my phone told me that BlackTack, according to the website, was a problem-solving company, emphasising discretion and confidentiality. *Former elite intelligence units offer tailor-made solutions to business challenges.* What kind of business challenge — at a low-security prison farm — required the services of ex-intelligence operatives? Enrique Nunzio, architect of a state-of-the-art agri-tech program, had paid them a lazy one hundred and fifty thousand bucks. Business challenges requiring that kind of money for the services of elite operatives were at the extreme end of the scale.

A weird nervy sensation came over me — call it fear or paranoia or white cold terror — and I deleted the photos. I couldn't say exactly whom or what I feared, but these days you can't be too careful. All I had to do was find out who murdered Joe. Any corruption, any scams, all the rest of it, that was none of my business. I needed to distract myself, and eating was by far the best diversion.

The night was not exactly young, more middle-aged, but with great skin and a positive attitude. So I rang Brophy to see if he'd eaten. He had, with Marigold, at Subway. I felt sorry for him — the things parents had to do.

'Come over anyway,' Brophy said, sounding a little desperate. 'We're watching *The Bachelor*. I'll make you a cheese toastie.'

'Tempting, but no. You and Marigold enjoy some quality time together,' I said. 'We'll cheese toastie another day.'

Tonight's dinner would be solo. I scanned the cupboards to see what I could come up with. I came up with nachos delivered to my door at the tap of my phone. While I waited, I remembered to check Kylie's paperwork. When Ben was involved, you couldn't be too careful. Just as he'd said, he'd initialled every page. What a noob. With any luck, it wouldn't void the contract. Thankfully, his babyish signature in full was also in the right place. At least Kylie's ridiculous paperwork was off my to-do list.

A scrap of paper was wedged into the contract, and as I detached everything from the clipboard, it fell to the carpet. Ben had written one word on it: *DUFF!!!*

Duff? Or D-U-F-F? What on earth was he trying to tell me? Did he mean 'up the duff', as in, Loretta was pregnant? That, I already knew. The three exclamation marks were excessive. Surely he didn't mean the brand of beer on *The Simpsons*. It was never beneficial to spend mental energy on anything Ben said, or wrote for that matter, so I binned it.

One hour later, leftover cheesy corn chips were stuck to the cardboard box they'd arrived in and had tasted indistinguishable from, a half-cask of wine had been drunk, and my mood was one of bruised regret. Sure, I regretted the nachos and the wine, that was a given. It was as normal as getting wet in the shower. Order food, regret food. Drink alcohol, regret alcohol. No, this was a rare form of sweeping regret, occurring like a comet or a total eclipse, every few years or so. The regret of my lifelong everything, my nervous curiosity, my sideways distractibility, my drifting plan-less existence. My life was a disaster, the result of folly, greed, and a lack of impulse control. And now, in order to avoid jail, I needed a hair. A *hair*.

I was at the point in a regret-a-thon where my thoughts turned once again to running away. I loved the escape fantasy. It held so much promise. It starred me, only slimmer, frolicking on a deserted beach, perhaps holding hands with Brophy. Running solved *every* problem. Phuong couldn't send me to jail, Percy Brash couldn't kill me, and Hardy-family shenanigans would cease to be my concern. A phone call rudely derailed my train of thought. The numbers said it was nearly midnight — I'd been in my head for hours.

'What'sssup, girl,' I sang, assuming it was Marigold, the only person who would call this late.

'Velvet Stone of The Best Bits, returning your call.' All business, this curt female voice.

'A bit late, isn't it?'

'Is it? I was working and time got away from me. I regret any inconvenience.'

'Don't worry, I was up.'

'Right. What can I do for you?'

I glanced at Joe's phone. Lovage and basil were code for something. Like a kid at a party holding a tail with a pin, I went in blind but hopeful. 'I'm looking for some … lovage seeds.'

'Who is this?' Sudden menace in the voice.

'Samantha Stevens.' I needed a hook. 'From Athol Goldwater.'

'You a cop?'

I was too exhausted to laugh. 'As if. I'm a friend of Joe's.'

'What do you want?'

'I want to pick up where Joe Phelan left off.'

Irritated snort on the line. 'Ten thousand, and I'll tell you everything.'

'Dollars?'

'No, lovage seeds.'

'When and where?'

'Be at Rock With You at five tomorrow afternoon.'

Naturally, the meeting was to be at Phuong's new favourite place. 'How will I know you?'

'Lots of tattoos — both sleeves, legs, neck.'

'That doesn't exactly narrow it down.'

'Shaved head.'

'Still not helping.'

'A pet rat will be on my shoulder.'

'Okay, that's good,' I said. 'See you tomorrow.'

13

ROCK WITH You had been easy to find. It was the first two floors of an apartment tower, billed as luxury, modern, serviced. The climbing wall was tall, mostly straight except for random scary slants and was dotted with faux-rock-like objects, onto which mad Saturday-morning urban adventurers were grabbing hold. The wall faced a vast window onto the street, affording witnesses in the building across the road an uninterrupted view of folks plummeting to their death. I'd had a hard time explaining to the woman at the counter that I didn't want to climb. She wanted me up there, panicking, holding a signed public-liability waiver.

'Sick view out the windows when you're at the top.'

Sick indeed.

I whiled away the minutes waiting for Velvet Stone to drop, thinking about what Loretta had said when she came home last night. She'd taken one look at the phone and pronounced it a dual SIM.

'Some companies offer free texts, some have free calls. If you use a dual SIM, you get both deals. Save heaps, like thirty bucks a month. If you're on the dole, it all helps.'

'How do you switch between SIMs?'

Lightning-thumbs tapped, and she'd handed it back to me. 'Second SIM.'

It was another phone entirely. I'd checked the phone-call log and messages, but found nothing. It had some apps, though. Tradie tools, mostly, like a spirit level and a laser measure, as well as a weather app, cricket scores, a voice recorder, a clock, notes.

'If you're not using it, can I have it?' she'd asked. 'Better than my shit phone.'

I thought about it. Her phone was more cracks than screen. I had the Best Bits contact, that was the windfall. 'We'll see.'

She hugged me hard with her bony arms, her protruding belly pressing on my hip.

'Ben says hi.'

Her face lit up. 'Did he? What did he say?'

'He asked how you are, and how the baby was. He was very concerned.'

Loretta beamed, teared up a bit. 'He's a keeper,' she said, heading for my bedroom.

'Where were you tonight?' I called after her.

She closed the door.

Velvet Stone was swinging across the fake rock face like a chimpanzee. As discussed, I knew it was her from the masses of tattoos, the shaved head, and the small grey thing that scampered from her head to her arm. She glanced down and must have seen me wave, because she immediately began to rappel to ground level.

'Samantha Stevens.'

She looked at me without blinking. 'Let's go, Samantha,' she said. 'My place is just around the corner.'

A surprise move. A change of location was not part of the arrangement, but I went along with it, grateful Phuong hadn't shown up. Hopefully no crazy accomplice was waiting there with a baseball bat. We walked around the corner, away from the buzz of the main city street and into a quiet lane behind the centre. We were walking along a row of red-brick warehouses, possibly the only un-renovated buildings in the city and no doubt marked for demolition. We reached a door at the end of the lane with a faded sign that said, *Bell Please Ring*, with an arrow pointing to nothing.

Velvet undid a padlock and moved the door back, the rat sitting still on her shoulder.

Inside was a squat with a mattress on the floor, a makeshift sink, and a camp stove. A table was spread with monitors and keyboards. Dozens of cables led away from them, no doubt filching power from elsewhere. The windows were painted over, a small lamp the only light source.

Her unblinking stare remained fixed on me, though her manner was weirdly detached, as if I was a specimen in a jar.

'Nice place,' I said.

'It's only temporary. Until I get my money.' She dropped her gaze to my handbag. I held the strap a little tighter.

She lit the stove and her aloofness gave way to charm. 'Tea, Samantha?'

'Thanks.' A choice between an old tyre, a milk crate, or the mattress. I sat on the tyre.

She produced a small teapot, spooned in something from a tin. 'What's your story, then?'

'I don't —'

Impatient sigh. 'Who are you, and how did you get the phone?'

'My brother's in Athol Goldwater. Ben. Did Joe ever mention him?'

She shrugged. 'Never.' Her tattoos were a tangle of vines along both arms with large rat-like creatures in them. The rat on her shoulder adjusted whenever she moved, and kept its perch.

'Joe's death was suspicious.'

She remained impassive and fed the rat a piece of biscuit. 'How did you get the phone?'

I hesitated.

'Not telling?' She tickled the rat under its chin.

'What's the rat's name?'

'Gnawer Barnacle. Gnawer with a "g".'

She brought it closer to me. I patted its head.

'Was it your brother?' she asked. 'He found the phone somewhere?'

'I'm the one with the money, you give *me* information.'

Her eyes moved to mine. She could outstare the Eye of Sauron. 'Hand it over.'

The money sat in an envelope in my bag. I'd come via a detour to the storage facility. It was a wildly inflated price for information, but I was bad at this sort of thing. I hadn't even haggled, and, consequently, I'd reduced the fund by ten thousand dollars. The moment had been a difficult one. My inner dragon had spread a leathery wing over the loot and wanted to guard it jealously. Dipping in at times was going be necessary, but it hurt my dragon feelings.

I placed the envelope on my lap. 'What's your business with Joe?'

A flick of her arm and the rat jumped away into the dark. 'Couple of months ago, I received an email about my services. Substantial payment on offer, all on the quiet.'

'Who was it?'

'Anonymous. Untraceable.' She went quiet.

'What services, exactly, Velvet?'

The kettle boiled. She poured water in the pot. 'Patience, sweetie. I'm getting to that.'

This didn't feel right. First she was icy, now warm. And this exchange was taking too long, it felt like she was stalling for time. I scanned the squat for exits. It was too dark to see. 'What did the email say?'

'The time and place for the first meeting with Joe,' she said. 'We met every month at the Talbot farmers' market. The prisoners have a regular stall selling herbs there.'

'Are you a foodie? A gardener?'

She stirred the pot, a slow mingling with a teaspoon, taking her time to answer. 'I can't grow shit.' She laughed. 'The herbs were a way to talk to Joe without drawing suspicion. The orders were code in case the phone was ever found.' She handed me a small ceramic cup. 'Got the phone?'

'It's safe.'

She nodded. 'At your place?'

My face did nothing, but she nodded again. 'Yeah. Who else knows you have it?'

'No one.' Except Loretta.

I sipped the tea, pleasant enough. But Velvet was clearly stalling now, and I didn't like that.

'What services did Joe want? Tell me or I leave. With the money.'

In one easy sweep, she leapt up into the air. I flinched. But she'd grabbed hold of two hoops suspended from the ceiling that I hadn't seen in the dimness and was pulling herself up with her arms. 'Last year, I hacked an ankle bracelet and put the demo online.' She hung upside-down like a bat.

'A home-detention bracelet? Like prisoners wear?'

'Yep. Look it up on YouTube. It's under my internet name: Foxy Meow.'

I tried to memorise the name, repeating it silently to myself. 'How hard is a detention bracelet to hack?'

'Easy,' she said. 'Just put foil over the bracelet and spoof the network.'

'Spoof?'

'Copy the bracelet signal on a laptop. You need software and a transmitter. Super easy. Not expensive, five hundred bucks for the transmitter.' Her laughter was cool and restrained.

To my confusion, I found myself laughing with her. I dimly registered a lift in my mood and a decline in the clarity of my thinking.

'Corrections think their prisoner is at home. Meanwhile, he's roaming free.'

'Joe didn't have an ankle bracelet. Whose ankle bracelet did he want you to hack?'

She dropped to the ground, dragged a crate over, and sat opposite me. 'Not who. What.'

'Sorry, I'm not following.' I was struggling to maintain focus; my mind was becoming murky.

Velvet checked her watch. 'GPS tags. The kind they use on cattle.'

'Cattle?' Again with the cattle. This was getting me nowhere. 'Velvet, tell me, did Joe ever say he was afraid someone might kill him? Did he name anyone?'

She shrugged. 'It doesn't matter if I tell you the whole thing, I suppose. So, the approach email offered me money to meet Joe at the market and to bring a mobile phone for him to communicate with. I had an old android I wasn't using.'

'The dual SIM?'

She smiled. 'Clever. Yes. If you're poor, they're great 'cause you can switch deals ...'

'I know. What happened with Joe?'

'Things went okay first few meetings — but no money. I get pissed off. He goes, "Don't worry, with this scheme, we'll rake in a shitload." He asks me about tags, then asks if I can hack a tag system. It's getting stranger, but okay. I can hack anything. Of course, that system doesn't use phone networks, so it's a lot harder to get in.'

I was feeling sick and wishing she'd get to the point. 'Velvet! What happened to Joe?'

'Wait, I'm getting to that. Then his texting code changed. It's a warning. I meet him for the last time. He wants me to take back the phone, take it to the cops. I say no.

'I'm on the train coming back from Talbot and thinking, *this is fucked*. I send the last text and cancel next month's meeting. Then, out of the blue, on the damn train, this guy approaches me. Big military type. He offers money, up front, for information on what Joe is doing. I get cash, over a grand. I tell him about the phone.'

Suddenly, I slid sideways and fell off the tyre. I couldn't move fast enough to catch myself, landed hard on my side, and rolled onto my back. The envelope of money skittered across the floor. Waves of giddiness and nausea exploded through me.

Without pausing, Velvet continued with her story. 'Few days later the same bloke turns up here, says, "Get back in touch with Joe and say yes. Get the phone for us."'

I was on the floor, staring up at her, aghast. What the hell was this?

'He's standing right here, waiting for me to do it. I get out my phone to text Joe again, say I'll meet him. But then the guy gets a call. It's too late. Joe was dead.'

I'd lost the ability to get up, to stand. My brain spoke to me in short sentences: *Tea, dodgy. Life, risked. Stella, fucked.*

The sound of a car engine came from outside in the alley. Velvet snatched up the envelope with my ten grand in it and shoved it in a desk drawer. She took a roll of tape, pulled out a long strip, and tore it off with her teeth. She came over to me, looked me in the eye, and held up her wrists together in front of her. I followed her example, and she wrapped the tape around my wrists. Pulled more tape and bound my ankles. I stayed on the concrete, unable to lift my head.

'*You shouldn't have come here,*' she whispered into my ear.

Then she dragged open the door. I heard pieces of conversation. A man's voice. I rolled onto my side with the last of my energy. By the look of him, my guess was a divorced personal trainer. Late forties, grey crew cut, fake tan, air of resentment that seemed permanent. Giant biceps and quads flexed out of his shorts and singlet. Military tatts: a sword with wings on one forearm, a Roman helmet on the other.

'She's got Joe's phone,' she said. 'At her place.'

'Brilliant,' he said to Velvet in a faintly British accent. 'Well done.'

'Don't patronise me. I was told to call if anyone used the phone. She did, so I called.'

'Can't a man express his gratitude?'

'I don't want your gratitude. I want to get paid.'

He sighed and walked around me. 'I don't get young women. They're angry all the time. Can't make an innocent joke.'

'I never want to hear from you people again,' Velvet was saying.

'I'm sorry you feel that way. Did she say if she found anything on the phone?'

'The texts.'

'Nothing else?'

'Like what?'

He sniffed. 'Very good.'

'Fine, whatever. Where's my money?'

'Not long now.' He glanced at me. 'Name?'

'Samantha Stevens.'

He snorted. 'And I'm Doctor-fucking-Bombay. Licence on her?'

Velvet opened my handbag and gave him my wallet. He went through my cards. 'Stella Hardy. Social worker.' He sneered at me. 'Big fucking wazzock, more like it.'

'Stella Hardy, you tricked me,' Velvet said, disgusted.

The man laughed. 'You never watched TV in the seventies?'

'I wasn't fucking born.'

'Foxy Meow,' I said.

He looked quizzically at Velvet.

'Quaalude cocktail. So she doesn't give you any trouble.'

'Look at her. Now look at me. Think she'd give me trouble?'

Velvet scowled. 'You're welcome.'

'Can she understand me in her condition?'

She shrugged. 'Sort of.'

'Stella?' He waved a hand in my face. 'Wakey-wakey.'

I was awake. 'Foxy Meow,' I said. Comprehension functional, language not so much.

He pulled out his phone, turned his back. 'I have a positive,' he said in a low voice. Pause. 'Not here.' Pause. 'Bloody social worker.' Pause. 'Yes, Hardy.' Pause. 'No? You sure?' Pause. 'You're the boss.' He put his phone in his pocket and frowned at me. 'Let's go.'

The muscle threw my slack body over his shoulder like a sack of spuds and carried me to a monster vehicle that took up most of the alley — four doors, a tray in the back. He opened the rear door, and

I fell across the back seat. He threw in my handbag, and it landed on the car floor, next to a discarded McDonald's McNuggets package. He reversed out of the alley.

'What do you know about that phone, Hardy?' he said.

I didn't know what to say. 'Text exchange ... Velvet Stone.'

'That's it?'

'What else ...?'

'Lucky for you.' He spoke no more until we stopped twenty minutes later. 'Out you get.'

'Can't.'

He came around and opened the back door. I was on my back like an upended turtle. He pulled a small object from his sock and unfolded a blade. He cut the tape on my ankles, then cut my wrists free. He snapped the blade into its Swiss Army case and tossed it on the floor of the car. My legs stretched. He grabbed a hand and a foot and dragged me from the car. I landed with a thud on the nature strip.

Ascot Vale, Roxburgh Street. The fresh air cleared my head. I had words. 'Fuck you.'

'And that's the thanks I get.'

I struggled upright. Walking was another matter. He supported me up the stairs. At the top, he opened my handbag, and held up my keyring. 'Which one?'

I pointed to my flat key. He unlocked the door, and immediately Nigel started to bark. That beautiful Alaskan Malamute could be a watchdog when he wanted to.

'Tell the dog to shut it, or I'll kick the fucking thing.'

'HiyaNigel,' I whispered. 'Shushup.'

The dog sniffed me and then continued barking.

'Get the phone,' he said.

'Stella? Is that you?' Loretta came out of the bedroom in a pair of my pyjamas.

'Go back to sleep, hon,' I slurred.

'Who is this bloke?'

'Shut the dog up,' the muscle growled.

'Nigel!' Loretta raised a flat palm. Nigel sat and licked her hand.

'Stella, I need you to focus,' the man said. 'Think carefully. Where is Joe's phone?'

I shrugged. He went to the kitchen, looked on the table, started opening drawers.

'What did you do to her?' Loretta demanded. 'I've never seen her this weird.'

'You are?' he demanded.

'Stella's sister-in-law.'

He frowned. 'Right. Go to bed, like Stella told you.'

Loretta planted her feet. 'I'll get you the stupid phone.'

'No, Loretta. I'll get it.' I crawled around, then stopped. 'What am I looking for again?'

'Joe's phone,' he said, exasperated.

Loretta pushed aside a pile of rubbish on the coffee table, picked up a phone. 'Here.'

He held Loretta's mobile with the smashed screen, near my face. 'This it?'

'Yes. Joe's phone. Yes,' said Loretta.

He gave her a long appraising look. 'You know what's on it?'

Nigel watched us like a tennis fan, his head moving from the man to Loretta and back. No teeth, no hackles, but at the ready. If she said 'Kill', I had no doubt he'd go for the man's throat.

'No,' Loretta said. 'Don't care, either. Not interested.'

He seemed relieved. And then, incredibly, he turned and left. I was alive, and he was gone. It seemed a kind of miracle.

The show over, Nigel went to bed. I crawled to the bathroom, pulled myself up to the sink, and splashed water on my face. I was staring at my reflection when I realised the miracle was only temporary. I came back and sat on the coffee table. 'That was your phone,' I said. 'When he realises that, he'll come straight back.'

Loretta threw herself on the sofa, laughing. 'Nope. I swapped the SIMs.'

'What?'

'I told you I needed a phone that worked. So I took out one of the other phone's SIMs and put my SIM in instead — into Joe's phone? — and it works!'

'Um … okay.' Suddenly, I felt extremely tired. I got down on the carpet; I felt more secure lying on the floor.

'One of Joe's SIMs is in my old phone. So they'll definitely think it's Joe's phone. Get it?'

'Yep!' I said. But I didn't really.

'But — like I told you — Joe's phone is a dual SIM. So your guy has a phone that he will think is Joe's, but it's actually mine with one of Joe's SIMs. But you still get to keep his other SIM in his real phone.'

'The one you are using now?'

'Yes. It worked out great, right? I kept the good SIM with all the apps. But to have Joe's phone, that's important to you for some reason, right?'

'Yep!' Was it? Perhaps it was. I'd gone over the first one and found only the texts to Velvet. The second SIM, the one with the apps, had no call or text history. Either way, Loretta had indeed saved my arse — even if it had purely been an act of self-interest to get herself a better phone. Whatever her motives, I didn't care. Hopefully that man, whoever he was, would now leave me alone.

I rolled onto my back, closed my eyes, and tuned her out. I drifted, weightless, not bothered by anything. On and on, I would have gone, drifting forever, if she hadn't been repeating my name. 'What?'

'Who *was* that man?'

'Velvet called him. And she never wants to hear from him again.'

She took that in without question. 'You okay?'

'Never better.'

She took a blanket from the sofa and tucked me in on the floor, put the pillow under my head. 'Night, Stella.'

For the first time in a long time, I was lying down, and yet I wasn't ruminating on my list of fears. Nor was I reliving my worst mistakes and mulling over the fact that each one was a turning point that led to this ludicrous moment. There was no angst at all, only a dull lower-back ache and a pleasant floating sensation. This rare halt in my constant worrying gave me pause. Was it possible to live without constant mental torment? Did people actually live like this, more-or-less content? When was the last time I was carefree? Clearly, I had become accustomed to an extreme level of tension. Perhaps I was not living my best life.

I rolled over as new disturbing thought bubbles rippled my mental waters. For one thing, Velvet Stone had drugged me, taken my money, and brought in a thug to assault me. I had to be more careful.

For another, what the heck was up with everyone's interest in cattle tags these days?

And one more thing: Joe had wanted the cops to have the phone. Why? Maybe he'd got scared, was in over his head and panicked. So what exactly was the crucial thing on it? So far, I'd only found the texts with Velvet that, by themselves, didn't amount to anything. Unless ... unless Joe Phelan had something much more important on the second SIM — the one with no calls and no text history on it. Something that had gotten him killed.

'That's curious,' I said to the carpet. 'Isn't it?'

14

SUNDAY MORNING and I didn't get along. I usually avoided it. I'd moved from the floor to the sofa in the night, and I stayed there under the blanket, even while Loretta made a racket in the kitchen. She'd burned the toast and let the kettle scream. But I stayed put, fingers in my ears. Finally, she took Nigel out, and I went back to sleep.

At midday I walked to Union Road for eggs and coffee, a little unsteady, but not hungover as such. I sat at an outside table at Buffy's with my ugly sunglasses on and a cloak of hostility, warding off any-one who might want a chat — even Lucas, who brought me my food with a cheery remark about the weather. I cut him off. Sunshine was not to be remarked upon. This was Australia, what did he expect? A blizzard?

My mobile vibrated. Kylie. I tried to dismiss the call, but hit the wrong button.

'Stella! Just got your message! Well done on the contract.'

'Oh, right. Sure. Ben was —'

'So you're coming up next weekend?'

'How did you know?'

'Mum. Are we finally going to meet the mysterious Peter Brophy?'

What was she on about? 'Um, I guess.'

'Don't forget to bring the paperwork with you.'

'No, sorry, I plan to leave it behind.'

'But I need that for the —'

'I'm joking.'

'Oh, ha ha! Good one! So, I've been reading about Dexters, did you know they thrive on all kinds of pastures? They're great doers, a real talent for foraging. That'll save us heaps. We're still working out the stocking rates, but the kangaroo numbers have gone up around here, bit of competition so —'

'Sorry, Kylie, got another call. See you next weekend.'

I ended the call and stabbed my yolk.

Full of protein, I ordered another coffee and read the Sunday paper. I skipped the depressing piece about businesses underpaying employees and skimmed a finance article about how the United States Federal Reserve intended to stop feeding free money into their economy. Global apocalypse would follow. Lucas would be thrilled. And he was right, it really was a beautiful day. The wind had eased, providing Melbourne with a rare moment of stillness.

A piece on private prisons caught my attention. It was by Father Rupert Baig, a Catholic priest and former prison chaplain. Certain private operators were so concerned with profits, he said, that they might put financial concerns ahead of their contractual obligations and the interests of citizens.

My coffee was cold when I sat back to think, observing my fellow citizens going about their business. Did they care about the welfare of prisoners? Or the impending economic collapse? Or the under-payment of overworked employees at the local convenience store? I liked to think that they did. Most of them. Some of them. I was a starry-eyed loon.

Back at the flat, I opened my laptop and wrote to Fr Baig, whose email address was printed at the end of the article. I mentioned my brother, Joe Phelan's mother, and asked if he would have time to help me understand the issues in his essay.

I googled BS12. Worldwide, they operated a lot of prisons. The company also provided security services. And they faced criminal charges in the UK over a failure to meet its contractual requirements at several events. Meanwhile, their website boasted:

With employees numbering over 60,000, our international operation spans four continents: Europe, North America, Asia, and Australia and provides services in the sectors of private security, immigration, transport, and civic services. At BS12 our motto is, essential public services? It's all BS!

From further reading, it would appear that BS12 was so poorly managed it was barely functional. The company also gave large donations to both major Australian political parties. Of course, that was mandatory when bidding for million-dollar contracts in this country. *Track record? Who cares, they gave us money.* No wonder they flourished here.

I left the laptop and picked up the dual-SIM phone that Loretta now thought of as hers. I tried to access the second SIM. The trick eluded me. I'd have to wait for Loretta to return and show me.

A ding on my phone.

Brash: *G'day Hardy! News? Time's a-wasting! One week to go.*

I replied: *I've made a good start. Your texting is unnecessary.*

Ha ha. Get going!

Another ding, this time my laptop. Father Baig had replied. He was at a conference in Auckland. But he could meet me on Wednesday evening after work, if that suited.

I said it would. And I mentally took back every mean thing I'd ever said about priests, nuns, the Pope, the Vatican, Opus Dei, the Catholic Church, and Christianity in general.

Instead of hanging around the flat waiting for Loretta, I went to the supermarket. I intended to make a curry for dinner tomorrow night. Brophy was coming, so it had to be special. At the checkout, I saw some cheap smartphones with a decent prepay deal. I bought one, plus an extra SIM card, and headed home.

When I got in, the TV was on, but Loretta was on Joe's mobile, crossed-legged on the sofa with Nigel.

'How's it all going in there?'

She patted her belly. 'Grouse. He's moving around all the time.'

'He?'

'Yeah. I reckon.' She noticed the bags. 'What's all that?'

'I'm cooking a veggie curry.'

She looked genuinely horrified. 'What about pizza again? I don't mind. For tonight, too — order one extra, and have leftovers tomorrow.'

On the matter of home-cooked curry, I would not be moved. She'd want to eat it when she inhaled the aromas. 'It's for tomorrow. I can't serve Brophy leftovers.'

She sat up. 'Who's Brophy?'

'My boyfriend. You've met him. Remember? The other night when you came home late.'

She slumped back down. 'Oh. That guy.'

I unpacked the groceries.

After a moment, she said, 'You feeling better, Stella? You were off your nut last night.'

'It was nothing. Must've eaten something that didn't agree with me. I'm fine.'

She was dubious. 'But who was that horrible man? Bastard was going to kick Nigel.'

I ignored the question and pulled out the mobile, still in its box. 'Hey, Loretta, I bought you a phone.'

'Oh my God.' She stared in disbelief, tears on her face. 'Thank you so, so, so much.'

Her gratitude made me uncomfortable. 'It's nothing, a cheapie. Don't mention it.'

'Stella, you're amazing.' She leapt up and gave me one of her bone-breaking hugs.

'No. I'm really not.' I patted her on the back. 'I wonder if you could change the SIM to your new phone now? I'd like to take a look at the other phone.'

She prised her SIM out of Joe's phone. Then she ripped open the box and inserted her old SIM in her new phone. 'Here you go.' She gave me the dual-SIM phone. I had Joe's second SIM. It would give up its secrets. The other part of my plan was to put a new clean SIM in it and use it when necessary to make untraceable calls. Loretta watched me try to insert the SIM without success. She took it from me and immediately slotted in the plastic bit of card.

'Show me again how to swap between SIMs.'

'You just go ...' She performed a rapid demonstration, which I failed to follow. She repeated the steps slowly. 'Go to *Settings*, tap *Connections*, tap *SIM Card Manager*, in general settings tap *Other SIM*. Select *On* and you're good.'

Then she took her new phone to the bedroom, which she called 'my room', and closed the door. Nigel went to his corner, turned in a small circle, and settled down to sleep.

I practised changing SIMs until I had the hang of it. Then I opened every app on Joe's second SIM, and began searching for anything unusual. The tradie apps had zero. The notes app was unused. The voice recorder opened with a red blink: *ready*. Two items in the app menu. *Home* and *History*. In the history was a fifty-four-second recording. I hit *Play*.

There was a hiss, then a man's voice, faint, distant. His tone of voice was plaintive:

In the blink of an eye, he got away ... I tear up now just thinking about it ... The thing was out of control. Bids going up and up ... It kicked alright, the market I mean. He was a stunner, too. Heavily muscled. Sky was antsy ... All of a sudden, it got away. Bids over the three hundred and I just, I panicked. Vincent got away. I said, 'Don't worry, love. I'll talk to Al.'

I sat back, stunned. Was *that* such a big deal? A whinge about missing out on a 'Vincent' at auction. What was so earth-shattering about that? What was on it that needed to be suppressed? The names of the people? Al and Vincent. Not much to go on. The identity of the speaker, maybe? The voice was faint and a bit distorted. I turned up the volume and replayed it a few times. Something familiar about the tone. I replayed it again. Yes. It was the plummy screed of Marcus Pugh.

15

'AND THAT'S finance.'

I aimed the remote at the TV and killed the Monday night news before it concluded. Sport was not essential, and the weather was no mystery. Any nong with a window knew it was nice out. Why stay for the finance? Because I'd been trying to educate myself on commodities and dollar fluctuations. I was in possession of a small fortune and was in want of a plan. Nibbles of miscellaneous expenditure had reduced the fund marginally, but there was still roughly four hundred thousand dollars in storage, and I needed to be sensible with it.

Loretta sat in her usual spot on the couch with Nigel, scrolling on her phone with earbuds in. She was valiantly tolerating my TV preferences and had even promised to *try* a vegetable. With the caveat that she could make herself cheese on toast if she determined my cooking inedible.

Earlier, at work, I'd been speaking to my colleague Shaninder. She'd asked after my sister-in-law, as Loretta had called herself when arriving at WORMS. I'd said, 'Who knows?'

At that, Shaninder had frowned. There were not many people whose good opinion I sought. Much of the time, I had no hoots to give. But this hardworking mother of three had a moral authority found elsewhere only in Toni Morrison and the Dalai Lama. Chastened, I'd said, 'I've given her my bed, I ask how she is, she says she's fine. I have no reason to —'

'What about the scans?'

'Scans?'

'Ultrasound, Stella. How is that baby developing?'

I thought of Loretta as an extension of Ben, and therefore, as a pain in the arse. But she was a vulnerable young woman, and there were potential risks around pregnancy that I had failed to consider. I was ignorant of the routine health checks. Scans were routine, apparently.

While I was cooking, I gestured to Loretta to take out the earbuds. When she complied, I started chopping and casually said, 'Had any scans?'

'Of this?' she pointed to her belly.

'The baby, yes.'

'Nah, it's all good.' To my sceptical look she added, 'I can just tell.'

'Do you have a doctor?'

'Nah, don't need one.'

The girl had been homeless, her worldly possessions amounted to a shopping trolley. 'Do you have a Medicare card?'

Her eyes narrowed. 'What's this about?'

'It's about you and your baby and giving birth, and both of you being around afterwards.'

A little dramatic, sure. But it worked.

'How do I get one?'

I didn't know, but I assumed it required several types of ID, something she might not have. On my laptop, we slogged our way through government websites trying to figure out how to replace a lost Medicare card and succeeded in getting the system to identify Loretta. This alone was a triumph. She was indeed Loretta Patsy Dolly Swindon. Twenty years of age. Australian citizen. And therefore entitled to benefits of our universal health care system.

I made rice in the microwave and set the table. When the curry was simmering on the stove, I went to shower and change. With my bedroom to myself at last I reverted to habit: uncomfortable work clothes were put away on the floordrobe. The benefits of the floordrobe were many. You could see at a glance what was there, what was creased, what was covered in sour cream from a losing battle with an aggressive serving of nachos. I reclaimed a skirt and t-shirt and brushed my hair, my damned incriminating hair. I should shave it all off, Phuong would never find a match then.

I put the TV on again, ready to flick around to something more to Loretta's taste — World's Greatest Farts or something. The ABC had an in-depth special on the upcoming state election. Pugh faced a plethora of microphones and repeated his 'do the crime, do the time' law-and-order line. A journalist in front of state parliament said, somewhat wearily, that both sides were saying the other side's promises weren't costed. I would have turned it off, but the next piece started with a graphic of prison bars. I stayed tuned.

A journalist walked through a stark prison common room. 'This is Victoria's newest prison. Soon, Grainger Prison will be home to a thousand inmates. For the medium-security jail's official opening, the Minister for Justice went behind prison walls.'

Cut to Pugh inside a cell. 'This is a very exciting moment for Victorians. From now on, the prison system in this state will be managed more effectively.'

Journalist voiceover: 'Inmates will be housed in single cells or multi-bed dormitories. Remand prisoners will be segregated from those serving sentences, and the building features new technology designed to prevent any costly prison riots.'

Pugh: 'We have a state-of-the-art biometric system, pioneered by BS12, so prisoners can't move around the facility unless authorised to do so. This is part of our expanded partnership with BS12.'

Journalist to camera: 'In a first for this state, the consortium running the prison could be paid millions of dollars in bonuses if the recidivism rate for released prisoners is fifteen per cent lower than the current rate in other jails. But prisoner advocacy groups have warned that, even with this new facility, the state's prisons will be at capacity in a matter of a few years.'

Cut to Meredith Phelan: 'This new prison will be as over-crowded as many others in this state. The government can relieve the pressure of over-crowding today by removing children from jail. The justice system is failing our children. We call for the immediate release from custody of children on drug-related offences. They need support and rehabilitation.'

Pugh: 'We are aware of the capacity constraints, and this government has already commissioned a report on the matter. Everything is on the table, including home-detention bracelets. And we intend to fully implement the recommendations.'

Journalist: 'Whoever wins the election, prisoners will be in Grainger Prison by the end of the year.'

Brophy arrived with a kiss, a bottle of wine, and a box of cannoli from Footscray. He looked wild, like a nineties feral, gaunt and unshaven.

'Not feeling any better?'

'Tired. Working nights. I'm fine.'

That didn't ring true. Nights for a night owl like Brophy were his best hours. The productive sweet spot between midnight and dawn, when the world was silent-ish. Hours that were uninterruptable, with clear space to follow through on an idea. Maybe his work at the market was more physically demanding than I'd realised. I let it go.

Brophy, Loretta, and I ate at my kitchen table, like a functional family. Unfortunately, I'd misread the recipe. There was too much chilli, and the curry was off the end of the Scoville scale. We piled on the yoghurt to take the heat down, but it was pretty much inedible. Brophy made appreciative noises. Loretta ate the rice, scoffed the cannoli, and went to bed.

Brophy and I did the dishes and binged on Scandinavian murder, until midnight when he got ready to go to work. He sniffed and honked into a disgusting handkerchief.

'Call in sick,' I said holding him around his skinny waist.

He rolled his eyes. 'Can't afford to.'

Again, I had an impression that he was not being completely straight with me. Where was his money going? He seemed as broke as ever. I hated to doubt him. I'd been wrong about him before, suspected his fidelity, and it didn't feel very good. This was the lovely, loyal Brophy — a man who loved me and took care of his daughter and lived for his art. There wasn't much else to it. He wasn't a showy type who blew money. It was probably mounting up in a secret account for a rainy day.

I pushed the doubts away and returned to the recording of Marcus Pugh. It was an anecdote of failure. Only Pugh could make failure sound like a brag. Code words and all.

Don't worry, love. I'll talk to Al. Name-dropping and crowing about influence.

… Sky was getting antsy. A koan to cause a Zen master's head to explode.

Brash hadn't texted me today, but he didn't need to any more. As I went to bed, I mentally ticked off another day without getting any closer to finding who had killed Joe Phelan.

16

I TOOK Tuesday afternoon off, with Fatima's blessing, and Loretta and I took the tram to the Royal Women's hospital for her first appointment with a doctor.

We were seen within the hour. The doctor pressed her hands on Loretta's belly, took her blood pressure, and took various samples for other tests. Loretta was slightly underweight, but otherwise healthy. Due to the late stage of this first contact with a health professional, we were given an 'urgent' status for immediate ultrasound. There'd been a cancellation, so we went straight up. That led to another hour in another waiting room. Loretta and I were the last people left. I flipped through a two-year-old *Hello* and jotted down recipes from a *New Idea*. She was glued to her phone.

A squirt of lube on her belly and a wave of the magic scanning device, and presto, a foetus popped up on the screen. A baby girl, growing normally, heart beating rapid and strong. Tears streamed from my eyes, I'd never seen anything so remarkable. Perhaps I was tired, or the events of the last few days were weighing on me, because a loud sob escaped. Loretta patted my shoulder and smiled. I admired the tough little elf.

Now that Loretta was considered a patient of the hospital, we were encouraged to attend antenatal classes and take the tour of the maternity wards. We both knew it was more likely that the birth would happen in a hospital near Woolburn, probably Mildura Base Hospital. But at least she was in the system, and the health of mother and child was established. Arranging the right hospital was a bridge we could jump off when we came to it.

We celebrated with tea and cake in the hospital café. On the tram journey home, she thanked me.

'Don't mention it.' My emotions were back in check.

'Ben told me you were caring. You act like you don't care, but really you do.'

'Of course I do. I'm going to take care of you until you're safely in Woolburn, and then my mother will care for you.'

'What's she like?'

'Delia?' An irascible, hyper-critical, conservative non-sufferer of fools or anyone not bestowed with a punishing work ethic. 'Oh, you'll love her, she's a warm-hearted, generous, sweet old lady.' One word of truth in there: old.

As Tuesday came to an end, I fell asleep on the sofa, pleased that Loretta was having proper prenatal care. I also noted with some relief that, once again, I had not heard from Brash all day. But I didn't need a text to know that, having made zero progress on Joe Phelan's murder, I was one day closer to mush.

After work on Wednesday, I came out of the office, got in the Mazda, and drove east. A moronic idea at that time of day. The congestion seemed to send some drivers mad, resulting in deranged lane-hopping. Peak hour was a test of character, and unless swearing and murderous rage was considered good character, I failed. Dripping with sweat, I continued down the Maroondah Highway, suburb after suburb, until the urge to kill someone became overwhelming.

Over the next hill, I saw the problem, roadworks, with one lane closed. I was in for a long evening. I cracked a window. The stop-starting and the stale air in the car combined made me woozy.

I fell into ruminating on what Velvet Stone had told me. I'd gone over it and over it, and hadn't gotten anywhere. Someone anonymous had sent Velvet that first email, the one setting up the meeting with

Joe. That person had seen her YouTube demonstration on the ease of detention-bracelet hacking. They'd probably searched for *hacking*. They wanted to know about how to hack cattle tags. That was the reason for the phone, the meetings. But something had changed when Joe managed to record Pugh. Suddenly he wanted Velvet to go to the cops. He knew he was in danger. Would the Pugh recording save him?

Maybe he'd told Velvet why the recording was so important. She was still my only lead. She'd given me a few morsels, but she knew plenty more. Plus, she'd set me up, drugged my tea, and called in some muscle — muscle she never wanted to see again. She owed me. I decided that after my meeting with the priest, I'd give Ms Stone a tingle on the blower and demand the full story. Threaten to go to the cops if she didn't deliver. An empty threat, but it might work.

A stern voice was telling me to turn left. I'd forgotten I'd set a course with the GPS. What a blessing and a curse these things were. Tracking, watching, and recording. Always watching. Remembering my every move, my steps, my thought patterns.

I entered the sweeping circular drive of the Villa St Joseph. Elderly Catholic priests, those who were not in jail, retired to church-run nursing homes like Villa St Joseph.

A senior nun led me to a sunny veranda with a view of a green lawn. Some distance away, a woman in green overalls was pruning a rose bush. Further along, a row of priests were enjoying an early dinner, scooting their plastic chairs up to small metallic tables. The nun pointed out Father Baig. His dinner had just arrived on a tray. A plate of lamb chops, gravy, and steamed vegetables next to a large glass of red. Not bad, Catholics, not bad.

He wore no glasses and squinted at me. 'Who are you?'

'Stella Hardy. We had a meeting. Sorry I'm late, the traffic …'

'Ah, you wrote to me about that article.' He smiled and pointed to a spare chair with a trembling hand. 'Excuse my eating in front of you, Stella. We dine early here,' he said.

I pulled up the chair and sat. The nun returned with a mug of strong Earl Grey with milk. One sip and I felt a lot better.

'Where is your brother incarcerated?'

'Athol Goldwater. Minimum security. Fresh air. Could be worse.'

'Could be worse?' the priest mused. 'Run by that BS crowd, mug contractors.'

'How bad are they?'

'Public has problems, but private … all the same. Unmitigated disaster. Here and overseas.' The priest chewed rapidly. 'Private consortiums scout the globe for opportunities. When a state has problems with their prison system, they offer fast, temporary solutions.'

'Problems like what? Overcrowding?'

'Everything: drug taking, deaths, behaviour control, high recidivism. Governments of both stripes say, "Ooh, isn't this marvellous."' He clapped his hands. 'They come to depend on these smooth-talking private setups.'

I sipped the milky tea. 'Makes their jobs easier.'

'*Much* easier. And that means governments aren't motivated to monitor them properly, let alone address the causes of overcrowding or crime or social issues —'

His criticism had the effect of pushing me to the centre. I felt a weird urge to defend the government. Crazy. 'But surely some people in government still develop policies —'

'Social policy? No votes in it. Election rhetoric is all about punishment and cruelty.'

I ventured a contrary view. 'But the fair-go thing. Australians aren't that harsh.'

'Rose-coloured nonsense. Australians abhor what they see as handouts. And punishment is part of our national identity. Goes back to the early days — vicious penalties dished out in the colonies for the slightest infraction. That continues right through to Aboriginal deaths in custody, asylum seekers, child incarceration, mandatory sentences. Harsher the better.'

I began to feel ill again, and drank some tea.

'In any case, these companies are the direct cause of excessive pressures on the prison system. A private prison operator in the US lobbied for greater prison sentences, mandatory sentences, successfully increasing incarcerations rates. They told their shareholders they had every reason to be,' he made quote fingers, '"optimistic about the future".'

'Yeah, but that's America. Here they can't get away with —'

'They're experts in aggressive marketing and lobbying. They donate, schmooze, flatter.'

'Flatter?'

A solemn nod.

How would one flatter Pugh? *Nice watch? I like your tie?*

He wasn't finished, not by a long chalk. 'If you invested money in incarceration, would you allow a government to develop programs to address poverty?'

The question caught me off-guard. My investment plans were private. 'Me? Certainly not. I mean, I wouldn't invest in jails. There are ethical investments funds, aren't there?'

A pause at last. He laid down his cutlery and sipped his wine.

'What about the counter-pressure from advocacy groups?' I said, thinking of Meredith.

'Private operators are the greatest obstacle to policies of justice and fairness. Prison-reform advocates know this.'

I wondered if Meredith blamed BS12 or Pugh for the policies that kept kids in jail.

He sipped his wine. 'Oh, strategies do exist to neutralise their influence.'

'Such as?' Against all expectations, I liked this commie priest.

'You can highlight their utter mismanagement and their financial scandals.'

'What scandals?'

'A classic was the company that charged the UK government for a long list of prisoners wearing their detention tags. Problem was, some of the prisoners on the list were dead.'

I nearly sprayed him with tea.

'Oh yes, this mob, the UK arm of BS12, they've been caught in more financial scandals than Bernie Madoff. Debts, mismanagement. A contract for prisoner escort services was rorted to the tune of two million pounds. Prisoners were said to have been delivered, but were not. A cursory glance at online newspaper articles would tell you these things.'

Would the government of this state do that? Look into BS12 and assess their competence as a contractor? Perform basic due diligence? Evidently they had not.

'Justice cannot be privatised, it simply doesn't work.'

I agreed with him and took my leave.

'Good luck,' Father Baig said.

With what, I didn't ask.

Traffic flowed freely as I headed towards the city, blinded by a fiery sunset. There was plenty to be concerned about with BS12. But was it as bad at Athol Goldwater as Father Baig had implied? They were open about their work with cattle tags. It made sense to use the prison farm facility for research. But what of the recording? Velvet Stone and the hacking? Something was definitely up with that. Plan: call Velvet as soon as I got home.

I switched on the radio to listen to the news.

A woman has died of suspected gunshot wounds following an incident at Dights Falls in Melbourne's north. Homicide squad detectives are investigating after Victoria Police were called to the area just after two p.m. A member of the public, who did not want to be named, said she heard the woman scream.

An ambulance spokesman said CPR was in progress on arrival, but ambulance officers soon declared the woman dead. Local residents first on the scene have told the ABC the woman had a number of tattoos, including distinctive vines on both arms, and cropped hair. Police forensic officers collected evidence throughout the morning. A section of the area remains closed to the public while police continue their investigations.

New plan: drive straight to Velvet Stone's squat.

17

A PARKING bay in the centre of Queen Street had twenty minutes left on the meter. I topped it up with a gold coin and ran up Lonsdale Street to Velvet Stone's laneway. The padlock was missing, and the door gave little resistance to my shove. The place was in darkness except for the light from the monitors.

'Who's there?' A woman's voice from the recesses of the squat.

'A friend of Velvet's.'

She came into the light. Young, tattoos, dreadlocks. 'The new girlfriend?' she asked.

'Just a friend.'

She sniffed. 'I'm taking custody of Gnawer Barnacle. She's my rat really.'

'Good for you.' I went to Velvet's desk and shone my phone into the top drawer.

'Don't do that.'

I ignored her. 'Where's Velvet?'

'She left with some bloke.'

The envelope was there. I slipped it into my handbag. 'What did he look like?'

'Dunno. I was crawling in the back there, looking for Gnawer.'

'Did he say anything?'

'He said for her to come with him and he'd drop her back in half an hour. I've been waiting around here all day, but she hasn't come back.' She thought for a moment. 'Very weird for Velvet to go with some guy, just because he asked her to. Why would she do that?'

I had an idea. 'What did he sound like?'

'*There* you are, Gnawer.' The rat ran up her arm. She fed it a piece of cracker.

'Hey!' I yelled. 'This is important. Did he have an accent?'

'Yeah. Like on the *EastEnders*. You know that show?'

'I was never here,' I said and staggered away, backwards, retracing my steps. I was in shock, but also aware that this, too, was now a crime scene, and my hair had a tendency to shed.

I wandered down Swanston Street, looking over my shoulder, into the milling Wednesday-night crowds. Students, office workers, throngs of young men and women ready for a night on the tiles. I saw a bar and went in. It was dark, with upholstered chairs and fringed lampshades. I ordered a plum Giddy Aunt from a pink-haired woman in a blue wife-beater and Warner Bros. cartoon tatts. I took it to a table in the darkest corner. From there, like a bird of prey, I fixed my gaze on the entrance. A short man with a handlebar moustache in a leather hoodie came in, ordered a beer, and drank it at the bar. I watched him with increasing paranoia. His friend with a Ned Kelly beard showed up, and they embraced. Phew. Next, three middle-aged women entered, one bought a jug of something, another took three glasses, and they repaired to a booth by the window, the impression of habit in every gesture. They were only concerned with themselves. At last, I exhaled. My heartbeat slowed. I consumed the cocktail in two swallows and signalled to the bar for another.

I got out my phone and started to check media sites for news of Velvet. When it rang in my hand, I nearly had a fit. Kylie again, and again, stupidly, I answered.

'Stella! That was quick! How are you?'

'Great.'

'Just wanted to let you know the good news.'

Oh merciful goddess, good news at last. 'What's happened?'

'Live cattle exports are up twenty-two per cent on last year.'

Until now, I hadn't made the connection. Kylie intended to join in the horror of the live cattle export. Beef cattle was one thing, but herding frightened cattle onto a ship was quite another. At their destination, depending on the abattoir, they could expect, among other possibilities, to be bludgeoned to death with a sledgehammer. It was barbaric. And I had helped her.

'Asian demand. That's the key. Boosted the total value to one point two billion.'

'Awesome.'

'I did the maths — number of cattle against the value. Guess what? That's around a thousand dollars for each cow.'

My second Giddy Aunt was taking too long. '*Per head*, not "each cow". And I'm not sure that's how —'

'Just think what we stand to make here! Once their weight is up —'

'Terrific. Listen, Kylie, I have to go, my toast just popped.'

I put my empty glass on the bar in front of the pink-haired bartender. 'Another, please.'

'Is that what you wanted? I thought you were telling me to turn the music up.'

'Oh, come on! Has anyone *ever* asked you to turn the music up?'

'No.' She put a scoop of ice in a large wine glass, added one part plum schnapps, one part plum brandy, a splash of champagne, garnished with a red plum segment on a toothpick.

I gave her a lobster for the cocktail.

'Are you okay, sweetie?'

The kindness undid me. Tears escaped. 'I'm fine,' I whispered and fled to the darkness.

I sipped my drink and tried to think. They wanted the phone. They had the phone. No, only half a phone. One SIM of a dual-SIM phone. They knew something else was on it — the recording of Pugh. The thug had asked Loretta and I if we knew what was on it. Velvet didn't know about that, she didn't know the recording existed. They killed her because she knew one small fact, that they wanted the phone. *They. They* killed Joe, and *they* killed Velvet.

I rang Loretta, terrified she'd be wandering the streets instead of where I needed her to be, vigilantly checking the street for violent men.

'Mate, where are ya? Been waiting here all day. I'm starving.'

'Thank God you're at home. Listen, can you do me a favour? Check the street — don't go out, do it from the window — and see if that bloke from the other night is waiting around. He might be in a car, one of those four cab things, like a ute but bigger.'

A pause. 'Yep. There's a car like that out the front. Want me to check if it's him?'

'No. Just wait there, Loretta, while I think of something. I'll call you back.'

I put down the phone and twirled my plum. What to do? I had an idea. No, it was crazy. But I was desperate. I picked up my phone and rang the only person I knew could help.

After a short conversation I ran to my car and drove to Ascot Vale in a gear-grinding, lane-swapping frenzy. A few streets from home, I turned, went up to Mount Alexander Road, and came down Roxburgh Street from the east. I parked on a hill about a block from Pine View.

I checked my phone and waited. At nine o'clock I rang triple zero on Joe's phone, and told the operator that a man had collapsed outside my building. She put me through to the ambos. I fibbed to them at length about a person on the nature strip, suffering from severe chest pains, must be a possible heart attack. 'Oh no,' I said. 'He's stopped breathing!'

Then I got out and walked down towards my building. The monster ute was there. The same one he'd driven from Velvet Stone's squat. Inside it, someone lit a cigarette.

I walked up to the driver's window and knocked. 'Looking for me?'

Startled, but pretending not to be, he lowered the window and flicked the smoke into the darkness. He took an object from the centre console, raised it to the window for me to see. A handgun. 'Where's the phone?'

'I gave it to you.'

'I don't think you did. Not all of it, the rest of it, whatever.'

I shrugged.

'It's been a long day,' he sighed. 'Go get the fucking phone.'

'I'm afraid,' I said. 'After I do, you'll kill me. You killed Velvet Stone today, didn't you?'

'I won't hurt *you*. I had the chance, and I didn't. Doesn't that tell you something?'

I hesitated. He glanced down the street. I turned to look. Quick as lightning, his hand darted out the window, wrapped around my neck, and pulled me in towards him in a headlock, lifting me almost off the ground. With his other hand, he pressed the gun hard against my cheek.

'Okay,' I said, through gritted teeth. 'The rest of it is upstairs, in a safe place.'

He released me. 'Wait there. I'm coming with you.'

Movement in my peripheral vision, a shadow crossed the lawn in front of my building. I walked slowly around the car, then sprinted up the path to my building. He sprang from the car and sprinted after me. I was nearly at the door to the foyer. His hand caught a piece of my shirt, and I was yanked back. I heard a rip. 'Hurry up!' I yelled.

From behind the Norfolk pine, Percy Brash stepped out and nonchalantly connected a taser to the man's neck. The man grunted in pain and shock, but was immobile, till Brash stopped the charge — then his legs gave way and he dropped. Brash bent, pried the handgun from his fingers, and said in his ear. 'Stay put, mate, or the next one goes into your balls.'

Sirens, beautiful deafening sirens. A long woooo and some short wah wah wahs came up from Union Road.

Brash and I ran up the street to my car. 'Took your time,' I said. 'Nearly died back there.'

He ignored me. Blue and red lights strobing, the ambulance flew up Roxburgh Street and parked in the Pine View driveway. Two people in uniform ran up the path. Brash pulled out a small tin and shook a mint into his hand. We watched the ambos take a gurney from the back of the ambulance.

'Been busy, Hardy. That's good. If the SAS come for you, you're on the right track.'

'SAS?'

'He had the tatt — sword and wings. That's SAS.'

'Shop and save?'

'Special Air Service. He's British army. Very tough. Trained killers.'

I thought of BlackTack, an organisation comprised of ex-army intelligence operatives, ready to solve your business challenges. Maybe they employed some ex-SAS guns-for-hire, too. 'That means —'

'That's serious. Means you've upset them. Give me a full report.'

I told him that I'd found Joe's phone, and it had two SIM cards, one of which led me to Velvet Stone. That a meeting had been set up with Velvet and Joe at the market to discuss hacking cattle tags.

'Who set up the meeting?'

'To be honest, I thought it was you.'

Brash shook his head, frowning. 'Go on.'

I said that I'd made contact with Velvet, and when I'd gone to see her, she'd told me that Joe had suddenly changed the plan and had asked her to take his phone to the cops. And when Velvet reached that part, that was when the SAS guy had turned up. He'd taken me home, and then Loretta, my lodger, had handed him a phone with only one of Joe's SIMs, the one with text messages to Velvet.

'He let you live after you gave him the phone?'

I nodded. 'I'm as flummoxed as you are.'

'No one is flummoxed, Hardy. Go on.'

I said after that I'd checked the other SIM and found a recording of Marcus Pugh talking about an auction and Vincent and someone named Al. *That*, I presumed, was what Joe had wanted the cops to have, and that was what the SAS guy had really wanted.

Brash chewed his mint. 'Interesting.'

Lastly, I told him that the SAS guy he'd just tasered had — I suspected — murdered Velvet. And that was everything, save some irrelevant details, like Gnawer Barnacle. He didn't need to know about the pet rat.

'You've exceeded my expectations, I'll tell you that much.'

'What'd you expect?'

'Dunno. That you'd get yourself killed or something.'

'Happy to disappoint you.'

'Yeah, you're in deep. Got a good sniff of the bastards.'

We were silent for a moment. 'Where'd you get the taser?'

'Mate gave it to me.'

'Can I see it?'

A yellow, hard-plastic gun-like thing came out of his jacket pocket. It reminded me of a kid's toy or a starting pistol. 'Got two shots. Or you can arc the current with this button.' He demonstrated, and a blue electric charge crackled across the points. 'Sometimes that's enough to get cooperation, just show them the arc.'

My shoulders did an involuntary shudder.

'Keep going, mate,' Brash said. 'You're a good little worker.'

It was the only praise I'd had for a while, and I enjoyed a warm inner glow. Sometimes a person needed a boost. Too bad it was patronising, and came from a murderous bogan thug.

'The recording is why they killed Joe,' I said.

'I daresay you're right. That's the *why*. Now give me the *who* — the *exact* who.'

I nodded. Here I was, discussing a possible hit with a member of an organised crime gang. Former, current, it didn't matter. It was a new low for me.

'They'll come at you again, Hardy. They want that phone back, so stay alert. And hold onto it tight — it must be fucking important.'

'Right.'

He jumped out, paused, and came back. 'Here, you might as well have this.' He threw the taser in the window, and it landed on my lap. 'Carry on. Time's running out, Hardy.'

He sauntered up the road in a confident, unhurried way and disappeared into the darkness.

18

I DROVE down the hill, parked the Mazda behind the monster ute, and took a photo of the number plate. The paramedics had the SAS guy on the gurney. He was conscious and belligerent, but weak, taking sloppy punches at them. They restrained him with straps, packed him away into the back, and made a quiet exit.

A crowd of neighbours milled about on the footpath like Brown's cows. These were good people, who liked a chat, but were usually too busy to stop and talk. The arrival of an ambulance was the perfect opportunity to stand in the street and discuss important local matters. A recent house sale, what was paid, what they'd done to the bathroom. What was not being done about speeding drivers, cracked footpaths, tardy rubbish collection. I acted calm, smiled at some of them, and using slow movements locked the car door with the key. Someone waved. I waved back, but kept going, slipping into the foyer and taking the stairs two at a time.

Loretta came away from the window as I entered.

'Electric shocked him! Sick!'

'Grab Nigel, get your stuff. We're going to Woolburn. My car's out the front.'

Without hesitation, she opened the tartan case and started to stuff dog toys into it. A seasoned practitioner of the midnight flit. In the bedroom, I fed clothes into my wheeled case. I grabbed the folder with Kylie's papers in it and shoved that in as well. We bumped into each other in the bathroom as we scrambled around.

Minutes later, the dog, the girl, and I flew down the three flights and ran to the car. I popped the Mazda's boot, threw in my suitcase, and then I unlocked the front passenger door and the dog leapt in. I shoved him between the seats and into the back. Loretta dumped the trolley in the boot, slammed it shut, and jumped in. I chucked a screaming U-ey, drove like a hoon through the backstreets, then turned onto Mount Alexander Road, then the freeway, then the Calder.

It was twenty minutes before one of us spoke. Then I grabbed my phone. 'Here,' I gave it to Loretta. 'Ring Brophy.'

She found the number and called. 'Hi, this is Loretta, Stella's sister-in-law.'

I emitted an audible breath, but didn't correct her.

'She says to tell you there's been a change of plan. We're on our way to Woolburn. Like, right now.'

I could hear his voice, but not the words. He sounded confused rather than disappointed.

'He wants to know why.'

'Tell him it was unavoidable, and I'll explain later.'

I waited. 'What did he say?'

'He said, "Fine, okay, see you when you get back."'

The thought of days at the farm with a bunch of Hardys and future Hardys and no Brophy was almost too much for me. 'Tell him to drive up with Marigold on Saturday as planned.'

'Who's Marigold?'

'Tell him!'

She told him, and she listened. Then she relayed. 'Drive up in what?'

'In the van,' I shouted, so she didn't have to repeat it. Brophy's beaten, rusted, barely roadworthy ex-telco van still functioned. Surely that would do?

She listened. He spoke for a long time.

'Okay,' Loretta said and ended the call.

'Well?'

'He said he'll see.'

He'll see? That meant no. Instead of quality time with Brophy, I could look forward to junk time with stupid. The one thing, the *only* fucking thing I wanted, was slipping from my grasp. In lieu of leisure and love, I had a pile of steaming cow poo.

We travelled in unfriendly silence, me with my head in a dark cloud of resentment, Loretta staring ahead with who knew what wheels turning in her elfin noggin.

We were two hours out of Melbourne on the Western Highway. Nigel was in the back, nose poking through a narrow window gap, happily cataloguing all manner of airborne odours. And I was ruminating on why an SAS soldier wanted to kill me. If he *was* connected to BlackTack to whom Enrique Nunzio had paid a hundred and fifty thousand dollars for 'services', then why was he working to recover Joe's phone? What did Nunzio care about Marcus Pugh and that recording? It did not fucking add up.

It was Nunzio I should have been focussed on, not Velvet Stone. I should have gone back into that tech shed for a proper look. Damn, I regretted deleting the photos I'd taken of the invoices. And of something else ... Oh my God, yes! I hit the steering wheel and cursed. Loretta glanced up, but said nothing. The email on Nunzio's screen in the shed — it had been from an 'Al' someone. *Al!* Could that be Pugh's Al — 'I'll talk to Al' — the one who was going to fix everything for him? I was willing to bet the whole fund that it was. Al who, though? I couldn't remember the surname. There was nothing I could do about it now, in the middle of driving Loretta to Woolburn. Not to mention, time was running out with Brash, and it wouldn't be long before that thug came looking for me again.

Loretta suddenly broke our long semi-hostile silence. 'I have a right to know what's going on.'

She had a point.

'Truth is, Loretta, even I don't know exactly what's going on.'

'You know *something*.'

Again, that was a valid argument. I gave up. She already knew too much, and she was bright and tech-savvy — maybe she could help me. And, as she said, given her life had been at risk and I was now hooning her up to Woolburn a week early, she had a right to know.

'Joe Phelan, a prisoner at Athol Goldwater where Ben is, was found dead two weeks ago. It was a suspect way to die, but it's being treated as an accident by both the department and the private prison operator. I'm helping the family look into it.'

'Why are you helping them?'

'Let's say, I'm obliged to. Anyway, his dual-SIM phone contained text messages with a woman called Velvet Stone who could hack those ankle bracelets they use for home detention. I spoke to Velvet, and she said Joe Phelan asked her if she could hack cattle tags.'

'Okay. Good ...' She sounded unconvinced.

I glanced at her in the dim interior. 'Any idea what tags he might be talking about?'

'NLIS tags maybe.'

'And they are?'

She shrugged. 'Just the usual cattle ID.'

'Cattle tags use a different network, right?'

'NLIS uses radio signals.'

That sounded like she knew what she was talking about. 'How does it work?'

'When the cattle leave a farm, their tags get read. There's a device you use to read them, tells you the breeder and that. Keeps track of them.'

I'd have to look into the NLIS tags myself. She might be right. But it seemed unlikely.

I suddenly realised I was exhausted, it was late, and we were only halfway to Woolburn. We pulled into the small town of Beaufort, and I paid cash for a twin room in a motel. The owner was a fan of the Alaskan Malamute and allowed us to keep Nigel tied up outside with one of our own blankets and a bowl of water.

'Look at his eyes. Alert, intelligent, loyal. Better than most people you meet,' she said appreciatively.

The local Chinese was still open, and we consumed passable takeaway while watching mindless reality TV in our room. Loretta worked her way through the soft drinks in the minibar. Coke, Fanta, anything sweet. I finished two bottles of Crown Lager and went outside for a breath of fresh air. I walked the length of a few blocks to stretch my legs. It was a quiet town. Not dead, but not living up to its full potential. I saw possibilities. Country life, would that be so bad? Friendly folk, traffic flowing freely, birds, trees. I shook myself out of it. Tropical islands, country retreats, my fantasies were escapist drivel. Marigold's mother would never allow her to leave, Brophy wouldn't go anywhere without her. I had to give it up.

Back in the room, Loretta was changing channels.

'Wait, stop,' I said. 'Go back.'

A woman in a pink Akubra in a dusty outback location was doing a piece to camera. 'Imagine you're riding a horse at the head of a herd of cattle. Not a few hundred head, but thousands and thousands of cattle.'

I knew that journalist. Bunny Slipper. She used to cover organised crime in Melbourne.

Background guitar music played over aerial shots of vast herds of rust-brown cattle moving across a desert landscape. The reporter's voiceover: 'You're watching *Rural Life*, an outback series on real Australia. This week: people.'

Back to Bunny, standing in a sea of red dunes. 'Here in the Kimberley, there's cattle stations that are too big to imagine. All across Australia's north there are stations bigger than most countries — Belgium, for instance. These are farms with more than fifty thousand head of cattle, and it can be hard work for station managers to keep track.'

Slide guitar over shots of a shed, a rusted windmill turning against a blue sky, water pumping into a trough, helicopters hovering, then flying directly at herds that scattered in panic, clouds of red dust pluming behind them.

'We've come a long way since the days of jackaroos on horseback droving cattle hundreds of kilometres to new pastures.'

Cut to Bunny, now wearing headphones inside a helicopter. 'Graziers swapped the horses for motorbikes, and then the motorbikes for helicopter mustering,' she shouted.

Shot of thousands of cattle crossing a shallow river.

'Some of the romance of the golden age of Australian cattle farming might be lost — the campfires, the long cattle drives — but the characters remain. Today, I speak to some of the people who live and work out here in the outback.'

Loretta threw the remote on the bed. 'This is boring.'

'Yes, it is. Turn it off.'

She went to the bathroom, and I heard the shower running.

I turned the TV back on.

A caption said *Station owner* under a shot of a woman in moleskins, boots, check shirt. 'It's a special part of the world up here, and the cattle trade is viable again. Live export will continue. I want the industry to be as viable as possible, and one day the people down south will understand that we love our cattle. Our cattle are our life, and we bend over backwards to look after those animals day in, day out. It breaks my heart when you get these people down south thinking otherwise, because we are our cattle, and that's all we do, that's all we live for.'

Cut to a shot of Bunny Slipper, as she tilted her pink Akubra and nodded.

Bunny and I had history. She'd given me valuable information to help me in that tricky situation involving the bikies. And I'd given her the scoop of the century. She was a hard-core investigative reporter. This *Rural Life* gig seemed pretty soft for someone of her calibre. I wondered if she would be willing to join forces with me again.

Her number was still in my phone. It went straight to her voice-mail. I said I had another amazing scoop.

At dawn, we set off again. It was a typical superb March morning; delicate pink wisps on mauve clouds made the world seem benign.

Loretta had woken up in a talkative mood. She prattled on about her childhood, travelling from farm to farm with her grandfather. He'd been a stockman, a shearer, a drover. He'd done branding and tagging. It explained a lot.

He'd been a station hand on a government farm when one of the workers there had shut the stock in a paddock, chained the gate, and knocked off without telling anyone. The cattle were cut off from their water trough and had died of thirst.

'That's horrible.'

'Grandad was ropable. Swearing and carrying on, but I reckon he was traumatised.'

'But they weren't his.'

'Didn't matter. It was the stupidity, the carelessness. And the poor cows suffering.'

I knew some farmers cared, some didn't. Most would have hated to see that.

'After the cattle died, that was it. We packed up one night. Went to Yuleba North.'

'Where's that? And don't say near Yuleba.'

'Near Wallumbilla.'

'Where's that?'

'Roma, on the stock route. Drover reckoned his calves got stolen. Grandad found them.'

My phone chimed, and I glanced at the screen.

Phuong: *Bit of commotion at your place last night!*

The small town of Great Western was coming up. I stopped in

140

the main street, outside the general store. Loretta and Nigel walked to the public facilities.

I called Phuong, and she picked up straight away. 'No big deal,' I said. 'A bloke had a heart attack. He's fine now.'

'Not cardiac arrest,' said Phuong. 'Doctors are speculating about taser exposure. If that's true, it's lucky he wasn't killed.'

She'd spoken to doctors at the hospital. She was super cop. 'What? That's weird.'

'Superficial burns to the neck, with small puncture wounds, consistent with taser-related injury. The guy wasn't cooperating, refused to give his name. Staff called police.'

That was good news. 'Was he arrested?'

'No, why would he be?'

'I mean, interviewed. Polite questioning.'

'No. He left before we arrived. Nothing the hospital could do.'

'You should follow that up. I took down his number plate, if you want it.'

A pause. 'You took the number plate?'

'As a concerned citizen, yes. Definitely his car. I saw him park it there.'

'You saw him?'

'That's right. I happened to be looking out the window. He parked in front of my building, next thing the same guy is strapped to an ambulance gurney.'

'Did you see anyone approach him? Who else was there?'

'No one.' I checked my photo. 'Nissan Navara ST-X, silver.' I read out the registration.

'Stella. Tell me the truth. Are you in trouble?'

'Trouble? Of course not.'

'Meet me for a drink later?'

'Can't today. I'm on my way to the farm.'

'Great! I'll see you up there. I'm going rock climbing near Woolburn on Saturday —'

Luckily another call sounded. 'Sorry Phuong, got another call. Talk to you later.'

I was so relieved to have her off the line that I swiped the other call without looking at who was calling.

'Stella? It's Thursday.' It was Fatima. What did that mean? Thursday was a workday, sure. 'Where on earth are you?' Fatima said, concern in her voice.

Where? In the vast splendour of the Wimmera, where glorious autumn sun shone on the golden landscape, and the majestic peaks of The Grampians rose up in the west. A magpie in a tree let forth a complex morning warble. In spite of the seriousness of my situation, a burst of happiness exploded in my heart.

'I'm at home,' I said.

'Everyone's here. The other agencies are all here. We're waiting for you.'

'Waiting for what?'

'... I can't believe I have to say this, Stella. For the *presentation*.' Her words were an ice-cold slap.

The presentation. Thursday. Today. I started to cough. 'I'm very sick. It's a bad cold. I think it's the flu.'

'You've already had one warning, Stella.' I'd never heard Fatima so angry. 'Consider this your second. One more stuff up like this and —'

'I know, I know. Can you reschedule?'

I heard a kind of hiss. That was not a good sign. 'For when?'

'Tuesday — after the long weekend. I'm sure I'll be right by then.'

She hung up without a word.

I went into the general store and bought two chocolate Big M's and two pineapple doughnuts. I ate mine waiting for Loretta and Nigel to return. I should have been worried about work. But I wasn't. I was having a moment.

This was the land of my childhood, and I almost didn't recognise it. The familiar was new again. I'd never noticed these subtle colours before, or experienced this feeling of an ancient land humming with truth. I'd driven on this road at Christmas, without a hint of possible communion, or sensing the danger of imminent transcendence. Yet now I finally understood this place was miraculous. The immensity of the sky, the waft of fragrant breeze. The magpie finished her song, and I almost burst into applause.

I resolved to lay off the doughnuts.

19

WE TURNED off the highway onto the Stawell-Warracknabeal Road. We passed through Minyip, then Warracknabeal, and drove for another two hours. Loretta leaned forward and pointed to a bump on the horizon.

'What's that?'

'Mount Woolburn,' I said. 'We're nearly there.'

Since we'd left Great Western, I'd been preparing my speech to my mother. It involved appeals to her better nature; it had to be in there somewhere. I presumed this on account of her Catholicism. However, I had yet to witness true acts of Christian kindness on her part. Sure, she pitched in when neighbours needed help. It was in her rural DNA. To people in crisis who were considered different, who lived outside her circle, to them she was harsh. Those individuals only had themselves to blame for their plight. What next? Allow people fleeing persecution into the country? Not on your nelly. This black-and-white world view formed the foundation of Delia's thinking. And it meant that Loretta would be a fifty-fifty call.

Delia might decide Loretta was family, and, provided she conformed utterly to Hardy family rules, she would be welcome to stay. Those rules included hard work, never talking about uncomfortable facts (like the plight of people fleeing persecution) or vegetarianism. Never talking politics; the National Party were just terrific thank you very much, if you ignore the sleaze, the rorts, and the hostility to vital river protection agreements. It included a directive to dress in a manner becoming of a 1950's woman. To know one's place. To know that capitalism, with a pinch of protectionism and a soupçon of agrarian socialism, was an unquestionable good. Delia was not to be challenged on any decision. She knew best, and everyone else was a fool or a nitwit. Or, after a few beers, a bloody ratbag troublemaker.

Alternatively, Delia might consider Loretta to be *not one of us*. She was not your clean-cut, tennis-playing, horse-riding, sponge-baking, quilt-(or other authorised craft)-making supporter of men. She was a young, unmarried, pregnant daughter of an itinerant worker. She spoke her mind. She certainly didn't follow any of the rules I had laid down. And she had a free-range Alaskan Malamute. Only cattle dogs and Shih tzus were acceptable dog breeds.

There were problems aplenty with either judgement. I tried to brace for every possible outcome.

At last we arrived. I drove slowly up the long driveway, avoiding two BMX bikes carelessly dropped on the road, a soccer ball, and a plastic basketball hoop in pieces, and stopped.

The garden beds were in a bad way. Plants drooped for want of a drink, weeds encroached. The lawn was not mowed, edges were not snipped with laser precision. It wasn't neglect as such, but I knew my mother, and anything other than flowerbed perfection was a sign of insanity on the part of the occupants. What, I wondered, had happened here?

Delia's car was not in the shed, nor that of my stepfather, Ted. Kylie's white RAV4 was in the driveway, and behind it, an unfamiliar Commodore. I tooted the Mazda's horn: the universal language for *put the kettle on*. Then I advised Loretta and Nigel to explore the garden.

I grabbed the folder holding Kylie's legal documents and walked up the front steps. A door-slam inside, then a thump, a person running. I heard Kylie say, 'Shit, it's Stella.'

A man swore, and it wasn't my brother-in-law, Tyler.

'What are you doing here?' Kylie said behind the closed door.

'Wasn't expecting you till Saturday.'

'Open the damn door, Kylie, we've been up driving since the crack of sparrows, and I need to use the loo.'

'Just a minute.'

More running and slamming. Finally, the door opened, and Kylie stood there, blocking my way, in an inside-out t-shirt, jeans, and bare feet, looking flushed and dishevelled. 'Hi.'

'Let me in.'

'Sure. Okay. I mean, the place is a little untidy.' She didn't move. 'Where's Mum?'

'They've moved. They're in the unit.'

'Already? No one told me.'

She smiled. 'Yeah, we've been here for weeks now.'

'You said you couldn't move in until you had the paperwork. You hassled me nonstop. I had to go back to the fucking prison.'

'It's called trust, Stella. Mum trusts me. I still require those documents, but in the meantime, we realised there was no reason to wait to take possession of the farm.'

'Let me the fuck in.'

She glanced behind her. Someone whispered. She stepped aside, and I started in. A shaved gorilla in a singlet pushed passed me. Shane Farquhar.

Shane. Fucking. Farquhar. This did not make sense. My old high school tormentor? The man who had hoped to buy the farm from my mother before Kylie got involved was having an affair with ... Kylie?

'Hardy.' More threat than salutation.

'Shane.'

'Your fucking timing is perfection as usual.' He stomped off to his car.

'How's your wife?' I called after him.

'I'll tell her you said that.' He revved the motor, spun the wheels on the gravel. He drove over the lawn, onto the driveway, and fish-tailed away.

I used the bathroom and had a quick check of the cabinet, found it stocked with expensive cleansers, exfoliants, and make-up. My mother had indeed left the building. Astonishing. I never thought I'd see the day.

My sister was in the kitchen, a room large enough for an old wood-fired stove in a brick alcove and an electric stove built into a long bench. My mother's ten-seater Laminex dining table was still in centre place. Delia had, I noticed, left a lot of furniture behind.

'What the hell are you playing at?'

Kylie smirked. 'Free country.'

'But Shane-fucking-Farquhar. He is the *worst* human being in human history.'

She filled the kettle. 'Tiger in the sack.'

I nearly gagged. 'He made my life a misery in high school.'

'Water under the bridge. You should move on.'

My bridge was clogged with garbage, dead fish, plastic bags. An abandoned car was under there, rotting corpses inside. Nothing was getting through.

'Who's your friend?' She pointed out the window to Loretta, who was struggling to get her trolley out of the Mazda's boot.

'Long story.'

Kylie turned slowly back to me, fierce expression, demanding obedience. She was the matriarch now. 'I've got time.'

Where to start? The lax supervision at the prison? Eww. In the lull, a brand-new side-by-side fridge began to vibrate impatiently. 'She's ... I mean. Her boyfriend. That is ...'

Enter Loretta, wheeling her trolley. 'I'm Loretta. Ben's wife.'

Kylie took in the belly, the grubby hands, the pixie face. 'Wait till Mum hears this.'

'Common-law wife,' I said. 'And it might be best to let me explain the situation.'

Kylie snorted. 'It won't make any difference who tells her.'

It pained me to admit it, but she was probably right about that.

147

Kylie seemed cheered by Loretta's arrival, and remembered her manners. 'You guys hungry?'

Loretta said she was. Kylie took a bowl from the fridge and nuked it in the microwave. She cleared the table of papers, and then distributed plates. The kettle sang, and she made three mugs of tea. She dumped some cutlery on the table and dropped into a chair, as though exhausted from the effort.

'Give us the papers, then.' She put her hand out. 'I'll call the lawyer this arvo, get this thing finalised.'

I opened the folder. It contained a copy of *Who Weekly*. I removed the magazine. Nothing. No contract.

A moment passed. The microwave dinged. Kylie put her head to the side, looking at me impassively. 'Am I missing something? Why are you here if you didn't bring the papers?'

'It's not Stella's fault,' Loretta piped up.

She ignored Loretta. Her eyes drilled into mine. 'Why are you here?'

'This bloke was going to *kill* us,' Loretta said. 'We had to run for our lives.'

Kylie's eyes widened in an expression of mock horror.

This was going to be torture. 'Um. It's true. Kind of.'

The fridge shuddered and became silent. Kylie's face and neck were pink. She retrieved the nuked bowl and slammed it on the table. Loretta started to spoon stew onto her plate.

'You're two days early,' Kylie started. 'Totally unannounced. One of Ben's skanks with you. And yet you didn't bring the papers, the *only* reason for you to come here.'

'So it would seem. I'm sorry,' I said, tapping the folder. 'I thought they were in here.'

'I really don't understand. I mean, I only reminded you to bring them a million times.'

'We left in such a rush —' Loretta began.

Kylie cut her off with a weaponised glare, then turned on me.

'You want to undermine the arrangement. Don't you?'

'Rooting Shane Farquhar is undermining the arrangement.'

Kylie *ha ha ha*-ed like a pantomime villain. 'Are *you* judging me? That's rich.'

I shook my head. But I was, and that made me an A-grade hypocrite. My past was as shady as an English country lane. A stupid dalliance with a married man called Jacob had ended badly and sent me down on a journey into the dark night of the soul, with a stopover at internal turmoil, and a tour of the ancient sites of self-hatred. The cost? It had nearly derailed my friendship with Phuong. Kylie didn't know that; none of the family knew. I liked to keep certain things from them. Like everything about me.

'I know what you're up to. You want the farm, don't you?'

Now I laughed. 'Not in a million years.'

'Then it's Ben, the treacherous little bastard.'

Loretta inhaled in horror. 'Never!'

'Relax, Kylie. No one wants the farm. But if Loretta could stay here for a while, that would be very much appreciated.'

Kylie blinked. 'Are you out of your mind?'

'Look at her,' I said. Meaning, see how pregnant and how harmless.

'Fuck you, Stella.'

'I'll take that as a no,' Loretta said.

'You're staying here,' I said with fresh determination. 'You can have my old room.'

'Er, no. She can't.'

'Let her stay, and you'll have the documents by next week.'

Kylie placed both hands on the table and raised herself to standing. 'What's this, some kind of slimy form of coercion? Your true colours at last.'

What were my colours? Grumpy purple, martyred orange, criminal-gang-money-stealing blue, maybe throw in some lilac for my excessive devotion to one Peter Brophy, and finish with a sprinkle of yellow for my constant state of fear.

'That your wolf?' she said to Loretta.

'Alaskan —'

'Lock it in the shed. My kids'll be home soon. If it so much as growls at them, you're out on your arse. Got that?'

Loretta was out like a shot, whistling for Nigel to come.

'I'll give you some money for food,' I said, opening my wallet. 'Damn thing eats like an elephant.'

'The dog or the girl?'

'Both.' I held out a colourful posy of legal tender.

She took a fifty. 'You staying, too?'

'Just a few days.' Velvet Stone's murderer would be in custody soon … I hoped. Phuong would trace the number plate. Witnesses at Dights Falls. Shouldn't be too long.

'Try the pub. We're out of bedrooms.'

She was a shocker. I nodded. 'Where's Tyler?'

'Livestock auction in Horsham, be back tonight.' She sighed. 'You might as well eat.'

I looked at the stew. 'I'm good.'

'No, Stella. You're really not.' A scowl, a toss of hair, and she glided away, head high, a Shakespearean monarch, all the way to the exit, stage right.

She was mean, she was greedy. But she knew how to leave a room. Respect, queen.

20

'BLOODY BULLSHIT is what it is.' Loretta came stomping in and straddled a kitchen chair.

'Easy, cowgirl. The world's drowning in bullshit. You're going to have to be more specific.'

'He's not a wolf and he's not aggressive.'

'True.' Nigel was a sweet-natured, loyal dog. He also weighed more than she did, and ate more in one sitting. 'But you're a guest here.' I lifted my shoulders, showed her my palms.

'Rules. Everyone's got rules. I get it.' She unhooked the tartan case from the trolley, flipped the catches, and took out the dog blanket and a chew toy.

'At least you've got a place to stay till the baby comes.'

'I do?' It appeared to slowly dawn on her that I'd delivered her to the farm, just as Ben had promised. 'Oh, Stella.' She dropped the dog's things and hugged my neck.

'Next time, just say thanks,' I gasped. 'I'm staying in the pub, but I'll be back tomorrow.'

Loretta released me and smiled sheepishly. Then she noticed the brochures Kylie had left on the sideboard. 'Annual Weaner Calf Sale? What's all this?'

'My sister plans to turn the farm into a Dexter stud.'

She raised an eyebrow.

'They're small —' I started to say.

'Irish. I know. Probably a good move. The meat is better. Better for the environment, too.'

'I find that hard to believe. A cow's a cow, right?'

'No way. The smaller breeds produce less methane, lighter on the land, less feed. A good idea, I reckon.'

She knew cattle breeds and their impacts, knew tag technology. I started to appreciate that Loretta was not a dippy elf, but an agricultural aficionado. 'Make sure you tell Kylie that.'

'Grandad reckons stockyards and agents don't like the small cattle and don't support them. Rumours are, the butchers don't like them either.'

'Maybe don't tell her that part.'

'But he says they're wrong. Small cattle make a quality steak, very tender and more flavour. They're smaller, but customers prefer that rather than a great slab that flops over the side of the plate. That's what he reckons.'

'Great,' I said. As a vegetarian, none of that mattered to me. 'See you tomorrow.'

I sent my mother a text to say I was coming. Then I drove to Ouyen, with directions to Delia's new unit in my phone. I wondered what state the farm would be in when I returned tomorrow. Kylie and Loretta on good terms, having bonded over the finer points of stock feed and worming? Experience had taught me to adjust my expectations lower. More likely, they'd both be dead, having murdered each other simultaneously. A hard thing to do, but they would find a way.

The phone told me I'd arrived at my destination. I looked around the street in confusion. Checked the number again.

Ted had called it a unit, and I'd pictured a tiny two-room affair. But my mother didn't buy a *unit*. It was a house. I had to adjust my expectations upwards.

It was a grand weatherboard residence on a huge block, with a green lawn and the garden of her dreams. Less attractive was the corflute sign hammered into the front yard featuring a rubicund male in a National Party hat, with a smirk that said *safe seat*. Under this

152

fetching portrait were the words *Kelton McHugh: a steady hand*. I loved my mother, but, boy, I didn't get her. And her retired real-estate-agent life partner, Ted, was even more unfathomable.

A path lined with standard roses led to the house, where they both waited on the veranda.

'Hello, love. How was the trip? We're just back from bowls. Come in. Mind how you go, we're still unpacking so the place is in a state, but I've got scones in the oven.'

Bowls then scones. She was more robot than human. But something about all this was wrong. She'd not criticised my appearance, my dead-end job, my lack of a wedding band.

I could only conclude that Delia was happy, content with her new life here, and no longer burdened by the years of weather and market unpredictability on the farm. And so was Ted. He gave me the tour and used words like 'character' and 'street appeal'. I didn't object because, well, this house had those things.

'And out here,' he real-estated, 'is a marvellous covered outdoor entertaining area.'

A cane outdoor dining setting near a matching lounge suite upholstered in a tropical print, a well-stocked bar, a vast wall-mounted TV, ceiling fans, and an open fire place. By the time he showed me the in-ground pool, I was considering tossing in my flat for street appeal like this.

When we were settled on the cane settee, with tea in a pot and a warm autumn breeze gently lifting sheets on the washing line, and with Delia slopping tablespoons of cream on my scone, I cleared my throat.

'I have a bit of news.' I smiled to reassure them that it wasn't of the bad variety.

Nonetheless, Delia's face hardened, lips pursed, eyes staring far-away. After my father died suddenly — his plane crashed while crop dusting when I was sixteen — she'd had that frozen look for years. A way of bracing herself, I imagined, against any further shocks that life might throw at her.

153

Ted chuckled. 'Here we go,' he said, stirring his tea.

'About that boyfriend of yours?' she asked.

'No. It's about Ben.'

'What's he done now?'

'He has a girlfriend. He was seeing her before ... well, before.'

'Before he got chucked in the clink!' Ted said. He may have been drinking.

'Let her finish.' Delia slapped him playfully on the knee. Eww.

'She's pregnant with his baby.'

Ted was quiet, and Delia paused with her cup near her lips. 'Can't be,' she said.

I didn't want to have this part of the conversation but there was no choice. 'During a prison visit. There's places prisoners can go, apparently, and the guards aren't too vigilant.'

Phew, with the nasty part out of the way, I told them about Loretta, starting with the fact that she was a country girl. Ben wanted to take care of her and the baby when he got out. She was staying at the Hardy farm in Woolburn with Kylie's blessing — I exaggerated that part.

Delia drew a tissue from her sleeve and dabbed an eye. 'I hope it's a girl.'

Ted was up and shaking my hand, though I assured him it was none of my doing. 'I'll ring Kylie,' he said. 'Tell her and Tyler to come for dinner, bring the girl.'

'Loretta.'

'I'll fire up the barbie.'

Delia was laughing. 'Sit down, you'll do your back again.'

They really were disgustingly happy.

Later, I heard Delia on the phone to Kylie. She'd heard the wonderful news, and she thanked Kylie for putting Loretta up, offered to help with anything, and invited them all to dinner.

Ted had his apron on and gave Delia a shopping list. 'Might as well pick up Kelton's letters while you're out, Del.'

Delia agreed and grabbed her keys. 'Stella, come with me. We can have a chat.'

A chat? Good. I clipped on my seatbelt. 'Did you and Dad use NLIS tags on the sheep?'

She adjusted the mirror. 'Of course. You have to. Why do you ask?'

'Kylie will need to do that for the cattle, won't she?'

'Obviously.' She reversed down the driveway and fanged down the road.

'How does it work?'

'Each farm has a code, and the tag has information about the animal and the farm. They keep track of the animal's history. Handy if there's an outbreak of disease. Exporters have to for the quality standards. But, even for local abattoirs, they want to know everything.'

'And they get that info with a scanner?'

'Yep. Same as they use in supermarkets. Info stored on a big database.'

'So someone could hack into that?'

She laughed. 'Who'd want to hack stock information?'

'I just want to know if it's possible.'

'Probably, love. I don't know, to be honest.' She parked in front of an empty shop.

'What's this place?'

'Kelton's campaign office, one of. Saves us driving up to Mildura all the time.'

This electoral district was big — thirty-five thousand square kilometres. Current incumbent Kelton 'a steady hand' McHugh had his office in Mildura, over an hour away. This little outpost made perfect sense. A state election was looming, and even the safest of seats could be lost to a cleanskin independent with an ability to speak, remain sober, and refuse money from nefarious mobsters. McHugh was not going to let power slip, not for a moment.

'Wait here,' Delia said. 'I need to whiz in for some leaflets.'

I unbuckled my seatbelt. 'I'll come, too.'

She looked askance at me. 'Promise you won't say anything.'

'Cross my heart.'

21

A WOMAN in a floral dress and pearls stood behind a counter. My mother called her Penny, she called my mother Del.

'Out the back, Del. Your name's on the box. Got you a map. If you like door-knocking, knock yourself out. Otherwise just letterboxes.'

Penny hit a buzzer, and the door made a mechanical click. High-tech security for a temporary election hub. McHugh obviously wanted to screen unannounced visitors. Delia pushed it open and went through to a back room. I smiled at Penny, who responded with a blank look.

'Is that your handbag?' I asked Penny, pointing at an object with a shoulder strap sitting on the counter. A slice of peach, but made of plastic, and yet it seemed real — except for being four times the size of an actual peach. The colours were beautiful: the orange flesh, the flush near the pit, which, with its Velcro flap, was a handy spot for a mobile.

She immediately moved the bag to a spot under the counter and out of my view. 'Yes.'

'Where'd you get it?'

Penny shook her head. 'A gift, from my cousin.'

She didn't want to say. So be it. But the proliferation of fruit handbags had me feeling inadequate. What did my dull, utilitarian handbag say about me? Nothing whimsical, that was for sure. And whimsy was, all of a sudden, crucial.

Next minute, Kelton McHugh himself came in from the street holding a briefcase and jiggling a set of keys with a BMW logo tag on the ring.

'Tell me, Penny, who might this young lady be?' Kelton said, looking me up and down.

Young? He was a skilled flatterer. Or lecherous old creep. Either one.

'Delia's girl. From Melbourne.'

'Kelton.' He held out a soft hand. This was no farmer. No tractor-driving, hay-bailing, sheep-wrangling, dam-building, caked-in-dirt type. Kelton wrangled numbers, was good on the phone.

'Stella Hardy. How's the campaign going?'

'Tremendous, Stella. Getting ready to do a doorstop. Keep these greenies in their place, with their claims about environmental destruction of rivers. Ordinary blokes need water-rights certainty, the system's unmanageable otherwise — honest farmers can't guarantee the land will produce. Entire community suffers. That kind of thing. Like it?' A show of white teeth.

'But most of those farms are run by overseas corporations, and the rivers *are* nearly dead.'

'Oh *nearly* dead, but not quite. Besides, cotton farmers draining water from rivers is perfectly natural.' He pulled out his mobile and started to read.

'Natural to drain rivers? Okay, I'll be sure to tell the voters you said that when Mum and I door knock for you.'

Penny gave me a sceptical look, but McHugh put the phone in his jacket pocket and seemed ecstatic. 'Hardy women are top quality. Your mother's a godsend.'

'Oh my word, Kelton.'

'What do you do, Stella?'

Delia interrupted, shouting from the back room that she couldn't find the right box. Penny hit the buzzer and went through.

'I'm helping Marcus Pugh's campaign.' A quarter truth. 'Trying to get this prison problem to go away, new narrative about transparency, independent inspections, all that.'

'Is that right? Sounds like quite a challenge.'

'Yes. It's a challenge just trying to understand the man. You know Marcus — he's so vague. He sends me these cryptic texts, voicemails that sound like a foreign language.'

He nodded. 'Busy man, Marcus. Not an easy portfolio, I can tell you.'

'I wonder if I could ask you to clarify something.'

He frowned. 'I doubt it. Separate parties. Apart from cabinet meetings, the odd dinner, I barely talk to him. Why don't you call his office?'

'Yes, I will. But while you're here … what does it mean if he said, "sky was antsy"?'

'Antsy? Not familiar with that. Not a donor, is it? Some lobby group?'

'No, it means fidgety or restless, something like that.'

'Really? American, is it?'

'I don't know the origin,' I said, getting antsy. What a dolt. 'Why would the sky be restless?'

He stared at the ceiling. 'Could be the eldest girl, from his first marriage. She married some chap from Hamilton, can't remember the name. Simon? Philip? Something like that.'

'Of course! *Skye* was upset about an auction and … *Vincent* got away?'

He shrugged. 'A painting?'

'Heavily muscled.'

'A horse, perhaps? The husband's Western District, grazier. Breeds things with muscles.'

'Probably a horse.'

Delia came out carrying two cardboard boxes.

'Let me help you, Mum.' I put my hands out to take a box.

She looked from Kelton McHugh to me, and the sight displeased her. 'Just get the door.'

I swung the door and allowed Delia to pass. I said to McHugh, 'Marcus said he'd talk to *Al* about it.'

'Al? Doesn't ring any bells.' McHugh knitted his brow. 'Blast Pugh, what's the context?'

I needed him calm and forgetful. 'No big deal, Al's probably an intern. I'd appreciate it if you keep this between us, don't want them thinking I'm incompetent.'

He was vexed now. 'What's Skye's auction got to do with the election?'

'Nothing. Don't worry about it. I'll talk to his office. Thanks, Kelton.'

I ran outside to help Delia get the boxes into the boot. I began to manoeuvre the boxes around in the small space, and she swatted my hands away.

'Told you not to say anything,' she hissed at me.

'He started it.'

Delia exhaled through her nose. 'Saying what?'

'Something about a horse called Vincent.'

Delia whizzed into the supermarket, then whizzed into the butchers, then whizzed into the bottle-o, then whizzed into the bakery. While she was whizzing, I called Brophy and left a message. I virtually begged him to come up. Then I booked a room at the Woolburn pub. And then I fell to contemplating what *Skye* wanted with a horse, and, once again, who Al might be.

By the time Delia whizzed us both back to her place, Ted had made a marinade for the chops, produced two salads, and mixed a jug of margaritas. Quite the catch, Ted.

My main objective now was decent wi-fi and a computer. My phone was an option, but I was over forty and preferred a proper keyboard and a full-sized screen. I knew Ted had an iPad, but there was no way I could use it and keep my enquiries private. According to my mother, the nearest computer with internet access was the public library a fifty-minute drive away in Red Cliffs.

I downed an excellent margarita and announced that I had to see a woman about a horse. I leapt into the Mazda, promising to be back by dinner time. The dead-straight road was a bit much, and I scanned the radio. Christian broadcasting, no, flicked again. A country station, oh yes indeed. I sang along with Patsy. Top of my lungs, all of my troubles, no one the wiser.

The library, when I found it, was a handsome single-storey art deco building named for an A.S. Kenyon. A portrait of Kenyon greeted me as I entered the building. A senior gentleman, with a white goatee and moustache, seated with one hand on a book and the other tucked into his waistcoat, he peered into the distance through round-framed spectacles.

Evidently he'd established Red Cliffs, and his innovative engineering had supplied water to the arid Mallee for fruit cultivation. He resembled a less flamboyant Colonel Sanders. Dried fruit trumped fried chicken any day of the week.

I signed up for a library card and logged on. Typing a search for 'Skye Pugh' produced a gossip website which told me that she had married Alistair Redbridge, a Geelong Grammar old boy. The piece included pictures of a ceremony in 2009 at Como House, a National Trust property on rolling green lawns in the heart of Toorak, Melbourne's poshest suburb.

'Skye Redbridge' and 'horse' yielded a picture of a young girl, about ten, in equestrian attire, standing with a slim woman, mid-forties, wearing a cream blouse and fawn jodhpurs, and with blonde hair escaping a soft French roll. Caption: *Arabella Redbridge with her mother, Skye, at pony club.*

The search for 'horse' and 'Vincent' and 'Skye Redbridge' came up empty.

There was a lot of information about Skye and Alistair and their farm, a sprawling cattle stud called Dougal Park. Four hundred and seventy hectares, or eleven hundred and sixty acres in the old measure. I digressed briefly into searching for the size of Australian farms to satisfy my curiosity and to put the Redbridge holding into perspective. It was one of the largest privately owned farms in the state. Farms owned by private equity were larger, like seven million hectares across numerous farms in Queensland and the Northern Territory.

The Redbridge farm's official website featured photos by a professional photographer. Cute, freckle-faced children sitting on post-and-rail fences. Photo after photo, I flipped through images of the children on horseback or arranged around a bull sporting the blue sash for first prize at the Royal Melbourne Show.

A bull. I sat back, wanting to shout, 'Hey everyone, Vincent is a bull! Skye is Pugh's daughter!'

Maybe not. I searched 'bull' and 'Vincent' and 'auction' and 'heavily muscled'.

Noise. Nothing useful. A sad tinkle of piano keys disturbed the quiet ennui of the library. I'd forgotten I'd set a Tom Waits song as my new ring tone. The hooker's sad words on her Christmas card came through. I waited till the last minute to answer so I could hear more of the song and almost missed the call. She'd quit drinking whiskey when I snatched it up.

It was Percy Brash. 'Make it out of Melbourne okay?'

'No,' I said. 'I died in a hail of bullets.'

'Where are you?'

'Right now?' Azerbaijan. Tierra del Fuego. Greenland … Lie, tell him anything. Oh, what was the point? 'Red Cliffs, near Mildura.'

'We need to talk.'

'We're talking now.'

'I'm coming up. Need to protect my investment.'

'I'm not your —'

'Give me an address.'

I hesitated. The last thing I needed was a man who looked like Al Capone showing up at Delia's. Or the farm. Or anywhere. 'It's a long way.'

'SAS, Hardy. He'll find you and kill you before you've had time to shit yourself.'

He had a point. Until Phuong arrested him, the SAS guy was at large and hunting me, though I doubted he'd find me out here. Reluctantly, I gave Brash directions to the Woolburn pub.

'See you tomorrow, Hardy. I'll be expecting all the specifics.'

Specifics? I had Skye Redbridge, daughter of Pugh, owner of Dougal Park stud, a vast tract of prime agricultural country near Hamilton. It wasn't much. I had other dots like Nunzio and Pugh, the hacking, and the probably-bull called Vincent. But I couldn't join them up into a clear picture. I wrote the address of Dougal Park stud on the back of my hand, and then used that hand to wave goodbye to the librarian and give a passing salute to Alfred Kenyon, dried fruit king.

The barbecue was underway when I returned. It was a clear, warm evening, and the Hardy clan were dining alfresco. Half the fare on offer was not compatible with a vegetarian diet. Instead, I enjoyed a hearty salad feast — mainly Ted's excellent potato salad. Kylie and Tyler had brought more meat and more salad. Their twins, Blair and Chad, had each added another five centimetres to their height since Christmas, and were bony, elongated teenage boys with skin stretched to the limit.

And Loretta was there, freshly showered, hair combed, and wearing a check shirt I recognised as Kylie's. The result fitted beautifully into Delia's ideals. In the kitchen, I asked Kylie if the clothes were her idea. She touched her nose; I tipped my hat. Kylie could be an utter bitch sometimes, but she wasn't stupid. She understood Delia had to be kept happy, because the deal was not fully done, and a grumpy Delia might pull the pin on Kylie and sell the place. It was one of those rare instances when her self-interest aligned with mine.

Tyler had his arm around Kylie and was telling Ted a yarn about the livestock auction he'd been to. Apparently, the old blokes reckoned they hadn't seen the like: prices up, good rain, pastures in great nick. Tyler was set to make a killing. I felt sorry for him.

The twins spent the evening bombing each other in the pool. Delia insisted Loretta stay off her legs. She piled a plate with meat and salad, and forced it on her, saying something about eating for two, and her future grandchild needing good Australian red meat, with a nod over her shoulder at me. I shrugged it off. It was Skye Redbridge who was on my mind.

Skye missed out on Vincent. Pugh had said, *I'll talk to Al.* What could Al do to get Vincent back for Skye, if the bull had already been sold at auction? Make an offer? Make a threat? The small pieces of the picture hinted at influence, unethical use of power perhaps. Hence the fear of exposure. But was that enough motive to have Joe Phelan killed? I disliked Pugh, but I couldn't conceive of him as the type to order a hit. It was possible Pugh didn't know the recording existed. Perhaps it was Al, whoever he or she was, rather than Pugh, who feared exposure. Nunzio knew Al. Or *an* Al. I tried to think of a ploy to ring Nunzio and fool him into revealing Al's identity. But the margaritas were strong, and I couldn't think straight.

By the end of the evening, I was quite unsteady. I left the Mazda at Delia's and squeezed in with Kylie and Tyler, the boys, and Loretta. The Woolburn pub was on their way.

Kylie told me to call her in the morning, something about driving me back to Mum's for my car, and something about ducks in a row. I gave her a thumbs up, went into the pub through the door marked *Accommodation*, and climbed the old staircase.

My room had been updated in the seventies. A two-by-ten-metre cell, with a grubby casement window with a torn blind looking onto the main street. Blue-patterned nylon carpet, orange candlewick bedspread over a single bed on sagging bedsprings. The small laminate bedside table with one draw contained no bible. One star.

I lay on the bed exhausted, drunk, sad, confused. Waves of loneliness crashing over me. Brophy had not yet returned my call. There was no point trying him again. He'd be working at the market now. Was it me, or was he distant lately? The permanent cold, the vagueness, the excuses, the missing accounts of his day. I didn't like to think about what it might mean. There was one possible, but unthinkable, explanation. I'd pushed it away time and again. A series of moments replayed in my mind. The time he'd borrowed money because his ATM card had been taken. Never paid me back. He was always either sick or tired or broke. I could remember so many times he'd been one or another of those.

A return to his former drug use was a deal-breaker. If Brophy was using again, we were through. I'd told him that early on. Surely, he wouldn't risk our relationship for that. At least, I didn't think he would. I refused to entertain the thought.

Instead, I put my arms behind my head and listened to the distant hum of trucks on the highway. Sheep, cattle, wheat — back and forth. Pasture to market to processing to plate. The world turned, the wind rattled the window. I turned, and the springs groaned and sagged under me. Downstairs, the cash register in the bar tolled a series of ka-chings, signalling last drinks.

22

THE SOLE guest in the Woolburn pub's dining room, I contemplated the cornflakes. They were the only cereal option. A girl came bursting through the swinging kitchen doors and topped up the milk jug.

'Sorry, not much choice,' she said. 'We found weevils in the Weet-Bix this morning. What about some eggs after?'

She took my order and left. After close inspection, the cornflakes seemed okay. I took the bowl to a table and checked to see if my phone worked. It was unlike Brophy to take so long to respond. It appeared to be working. I ate some cereal speculating about when Brash would show up. It was a good five-hour drive, and I figured he'd be along in the afternoon. I needed to have something solid to give him.

I pulled out Joe Phelan's phone to listen to the recording one more time. A sudden loud noise startled me, and I fumbled the phone and dropped it. As I bent to pick it up, my bag fell and spilled its contents, including the taser, on the floor. I quickly threw it in my bag and answered my still-ringing phone.

Phuong. 'That car you said the man drove? It's registered to a Shanelle Dawe, Ballarat address.'

I pushed my cornflakes away. 'Stolen?'

'Not reported as such. But I trusted your judgement and contacted Ms Dawe. She was very cooperative. Gave me a complete rundown of the car's movement's that night. She was with friends on Union Road, parked the car near your building, and walked down.'

'No, she's lying.'

'Or maybe you were mistaken. It was dark; you were looking from a third-floor window.'

'I *saw* him. Anyway, her story doesn't make sense.'

'It's about a hundred metres from your place to the corner. That's nothing. You're wrong and you can't admit it. It's not his car.'

'Okay, maybe the car isn't in his *name*, but he drove it. He's using it.'

'You don't know that.'

'You should take it in, compare the tyre tread, get fingerprints.'

'Stella.' A loud exhale. 'Tell me what you know.'

I thought for a moment. 'The hospital said he was tasered. Innocent people don't get tasered by random strangers. He must have a history, a past. He's probably dodgy.'

'How you could know that unless you're involved? Stella, I'm worried you're in danger.'

I forced air into my lungs and let it out. Phuong's friendship was a life-sustaining thing of joy for me. I owed her everything. Not like Brash, a sleazy gangster who'd probably kill me even if I somehow found Joe Phelan's killer. If I told Phuong everything, she'd have some concerns, legal and moral, but she'd back me. Just like she had when she'd given me a hint about the hair. It was time for the truth … not today necessarily … but pretty soon. Later.

'No danger at all,' I said. 'But who is this Shanelle Dawe? What does she do for a living?'

Phuong sighed. 'I have to go.' She ended the call.

I tapped on Joe's phone and played Pugh's stupid posh voice to the room.

The girl came out of the kitchen. 'Bloody yolks broke, both of them.'

I quickly turned the recording off and took the plate. Two fried eggs cooked to a brown crisp sat on toasted white bread, garnished with parsley, on an oval plate.

'Thanks,' I said to her. 'Looks delicious.'

'What's that tape you were playing?' The girl asked.

'Nothing.'

'About a bull, isn't it?'

I looked at her. She turned away. There was something slightly unfamiliar about her neutral expression. Nothing major. And her unusual frankness about weevils. I wondered.

'Yes. I think he's talking about a bull,' I said.

'Bids over the three hundred, he reckons.'

'Yep.'

'That's a huge price. Probably near the record.'

I scraped some egg on a segment of toast and ate it. 'Really?'

She started filling the salt shakers. 'Season's good. Stock prices are up. But three hundred? That's the highest I heard of.'

I sipped some tea to wash down the eggs. The pub offered no wi-fi, and Woolburn's network coverage was hopelessly dodgy. My phone registered a thin mark of connection. Perhaps there wasn't much competition for coverage on a quiet Friday morning. I tapped in a search for 'record price' and 'bull' and 'auction'. The results took a while and I sipped some more tea. And then … there it was. My young friend was right. The record holder of most expensive bull sold at auction was held by a beast with the unlikely name of Van Go Daddy.

Van Go Daddy. Vincent Van Go Daddy, to his friends.

A write-up praised his moderate frame, his muscle, and the phenotype that buyers were looking for. A more recent article said he was purchased by Roy and Leonie Kennedy from the Bostock stud in Meandarra, in the Western Downs Region of south-west Queensland. A smiling Roy and Leonie were pictured with glasses of champagne. The next article, dated two weeks ago, had an image of Leonie, her face in shadow under her battered Akubra, with the caption, *I just want him back.*

Leonie Kennedy, of Meandarra, is using social media to try to locate her bull. Van Go Daddy, purchased at auction last month by Ms Kennedy for a record three hundred and forty-five thousand dollars, was last seen on last Wednesday morning. The following day the bull was missing from the property. Detective Sergeant Jason Costa of the Stock and Rural Crime Investigation Squad (SARCIS) said it was unusual for such a high-profile bull to be stolen. 'Probably a prank. He'll turn up,' he said. 'Leonie's got the Facebook crowd on it.'

'My post was shared over five hundred times in three states,' Ms Kennedy said. 'If you know something, get in touch. No questions asked.'

The roar of a motor shook me out of my bull cogitation. It sounded like a Harley Davidson was revving in the dining room. A woman in a floral dress was thrusting an upright vacuum cleaner over the carpet. It appeared to have been manufactured when my late grandmother was a young woman. She registered my presence and shut the thing down.

'Sorry, love. She didn't tell me you were still here.'

'No problem,' I said, getting up.

'Don't go,' she said. 'I'll come back later.'

'I'm finished.' I headed for the stairs.

'She bothering you? Likes to talk, our girl.'

'Not at all. She's amazing.'

If it wasn't for her, I'd never have discovered that Van Go Daddy had been stolen. It was the breakthrough I'd been hoping for.

23

IT WAS a truth universally acknowledged that no one could steal a bull in modern-day Australia and use that bull for breeding. The NLIS tags, the tracking systems, the databases, the scrutiny — the oversight was too thorough to pull it off. This much I learned from a slapdash review of cattle-trade websites. I paced the blue carpet in my hotel room, tallying my speculation and conjecture against my guesswork in deciphering the recording.

Van Go Daddy was the most expensive bull in Australia. But once stolen, all he was good for was as a pet, or food. Maybe the whole thing *was* a prank.

Unless someone hacked the NLIS system and changed the bull's identity.

It seemed extraordinary to go to all that trouble for one bull. He was the phenotype buyers were looking for, sure. But there were other bulls, other legal means of getting that phenotype. Bull semen was big business in these parts.

Joe had asked Velvet Stone about hacking cattle-tag technology. And he'd had a recording of Pugh stating that he'd told his daughter, who'd just missed out on a bull at auction, that he would seek the help of 'Al' to rectify the situation. And now Vincent Van Go Daddy was missing. The thought that Joe Phelan was murdered over a fancy bull was appalling.

But if the theft was true, it obliquely implicated Pugh. In an election year, if there was proof that this Al hacked Vincent's tags and stole him for Skye at Pugh's request, it would be disastrous for him. Maybe Pugh *would* kill someone to keep his reputation intact.

I believed that Joe had been murdered. And now I was a potential target.

I went to the window and looked out at the main drag of Woolburn: a general store with a sideline in dry-cleaning and train tickets; a combination café, bank, and post office; a petrol station and hardware shop that also supplied paint. Not much foot traffic, or any traffic for that matter. Nor action of any kind — none. There was talk of a festival of some kind to get the town off its knees. No one could agree on what kind. Elvis impersonation was taken. So was watermelon.

A car drove down the empty street, slowly passed my window, indicated, and turned off.

I closed my eyes and exhaled. The hooker's Christmas card song played on my phone. Phuong.

'The car was brand new. She paid cash, no finance.'

'The Navara?'

'Yes. And something else. Dawe also goes by her married name, Shanelle Tuffnell.'

'Tuffnell? A Nell Tuffnell works at Athol Goldwater.'

'You're welcome.'

Tuffnell paid cash for a new car. Pugh wanted to know who had unaccounted-for money because he was suspicious of a fiddle at Athol Goldwater. The recording was so sensitive, it had me wondering, what if Pugh was being blackmailed? And when he asked me to look into the fiddle, maybe he also wanted to know who had the recording. In fact, it was possible the sole reason he'd sent me into Athol Goldwater was to find the phone. If Tuffnell was involved, how did she fit into all this? Was she part of the Nunzio technology scam? Or was she on her own, operating at a much smaller scale? At the prison, Tuffnell had said they'd already searched Joe's unit, and when I'd asked what they were looking for she'd become vague and said it was routine. But the more I thought about it, the more I suspected they were looking for the phone. Brash was right, it was absolutely crucial that I did not lose it. I needed a safe place to keep it.

'Thanks, Phuong, you're a legend.'

'You think that's all I did? Come on. Don't you know me by now?'

I squealed. 'What! Tell me!'

'I contacted Tuffnell. Said police were concerned, wanted to take a look at the Navara.'

I shrieked again. Phuong Nguyen was a magnificent human being. 'What'd she say?'

'She was reluctant. Always a good sign, reluctance. Makes me more insistent.'

'I know.'

A pause. 'Want to tell me what's going on?'

I hesitated. 'Any progress on the case of that woman murdered at Dights Falls?'

'Witness statements, a pretty good description of the man, his tattoos.'

'The tattoos will match the ones on the man who was tasered. Navara he was driving will show up on street cameras in the Dights Falls area.'

'Stella ...'

'I'm telling you things,' I said. 'And one day, I'll tell you everything.'

'Yes, you will. This weekend. I'm going rock climbing at Mount Arapiles, driving up tomorrow. Then I'll come across to Woolburn. And I will look you in the eye.'

'Um, okay. Great.'

She hung up, and I went back to the window. A woman pushed a stroller into the café-post-office, a large red post box out the front beside an old-fashioned phone booth, the kind with the folding glass door. I resumed my pacing. A public phone booth — that might come in handy.

Loud knocking halted me in my tracks. Like a dummy, I'd registered here under my own name. I quickly grabbed Joe's phone from the bed and hid it in the bedside table drawer.

The place was so old the door had no peephole, but it did have a keyhole. I put my eye to it. Darkness. 'Yes?'

'Housekeeping.'

I recognised the voice and opened the door. My friend from breakfast stood in the doorway with a trolley stacked with clean towels and a bucket of sprays and sponges. Behind her was the vacuum cleaner her mother had been using.

'Come in.'

She pushed the vacuum in front of her, leaving the trolley in the hallway.

'Hey,' I said, 'what's your name?'

'Freya.'

'Freya. Nordic. Very nice.'

'She has a cat-drawn chariot.'

'Really? Sounds hard to steer,' I said.

Freya frowned. 'No. She's a goddess, so it's easy. Her hobbies include flirting and leading the Valkyries.'

'Awesome. So, Freya, can I ask a favour? Would you mind my phone? I'm scared I'll lose it.'

A flicker disturbed the neutral expression. 'Why?'

I wasn't clear on what she was questioning. Possibly all of it. I certainly was.

'Just for a few days. Thing is, I'm forgetful. What if I put it down and forget where?'

'Yeah. I do that all the time. Okay. I'll put it in my Tardis pencil case. I don't use it that much now I finished school.'

I retrieved Joe's phone from the beside drawer. Freya put it in her back pocket, and then plugged the monster vacuum into a power point. It roared to life and started beating and sweeping the crap out of the nylon.

I went down the stairs and walked onto the street. The wind whipped my hair around my face as I crossed the road to the public phone. I used my mobile to look up the number for Queensland Police. I found the number for the Stock and Rural Crime Investigation Squad, based at Mount Isa. Probably a long way from Western Downs, the district where Van Go Daddy was stolen, but I was pretty sure those cops were used to driving vast distances around the state. I fed coins into the ancient mechanism. A woman answered on the first ring.

'Mount Isa Police, Constable Faraday speaking. Can I help you?'

'Yes, good morning. I'm calling from Victoria. Is Detective Sergeant Jason Costa, of the SARCIS, available?'

'Who's asking?'

'Dorothy Zbornak.'

'Regarding?'

'The theft of Van Go Daddy from the Bostock stud in Meandarra.'

A throaty cackle down the line. 'Muscles made it to Victoria, did he?'

'No. I mean, I don't know. Is Jason there?'

'Yeah, nah. Not yet. Due any tick of the clock. Get him to give you a call?'

'No, I'll call back.'

I hung up and glanced down the street. A Commodore pulled up outside the pub. Shane Farquhar got out, slammed the door, and walked like a man about to get the kid who keyed his car. He ignored the door to the bar and walked into the residential entrance. Damn. I turned my back to the pub and hunched into the shadow of the phone booth.

Slow count to fifty. Dropped more coins, hit the numbers.

'Jason Costa. Queensland Police.'

'Hi Jason. Dorothy Zbornak speaking. I'm calling about the theft of Van Go Daddy.'

'I used to watch *The Golden Girls*. Me mum loved it. Lots of menopause jokes, as I recall, and gags about elderly women grow-ing moustaches. Not real popular with teenage boys, that kind of humour. But the only other option was to read a book, so I saw a lot of it. Sophia was my favourite. Always said what she thought. I tried it once. The old man dragged me to the woodshed. Belt broke the skin. So, there you go, that's my sob story. How about you tell me your real name.'

'Anonymous Crime Stoppers tip-off person.'

'Fair enough. What's your tip?'

'A name. Actually, it's just the first name.'

'You fucking joking? Half the district going off their nut about their cattle going missing.'

'Wait. What cattle? How many?'

'Brahman. As many as fifty thousand, multiple stations, most of them around Middleton.'

Was Middleton near Meandarra, where Van Go Daddy was taken from? Queensland was a big place. 'Jason, Detective Sergeant, whatever, does the name Al mean anything to you?'

He put on a la-di-da voice, '*Does the name Al mean anything to you, love?* Go waste someone else's time, will ya?' Click.

'I never said, *love*,' I said to no one.

Well, that was me told. I replaced the receiver, and a coin fell from the change slot. I dropped it in my jeans pocket. When I looked up, I saw Shane Farquhar was back on the street and looking even more furious, scanning left and right. Then he jumped in the Commodore, performed a screeching U-turn, and sped away. The most likely explanation for his strange behaviour was that he was looking for someone. To settle some score or perceived slight. He was a score-settling type.

The day was getting on, and my car was still at Delia's place in Ouyen. Kylie had offered me a lift back there last night, I was sure — if her ducks were in a row. I called her mobile, but there was no answer. I tried Delia. She told me to catch the bus. The Mildura bus passed through Woolburn at nine-thirty every morning and arrived in Ouyen at eleven. It was ten past eight.

I had time to kill. The building I was standing in front of had a sign on the window offering computers with internet access at a two-dollar hourly rate. I bought my bus ticket and ordered one hour's internet access and a cappuccino from a friendly woman in a t-shirt that said *Woolburn Information Centre.*

I sat down, interlaced my fingers, and gave them a stretch.

24

EYE-LEVEL WITH truck drivers, gliding towards Ouyen, a gloriously large window to look out of. Being on a bus in these parts seemed a sort of miracle. I'd managed to catch the once-a-day service and was feeling pretty good. From my vantage point, I saw recently cleared land stretching back to the horizon and a lone gargantuan agricultural machine in a distant paddock. The entire expanse would be sowed with barley next month. That barley was destined to become next year's beer. I wiped a tear: circle of life.

Traffic was light, utes and delivery vans, trucks and campervans, the odd sedan. A RAV4 just like Kylie's. Wait a minute. Kylie? Yes. I could see her through the sunroof, bopping her head and passing the bus at a velocity NASA thought impossible. The stupid ducks had not aligned. The simplest things were seemingly impossible. Strangely, I wasn't that concerned. The bus had its consolations; at least I didn't have to listen to Hall and Oates.

And I had time to think.

My time at the Woolburn Information Centre had been productive. Detective Sergeant Jason Costa's earful had dispelled the myth of the easy-going country copper, but he had given me information about Brahman gone astray from more than one cattle station.

For the hell of it, I'd googled 'cattle' and 'stolen' and 'Al', as well as all the names starting with Al- that I could think of (Alan, Allen, Allan, Alistair, Allison, Alana, Alexandra ...) and got nowhere.

I'd been deep in internet worm holes when Bunny Slipper phoned.

'Sorry it took so long to call you back. Middle of fucking nowhere

here. No reception till we got back to Fitzroy Crossing. What's up?'

That was Bunny, social niceties were a waste of time. '*Rural Life*, is it now?'

'Yeah,' she'd said, a little ruefully. 'I burned out on the hard-core investigations. The bikies thing was intense. And dangerous.'

'That's a shame. I've got a story here. Danger is involved.'

Background noise on the line, shouting voices, machinery. 'A story?'

'Yep, it's a got a *Rural Life* angle, too.'

'I'm listening.'

'Cattle-tag technology.'

'Done it. Not sexy. I'm not feeling it.'

'Tags and a racket involving the company BS12. A prisoner who had proof was murdered.'

'The prisoner at Athol Goldwater? I heard about that.'

'I believe the murder is related to the execution-style hit on a rock-climbing computer hacker called Velvet Stone, also goes by Foxy Meow.'

'Okay, yes, that *is* sexy.'

'*And* I have a secret recording of a Victorian government minister alluding to a theft.'

'Oh baby, that's sexy as hell. Theft of what?'

'A record-breaking prize bull.'

Pause. Breathing. 'Stella. Are you okay? Taking your medication?'

'If you don't want it, I can go to commercial television — that *Herald-Sun*-for-TV current affairs show.'

'No, don't do that. I'm interested. Email me with everything you've got.'

I had, and Bunny had replied almost immediately:

Started digging. Meanwhile, since you're intent on looking into cattle tag and prisoner monitoring tech, get a load of this.

The attached video file had opened with an ABC logo and titles: *RURAL LIFE. EP 24: The Future of Mustering — Satellites.*

A shot of Bunny in the pink Akubra. 'The future is here, now,' Bunny said, and held up a large round object, similar to an old-fashioned leather harness for attaching a beast of burden to a plough, except it was made of plastic and had a small solar panel and an antenna.

Bunny to camera: 'This collar allows a farmer to be confident of the exact location of every steer, every cow, with the touch of her smartphone.'

Her smartphone. Nice one, Bunny.

A fly crawled up her nose. She put a finger to a nostril and violently snorted it out. Someone laughed off camera. Cut to another take, saying much the same thing.

'It's called iDrover,' she said. Flies tried to crawl into her mouth, but she continued to look down the barrel, like a pro. 'It's part of a complete system of cattle management and high-precision farming. It uses satellites to keep track of cattle's whereabouts, feed access, the water levels in dams, and they can even open and close gates. The device is solar-powered with a built-in GPS. It lets the grazier know exactly where each individual cow is, and, using sound, it can direct them in any direction you desire. No fences required.'

There was B-roll footage of a cow displaying the collar. It walked one way, then abruptly turned its head, as if shocked, and began to run in the opposite direction. The video ended.

I'd had a little more time before the bus was due, and had spent it looking up the iDrover system, the little that was publicly available information, and learned that the collars featured small solar panels to power them, and that, once locked, they were almost impossible to unlock without a keyless mechanism unique to each farmer. The iDrover system had been tested at several sites, including in Victoria, at a BS12 facility. The system had already been rolled out across hundreds of cattle stations in Queensland, the Northern Territory, and the Kimberly. Enrique Nunzio, the tech genius at Athol Goldwater was using facilities at the prison to test and trial agricultural technology. Was that technology like the iDrover? And was that what Joe had meant when he discussed hacking 'tags' with Velvet Stone. Tags or collars or both?

I mused on these things as the bus barrelled along the narrow strip of bitumen they called a highway. It cut a straight line through dry pastures full of dusty sheep and in and out of small Mallee towns full of dusty people. It was the perfect opportunity to simply take it all in.

But I didn't. I couldn't. I was too wound up. Instead, I used the time to look over a mental smorgasbord of facts. And the combinations were whacky. For example, Nell Tuffnell, prison worker, lending her car to the tattooed man who murdered Velvet Stone. Or Marcus Pugh's daughter turning out to be a Victorian farmer obsessed with Van Go Daddy, a bull from Queensland. Then there was the presumed theft of that bull by Pugh's mystery fixer, Al.

Joe had been killed. And Velvet had been killed. And I … I was on a bus headed for Ouyen, which was undeniably very similar.

Delia was waiting for me, standing by her car, which was parked near to the bus stop. When I stepped down, she embraced me. An actual hug. This was so unprecedented that I was tempted to pull at her face to see if it was a mask. Ted was out for the day, she told me, and Kylie was waiting for us at her place.

'Morning tea. Just us girls,' she said, smiling happily, as though this was the highlight of her day. Whatever she was taking, I wanted some.

But first, she said, she had to whiz in to the bank, the newsagents, and the bakery. Her whizzing was becoming exhausting. When we finally arrived, Kylie had made tea and set places for us outside. We ate vanilla slices and apple pies. When we were finished, I poured a second cup of tea, and Delia went inside to top up the milk jug.

'Saw you drive up here this morning,' I said to Kylie. 'From the *bus*.'

She shrugged. 'I rang the pub, and they said you'd left.'

I sipped, nodding. Why had she not called my mobile? She was frustratingly stubborn.

'No, honestly, I did. The woman who answered said you were popular. I go, what do you mean? She goes, two other people were looking for you.'

I gasped. 'Who?'

'A bloke dropped in for a visit, a Mr Shane Farquhar.' Her eyebrows rose to her hairline.

'I can't imagine why.'

The brows came down and knitted to become one. 'Really. You can't imagine?'

'If you think I fancy that ape, you are gravely mistaken. Who else?'

'Oh, I don't know, some bloke called from Melbourne. She said he had a British accent.'

The SAS hitman. I gasped again.

Delia returned with the milk and a newspaper under one arm.

'What's with you?' Kylie asked. 'You've gone pale.'

'Yes, pale green, actually,' My mother said. 'Was it the vanilla slice? The custard might have gone off.'

'I ... I'm fine,' I stammered.

'You're all sweaty,' Kylie went on, pretending to care. 'Could it be early menopause?'

'Yes. Probably that's all it is.'

'Got *The Weekly Times*,' Delia said. 'There's a lift-out on the Beef Expo in Queensland. Thought you might want a read, Kylie.'

'You don't need an expo, you've got Loretta,' I said. 'She's an expert. By the way, where is she?'

'She's gone,' said Kylie and picked up the glossy magazine.

'Gone where?'

'Dunno. Said she wanted to go. Tyler took her and the wolf to Horsham, dropped them off this morning.'

I was stunned. 'But she's alone and pregnant and —'

'She wanted to go, Stella,' Kylie said. 'I can't keep her against her will.'

I went in the house and called Loretta's number. No answer. I left a message.

When I returned to the garden, Kylie was in the midst of a low-grade tantrum. She threw the lift-out onto the table. 'Can't go to Queensland now, Mum. I'm flat out at the farm.'

'Flat out having lunch,' I said.

My mother cuffed the back of my head. 'Kylie's doing a great job.'

'Ignore her,' Kylie said. 'She's just jealous.'

Despite my anxiety, I chortled.

'You won't be laughing when I bring in ten million in the third year.'

That was hysterical. I hooted, held my sides. 'How will you do that? With the Dexters?'

Kylie cleared her throat. 'With our current purchasing and breeding program, we expect to have ten thousand head of cattle across both farms in that time frame.'

'*Both* farms?' I was stunned. 'Tell me you're not in league with Shane-fucking-Farquhar.'

My mother biffed the back of my head again. 'Language.'

Kylie ignored the question and carried on with her address to the nation. 'In the current live-export market, that's ten million Australian dollars.'

I did a quick calculation. Those missing fifty thousand Brahman in Middleton were worth fifty million dollars. A lot of money *if* you sold them on the export market. It was a big if.

Delia ate another vanilla slice and pulled the glossy lift-out from the paper. I couldn't believe she wasn't concerned about this. The partnership with another farm, the plans for live export. The ridiculous ambition of a ten-million-dollar payoff. I watched her turn the pages as she chewed vanilla custard in her new serene fashion. She appeared to have completely renounced her emotional connection to the Hardy farm. My mother, I realised with a start, was Zen. A rural, conservative, church-going version of Zen. The judging, suspicious person was gone. She was happy, relaxed, easygoing. At least my cursing had brought out the old Delia. I made a mental note to say something obscene in her presence on a regular basis.

I looked at Kylie. She was on her phone, sending a furtive text.

I stared into the distance and made up my mind. It was time I gave up worrying about the farm, too. If my mother no longer cared, why should I? What I needed to do was prepare for the threats to my existence. Like tattoo man. It would seem he'd tracked me to Woolburn. He was probably on his way to the Wimmera right now, while I was sitting around eating cakes. If he was in Nell Tuffnell's car, the Nissan Navara ST-X, I would know what to look out for. No. Every second car here was a four-cab monster.

Next threat, Farquhar. The testosterone-soaked Neanderthal wanted something from me.

I needed to get away, and I knew just the place. Dougal Park, Skye Redbridge's property. Did she have any unauthorised bulls in her paddocks? The plan was sound. I'd leave now. Well, after a vanilla slice. If I was going to die, I had no reason to worry about carbs.

I ate a slice and turned a page of the paper. Rural news from across the country, with syndicated stories from the major dailies. Most were puff pieces about a kid's first medal in show jumping, or cheesy profiles of a farming family's triplets who scored blue ribbons for their pigs. I took another bite of custard, turned another page, and paused mid-chew.

Allyson Coleman Buys Green Ships for Cattle Export.

Coleman. That was it. Coleman. I was sure the name I'd seen on the email on Enrique Nunzio's computer screen in the Athol

Goldwater shed was 'Al Coleman'.

Allyson with a *y*. Hadn't thought of that.

> Well-known entrepreneur Allyson Coleman announced today
> that she acquired a number of ships known as 'green' that
> are cattle-friendly for the live trade. Ms Coleman is acting in
> partnership with a consortium of overseas buyers, and has
> paid a $3.2 million deposit.
>
> She has worked as a deal broker for major cattle station
> acquisitions in recent years and is director of Taurus Beef
> Trust. She made the announcement from a Jakarta teleconfer-
> ence to journalists in Australia and overseas.

Pugh's accomplice. I needed to do research on Allyson Coleman.
'Where's Ted's iPad?'

Delia cackled. 'What's unravelled your knitting?'

'Mum, this is important.'

'Everything's important.'

'Just fucking tell me.'

She tried to strike me with the rolled-up supplement. I dodged.
'Please.'

'In the bedroom, top bedside-table drawer on his side. And mind
your damn language.'

25

A CASCADE of hits for 'Allyson Coleman' flowed onto Ted's iPad screen. One profile in *The Weekly Times* covered her life in business. Ms Coleman had grown up on a farm in Inglewood, Queensland, and had attended the prestigious boarding school Willowbrook Girls Grammar in North Sydney. Her mother, Harriet Marie Wills Coleman, was a patron of the arts. Her father, Gideon Coleman, was a cattle grazier and politician who served in the Australian Parliament and was renowned for his military feats in Africa during the Second World War. In the fifties, Gideon Coleman diversified the business and went into coal mining, creating a large family fortune.

Divorced twice, currently single, Allyson Coleman had been through good times and bad. She'd struck out on her own in a mining venture in the seventies, went bankrupt in the eighties, and then recovered and went on to found Oz Macadamia in 1997 and raise millions to launch a range of nut products. But the business never took off, leaving a lot of angry creditors. She went overseas for a while, then returned to Australia and to the BRW rich-list, with renewed vigour and foreign money, this time, in the cattle industry. She was a director in numerous companies: transport, agri-tech, private security. She divided her time between Jakarta and Darwin. She drove a powder-blue Karmann Ghia in town and a top-of-the-range Range Rover in the bush. She had ships and helicopters and land.

There was a piece in *Stock and Land* on her recent purchase of three large cattle stations, on behalf of an international consortium.

'Cool Runnings and Patricia Creek stations acquisitions are part of a strategic plan by Taurus Beef Trust, allowing us to continue to export healthy Australian-bred and -produced cattle into the expanding Asian market,' Ms Coleman said.

Two of the properties, Cool Runnings and Patricia Creek, are large-scale breeding properties situated within commercial proximity of multiple market facilities including feedlots, abattoirs, saleyards, and ports of the Gulf of Carpentaria in northern Queensland.

A third property, Fly Hole Station, stocked with sixty-five thousand Brahman, is a quality finishing property located near Mount Isa, Queensland.

'The superb pastures Fly Hole provides improved our fattening base,' Ms Coleman said.

'The three properties, and the purchase of the ships, provide a continuous, efficient, and reliable supply of young cattle to live-export markets in key trading nations.'

Some articles were flattering, highlighting her charity work. Others were less so. Verity Savage of *The Australian Financial Chronicle* wrote, 'Ms Coleman, 63, best known as a disastrously unsuccessful nut farmer, bought the properties last September.'

The last line took the vanilla-fucking-slice:

Youngest daughter of Sir Gideon Coleman, Allyson is known to keep influential company. She co-owns a horse with Victorian Justice Minister, Marcus Pugh.

Melbourne to Ouyen by car, without stopping, was more than a five-hour journey. If the British hitman had left the city this morning, he'd arrive in Woolburn around two in the afternoon. People needed to eat and relieve themselves, so more likely, he'd arrive around three.

But that was fine, because I would be otherwise occupied; I had to see a woman about a stolen bull.

It was one in the afternoon when I left Ouyen for Dougal Park, the Redbridge stud farm. A pleasant three-and-a-half-hour drive down along the western side of The Grampians. I'd be there, if all went well, by late afternoon. Instead of the most direct route, via Woolburn, I detoured through Sea Lake, adding thirty minutes to my travel time. I figured it was worth it. Since people were looking for me in Woolburn.

I stopped at a service station on the outskirts of Sea Lake to fill the tank.

As I stood at the bowser, pulling the nozzle's trigger, I thought about Allyson Coleman. She and Pugh co-owned a race horse, she was the only 'Al' on my list of likely Als. Could she yank Van Go Daddy, a large and distinctive bull, from his paddock in Meandarra, Queensland, and send him to Pugh's daughter, whose farm was — I checked the map app on my phone — seventeen hundred kilometres away in Victoria?

Someone called my name. I glanced up. It was Tyler, Kylie's long-suffering husband. He was getting into his ute and gave me a wave and a sad smile. *Poor man*, I thought, as I waved back.

Petrol splashed from the tank. I grabbed some paper and wiped the side of the Mazda and my jeans. I had no change of clothes, since I was planning to return to Woolburn the same day. A bell jangled on the shop door when I went to pay, summoning a youth. He asked me how I was, I replied I'd never been better and went to peruse the beverage options in the fridge. Copies of *Stock and Land*, *The Weekly Times*, *The Age*, and *The Australian Financial Chronicle* were stacked up near the counter. I picked up the *Chronicle*. Verity Savage had a front-page story about tax avoidance by major Australian companies.

'Petrol, the *Chronicle*, and this can of Coke.' I needed sugar and caffeine and denial.

He noted the petrol stain on my jeans, and suggested I take care when next I light a smoke. I laughed. Accidental self-immolation was not even in my top five most likely deaths.

Back on the highway for a while, then a detour through Birchip, population six hundred and sixty-two, going slow and checking the road behind me. The statue of a bull in the main drag was a highlight of this particular scenic route.

Out on the open road again, I put on my speed-dealer sunglasses and found a radio station playing classic soul. Sam Cooke and I passed a pleasant half-hour, crooning and cruising through a landscape of dry scrub under a clear sky. A warm northerly carried the familiar acrid smoke from a distant burn-off. All being well, I'd hit Warracknabeal in twenty minutes.

Brophy would love this: the quality of the light, these colours. I pictured us relaxing in some quiet rural shack around here. He'd be sceptical at first after all the unenthusiastic things I'd said over the years about growing up in this part of the world, but I'd win him over.

A large furry roadkill blocked half the road ahead. I swerved to avoid it and checked my mirror. A small white car was coming up fast. Not unusual, I told myself, the locals were impatient, and kids were outright reckless. Tourists could be a problem — stopping in the middle of the road to photograph sheep, driving on the wrong side. I decelerated and kept to the left of the lane, inviting it to pass me.

The car came close, slowed and kept a ten-metre gap. No one in the passenger seat. The driver a dark blur behind the tinted glass.

What fuckery was this?

I thought about stopping. Bad plan. Middle of nowhere, between towns, no one but sheep to witness whatever this was. What to do? Get to Warrack' as quickly as possible. No, that town was still a long way off. I crested a hill, the white car kept pace. On the other side, there were two vehicles coming up the other way. I waved at them, but the first, an old falcon just sped by. Behind it, a ute with a roll of hay tootled up the incline. I waved frantically. The old bloke at the wheel, elbow on the open window, just lifted a finger off the steering wheel and carried on. Once it passed, I whacked the Mazda into third, hit the accelerator, and gunned it. The white car took a moment to respond, a second later it had matched my speed.

All of a sudden the white car was right beside me, driving in the oncoming lane. Without warning, the driver swung the wheel left. I slammed down on the brakes, a centimetre between the cars. I slowed, panicked, trying to think. The white car slowed in front of me, moved to the left lane. I went right, accelerated, and sped by as it swung out at me again. No collision — a whisker in it. The white car swapped lanes once more, and came up fast.

Ahead, an old sign post pointed to a possible left turn.

I braked at the very last moment and took the turn doing fifty, back tyres skidding on the bitumen. Dust clouds billowed up behind me, and no white car appeared through them. I exhaled for what felt like the first time in a while. It wasn't a road, but a narrow dirt track with shallow channels on either side, close to the fences. I rocketed down the middle, lurching in every dip and crack, engine roaring, steering wheel shaking. I checked the surrounding paddocks for a driveway or a track — anything to escape down — but the fences on both sides continued to infinity. What I did see was a dark mass ballooning, coming across the scrub fast. The burn-off.

I checked the mirror. The white car was coming, flat stick, rebounding off the potholes.

The north wind was pushing the smoke across the paddock, and it started to blanket the road. A blur of dark shapes moved inside the smoke. What the heck was that? Then I knew. A mob of eastern greys were thundering away from the fire.

In a panic, I made a quarter-turn left, then swung the wheel hard to the right and stepped on the brake. Time seemed to slow. The Mazda slid sideways in the sand until a front tyre found purchase. It spun in a 180-degree arc to face back the way I'd come, and then continued skidding sideways down into the ditch. The passenger side of the Mazda slammed into fence posts and the windows cracked. A second later, the white car went past. A second after that, a sickening boom of impact, and the sound of shattering glass.

A moment passed. The Mazda had stalled. I sat, stunned, covered in glass and grit.

The radio was still on: 'Yeah, nothing can ever change the love we feel for you, Sam.'

I moved my arm, put my foot on the clutch, turned the key: it started. I tried to turn the wheel, but the wheels were jammed. I turned it off and unbuckled my seatbelt.

I seized my handbag and climbed out on unsteady legs. I walked twenty metres down the road. The white car was on its side in the opposite channel. The front was smashed in, red smears on bonnet. I watched the car for a moment, no movement inside.

Nearby, a tangle of grey fur was motionless on the track. Blood pooled under it. The rest of the mob had continued to move on to the next paddock, except for a joey. It hung around the body, sniffed the blood-soaked fur, lifted its head, and looked around. Slowly, it moved off, then in a rush, it caught the rest of the mob.

A groan from the white car. The crack of the door opening. I put my hand in my handbag. Through the smoke, I saw the driver door lifted upward. Heart racing, I took out the taser.

26

AN ARM came out from the car, and, putting the hand flat on the car body, tried to push. A howl of pain.

'You alright?' I shouted from a distance.

'Oh yeah, brilliant, completely fine. Proper jammy, me.' British accent. Of course.

I detected signs of injury, but I wasn't convinced that he was no longer a threat.

'Actually, no, to be totally honest with you, my knee's fucked. Call an ambulance?'

'No network.'

'Your car?'

'Stuffed.'

'Get me out, will you? The fire's coming.'

It was true, the fire was on its way. And not far, probably a couple of kilometres away. But it wasn't here yet. The smoke was well ahead of the fire front, making it seem closer.

'Show me both hands.'

Two hands came out, shaking with the effort.

'Alright. I'm going to help you. But you should know, I've got the taser. Remember the fun you had with that the last time you came for me? So don't try anything.'

'Cross my fucking heart.'

I looked inside the car. He blinked up at me, blood, tears, and red dust on his face. I took his trembling hand and tried to lift him. He shrieked in agony. I stopped.

'Do it!' he shouted. 'Get me out.'

I dropped the taser, took both his hands in mine and pulled again, getting him half way out. One more pull, and he slumped onto the road. He rolled on his back. He was bleeding from a cut on his forearm, near the sword and wings tattoo. He wore cargo shorts, and I could see one knee was purple and twice the usual size. Lower down, a bone pushed at the skin. It was a couple of kilometres back to the main road. In the other direction, the track curved to the left and rose up to a crest a hundred metres away. No farm house nearby. No passing helpful cocky on a tractor.

The man was panting and rocking and holding the knee.

'Show me some ID.'

He pulled a wallet from his back pocket. I took it from him and pulled out a UK licence.

'Colin Slade. First-aid kit in that car, Colin?'

'Hire car. Probably not.'

'Can you get up, put weight on your good leg?'

He shook his head.

Waves of thick smoke rolled over us. I sat beside him and went through the wallet. Plane ticket — Melbourne to Mildura — plastic cards, four hundred in cash, and a photo of a small child. Tucked behind the photo, a folded piece of paper. A BlackTack invoice.

The wind sent another wave of dark smoke over us, swirling red embers within it.

'Why aren't you getting out of here, Hardy?' Colin Slade said, stunned at my nonchalance.

I shrugged, like I was resigned to death. 'My car's stuffed. I'll never make it out.'

'You can run.'

'Outrun this? No. I'd die trying.' I pointed to my jeans. 'That's petrol you can smell. I'm covered in it. When the fire comes, I'll go up fast. Nice a quick. Can't say the same for you.'

'You're a fucking psycho.'

192

I shrugged.

'Fuck this. I'm not burning to death. Hardy, get the Jericho. It's in the car.'

'What's a Jericho?'

'Semi-automatic pistol.'

'So you can shoot me?'

He stared at me in disbelief. 'So you can shoot *me*.'

I waved the paper at him. 'You were sent here to kill me.'

'It's a job. Nothing personal.'

'You also do work for Enrique Nunzio and Allyson Coleman, am I right?'

He ignored the question. His only concern seemed to be obsessively watching for the fire. He was probably in shock. I went to the Mazda and found the can of Coke under the seat. I lifted the tab, foam sprayed out.

'Here.'

He drank half.

'Alright?'

'Bit better.'

I went to Slade's hire car. The Jericho was under the passenger seat. I brought it out and went to sit next to him.

'How does it work?'

He shifted on his arse, pulled a pained expression, and took the gun from me. He removed the clip and shoved it back. 'I love this gun,' he said. 'Very comfortable. See? Hold it.'

I took it in both hands, no idea what I was doing. It didn't feel comfortable. It was large and unwieldy. 'How do you fire it?' I handed it back.

'First, rack it. Grab this slide on the top and pull it back.' He demonstrated, and the top of the pistol shifted back and forward, making a scary *click*. I had a try. It moved fairly smoothly, and I heard the click.

'It's a right-hand pistol. This one is the forty. You've got your safety, here, and your slide catch.'

'Slow down,' I said.

'Doesn't matter. Look. It has a double-action trigger. Pull the trigger, it fires.' He pulled the trigger. I wasn't ready. The sharp crack shook me. And the gun kicked back in a way that frightened me.

He took out the clip. 'Twelve round magazine.' He slotted it. 'You try.'

I took out the clip, slotted it, pulled back the slide, and held it in both hands.

'Straight arms,' Slade said.

I straightened my arms, aimed into the nearest fence post, placed my finger on the trigger, and pulled. The force of the round leaving travelled through my hands and up my arms. I'm sure I blinked because I had no idea where the bullet went. But my work was done. I put the Jericho down carefully on the road.

'Look,' I said. 'I'll shoot you, Colin, if it's what you want. But you know, *quid pro quo*, I need to know what the deal is with Allyson and Marcus Pugh.'

He sighed. 'What's the point?'

'No point. Just that it seems excessive to kill Joe Phelan and Velvet Stone, and now me, all because of a bull.'

He looked confused.

'The recording on the phone — it's just Pugh talking about an auction. *Vincent got away.*'

He snorted with derision. 'A fucking bull, that's a laugh.'

'What then? Give me something.'

'Close to fifty million dollars, how's that for something.'

'But for what? What's the bloody deal, Colin?'

His eyes lit up as if he heard an angel singing. Then I heard it, too. The roar and sigh, roar and sigh, of a truck changing gears. Through the haze, I looked towards the crest of the hill, expecting a harvester. The front grill of a Mack motored up and climbed over the hill, two massive trailers, side mirrors a metre out on each side. The

194

horn started blasting to raise the dead as the truck began flying down the hill. The driver was under the mistaken impression that we could get out of the way.

I stood up, waving my arms and shouting stop.

The driver hit the airbrakes, releasing a monster's bellowing fart, and the whole thing shuddered and lurched to a halt with barely a metre to spare.

I ran to the driver. He had the door open and was climbing out. A youngish man, short and thick set. 'The fuck happened here?'

'I stacked into the fence. He hit a roo. Broke his leg. Get him to the hospital?'

He spat. 'I'm on a tight schedule.'

'Mate, look at him.'

Colin's face was the colour of wax. 'Don't leave us here to burn,' he pleaded.

'Shit, you're not going to burn, not unless the wind changes direction. Fire's heading west.'

Colin scowled at me. I grinned back at him.

'Go on,' I said to the driver. 'Give us a lift.'

He thought it over. 'Alright. Suppose I better. Give us a hand.'

He heaved Colin up from under the armpits, while I took his legs. He stepped backwards up the cabin steps, movements awkward from lifting, and hoisted Colin into a space behind the front seats.

Once he was settled, I glanced back to the long trailer. It was jammed with cattle, complaining about the discomfort and the smoke.

'You coming or what?' the truck driver said.

'Just a minute.' I ran around, picked up my handbag, and, with my back to the truck, I carefully placed the Jericho in it, then I threw the taser in there, too.

'All set,' I called and climbed into the cab. From that height the flare of yellow-orange firestorm coming down the paddock towards us was clear.

'How about that,' the truck driver said. 'The fire's changed directions. It's coming this way, would have come straight for youse.'

The Wimmera Base Hospital waiting area had hard plastic chairs. The cars had been left to burn, the Mazda and Slade's hire car — his excess would be eye-watering. I'd made enquiries about getting the Mazda taken to a wrecker as soon as it was safe to enter the fire-affected area. Ben may as well get something for it. The other task on my list was to keep a close eye on Colin Slade. I needed more information from him: names, dates, times, all the details of this cock-eyed caper. I alerted the nurses that he was not to try to slip out the back, like he did in Melbourne after the taser incident. A clock in the waiting room marked the slow, tedious passing of time while Slade had his X-rays, leg set, and whatever else. It was now four-thirty, and I'd spent nearly two hours of bum-numbing tedium watching a TV attached to the wall.

The news presenter called the burn-off a major fail — thousands of hectares of pasture had been burnt. Cut to a scientist: 'Bushfire season in Victoria is much longer now.' Images of CFA volunteers directing high-pressure hoses on walls of flame. Pictures of an untouched house in a sea of black paddocks.

Piano music came from my handbag. I moved the taser and Colin Slade's hand gun and took out my phone. ID: *Percy*.

'Yes?' I said, wearily.

'Mate, you alright? On me way, nearly in your shithole town.'

Shit, I'd forgotten Percy Brash was coming up. 'I'm not there.'

'May I ask where the fuck you are, then?'

'Horsham. At the hospital. The SAS bloke is getting his broken leg seen to.'

A change in tone for the brighter. 'Fuck me, what happened?'

I told him, and he sounded impressed. 'What happens to him now?'

'Nothing. I didn't report it. I'm going to buy him a drink, hoping to get him to talk.'

196

I heard a wheezing noise I took to be laughter. 'You couldn't get information out of a choir boy on truth serum. Which pub?'

'Don't know. Maybe The International.'

'Right.' He hung up.

What did that mean? I stared at the phone. It rang in my hand.

Bunny Slipper. 'I've gone over your transcript of the recording, and I'm afraid nothing directly connects Pugh to the fancy bull that's missing. He doesn't actually use the name of the bull. It's vague. It would be super easy to shoot down in court. Frankly, Stella, there isn't much there.'

'They are so concerned about that recording that they killed Joe Phelan.'

'Well, I can't see why. If you have anything more, let me know.'

'I've got more. Allyson Coleman and fifty million dollars.'

'That is a name and a number. Not evidence.'

I shifted my arse around on the hard plastic. 'Bunny, check her out for yourself. She's a notorious scam artist, takes investor money for risky ventures, goes bust, skips town. One journalist called her a *disastrously unsuccessful nut farmer*.'

Silence at her end.

'Okay, yes, I don't have evidence. *Yet*. But I'm sure this thing goes deeper than one bull. Otherwise, why is Pugh so paranoid about the recording?'

'This thing? What *is* this thing? Corruption? Theft? An actual crime? You don't know.'

'You're right, I don't know,' I said. 'But I do know that BS12 are involved in the cattle trade. Athol Goldwater is a prison farm, and they test agri-tech there. Tech like that iDrover you had in your show. Cattle tags, tracking, GPS, all that. And BS12 hired a BlackTack operative to murder two people who found out what they're up to.'

'Two people? Remind me?'

'Velvet Stone was killed because Joe Phelan had asked her about hacking cattle-monitoring technology.'

'A pretty long bow, Stella.' Bunny sighed. 'What's Pugh's connection to Coleman?'

'They own a race horse together. Allyson with a *y*. Look into it, Bunny, they're both in on it. They're all in on it together.'

'You sound paranoid. But I'll take a look.'

I pocketed the phone and walked around the waiting room, and then out into the foyer, glancing over at the nurse behind the counter. She smiled at me and shook her head. No news yet. I went outside, did a circuit of the block, and went back to my hard chair. According to Kylie, Loretta Swindon had left the Hardy farm and was somewhere in Horsham. I rang Loretta's number, and, to my relief, she picked up.

'Where are you?' I asked.

'A church.'

'What, again? You shouldn't have left the farm.'

'I had to leave,' Loretta said. 'I wasn't welcome. Your sister didn't want to talk about cattle farming with me. Her mind's made up. She's got some arrangement with that bloke.'

Shane-fucking-Farquhar. Despite my decision to stop worrying about the farm, the thought of him riled me up.

'You need to talk her out of it,' Loretta said. 'He's been misleading her about how great a merger will be for both farms. I tried. I told her that without the legal papers that Ben signed, she was in no position to make those kinds of deals. I think she heard me, but you have to talk her out of it. Stella, are you listening?'

I couldn't see why she was so upset about Kylie's crazy plans for the farm.

'I'll deal with that later,' I said. 'First, we need to get you out of this dire situation. You need food and a proper room for the night. I'll pay.'

'You don't need to do that.'

'Loretta, you can't sleep in a church. Come on, be sensible.'

She agreed to meet me. But she was so reluctant that I began to wonder if the pregnancy had affected her mental capacity.

27

COLIN SLADE, BlackTack operative and man who'd tried to kill me earlier in the day, hobbled through the swinging hospital doors. He was on crutches, with one leg in a moon boot and one knee heavily strapped. Band-Aids criss-crossed his face and forearm.

'You waited,' Colin said, amazed.

'Of course,' I said. 'We have a lot to talk about. How about a drink?'

We went out into the warm afternoon. It was an easy five-minute walk on flat roads to the Horsham International. For Slade, on crutches, it took twenty minutes. While I went to reception to book a room for Loretta and me, Slade went into the bar, or Baa, as it was called.

I found him settled on a stool, staring out at the steady flow of cars, utes, and trucks on the Western Highway. Ballarat to the left of us, Adelaide to the right.

The place was unusually quiet for a Sunday afternoon, with only two other people in the place, a grey-haired man and a younger woman. He was doing all the talking, and her only contribution seemed to be an occasional nod.

'Beer?' I asked Slade.

'And a whiskey.'

I ordered two beers, a whiskey, and some sweet-potato chips and garlic bread. Slade drank the whiskey in one shuddering gulp. I sipped my beer, and we both stared out at the street.

'When do the cops show up,' he said.

'I wouldn't call the cops on you.'

He let out a deep breath, picked up the beer, and drank half. 'What do you want?'

'Information.'

'You'll get me killed.'

'No one will know I've spoken to you.'

He grimaced into his beer. 'They'll know.'

'Colin, what are you doing here? Not you personally, I mean. BlackTack. What are you here to do, exactly?'

'The syndicate hired me. Their operation had been compromised. The prisoner with the phone, the recording. It had to be shut down. It was an unacceptable risk.'

Shut down? Quite the euphemism. 'So you killed the prisoner?'

'No.' He looked up at me, squinting. 'I advised against it until we had the phone. We still don't know who did that. After he died, I was ordered to find the phone. Destroy it.'

'You killed Velvet Stone. You admit that?'

'Yes. She knew of the phone's existence. I doubt she knew what was on it. But she had to be neutralised.'

If only Bunny Slipper were here, listening to all this eye-witness evidence. Slade casually admitting to killing Velvet Stone. Perhaps he was telling the truth about not killing Joe Phelan.

'That night with Velvet Stone, when you took me back to my apartment, you could have killed me, but you didn't. Why?'

He shrugged. 'There was a pathetic attempt at blackmail using the recording. The syndicate believes someone working on the inside was conspiring with the prisoner. They thought you might help to uncover who it was. You gave us the phone, said you didn't know what was on it. I believed you. And so did my contact. They let you have another chance of finding the infiltrator. Not anymore — now you're a liability.'

'You called me at the Woolburn Hotel. How did you know where I was?'

'Went back to your apartment: old bloke with a dog out the front says you're at your boyfriend's. Just offered it up.'

Brown Cardigan, for a paranoid security-conscious wimp, he sure was a blabbermouth. 'So then what? You don't know who my boyfriend is.'

'Old bloke said he's an artist, lives in Footscray.'

I needed to have words with that gossipy man. 'But you don't know which artist.'

'Bloke goes, *Peter Brophy, aged forty-eight. Lives above a shop, calls his place the Narcissistic Slacker.* Which is a laugh.'

I felt a chill. 'You spoke to him?'

'My word. And he gave you up easy, too. Said you were in Woolburn with your mum.'

I was too stunned to speak.

'I'll tell you something else for free, he's not a well man, your artist friend.'

'He has a cold,' I said.

'Yeah. That's it,' he said dryly. 'He's so thin he's transparent, a sorry sight.'

'He told you where I was?' I asked, ignoring the awful implications of that description.

'I said it was urgent, and he gave me the lot, even your car registration.' He drank some beer.

I sat in stunned silence. A stranger asks for your personal information and your significant other just coughs it up. It wasn't a betrayal, per se; it was really bad judgement. I knew Brown Cardigan was a fool and a jerk, but I thought Brophy was more canny than that.

Slade was opening up. Perhaps the beer and the whiskey had gone to his head, because he started telling me about how he'd flown in a light plane to Mildura and driven a hire car to Woolburn. He'd asked around in the pub, and a bloke told him he'd seen me getting petrol in Sea Lake.

Tyler. He probably thought he was being helpful. That was three men who'd freely offered information about me to a BlackTack operative. What was the world coming to? And Slade said they regarded me as a liability to be neutralised. They were coming for me. I needed to know my enemy. I needed to come for *them*.

'Tell me about the syndicate, who are they?'

He sighed, like it was inconsequential. The topic seemed uninteresting to him.

'Who's in the syndicate? Enrique Nunzio?'

'Yeah, him.'

'And Pugh and Allyson Coleman?'

'Probably.'

'What about Ranik, the prison manager?'

He shook his head and drained his glass.

'Some BS12 people at the prison are not in on it?'

'I suppose. Look, Hardy, it doesn't matter. I'm already dead, we both are.' He stared into his empty glass. Something had changed, perhaps the painkillers were wearing off. He was retreating into himself. 'Fuck this,' he said abruptly. 'Call me a taxi.'

I pulled out my phone. 'Going to?'

'Mildura airport.'

It took a bit of convincing to get the taxi company to believe that Colin wanted to travel three hundred kilometres. But he had the dough. After many assurances that this was not a prank, I was told the driver was on his way.

'What's the plan? Back to the UK? Get a job doing something less risky, North Sea fisherman or something?'

Dead bat, not even a smile. 'For what it's worth, my contact in the syndicate is Paul. No last name. Calls me Harry.'

'Did you ever meet Paul in person?'

'Yes, once. When I first arrived. The bar of the Darwin Hilton, a month ago.'

'Darwin?'

He nodded. 'This assignment, the client comes from Darwin.'

Allyson Coleman drove her Karmann Ghia around the streets of

Darwin. Darwin's a main port. Ships out of Darwin went to Egypt, Jakarta, Tripoli.

Slade coughed loudly, finished his beer. 'I'm off.'

'Wait, tell me about Paul. What's he look like?'

'Mid-forties, average height, thinning auburn hair, auburn moustache, freckled face.'

'What about Nell Tuffnell?'

'Who?'

'The prison guard. You drove her car that night with Velvet Stone. And again the night you came to my flat.'

'You say so. I was told to use that car, not a rental. Keep the operation untraceable.'

We stayed silent as a woman came from the kitchen carrying a tray. She placed the chips and bread on the table without a word. I picked up a garlicky triangle.

When she'd gone, I said, 'What's next? What's the syndicate planning? Any hints?'

'Hints?' He held my gaze. 'Take a guess. You're still alive.'

He gathered his crutches and, without a word, began making slow progress to the exit. The automatic door parted, but he turned and came back, dropped one of the crutches, and put out his hand. 'Thanks for … the drink.'

I shook his hand. 'Don't mention it.'

'I mean, for everything. Considering …'

'Considering you were trying to kill me? Forget it, people try that a lot.'

'I'm not surprised.' He tucked the crutches under his armpits.

An uneasy feeling descended upon me.

I took out my phone to call Brophy. Minutes passed. I stared out the window without seeing, phone at the ready in my sweaty hand. More minutes passed. I couldn't make the call.

A man in a blue shirt with insignia on the shoulders walked into the Baa.

'Someone call a taxi to Mildura?' he shouted.

'He's out the front,' I said. 'The bloke on crutches.'

'No one's there. No crutches.'

'Maybe he flagged down a passing cab,' I said.

'Knew it was a prank,' he said and marched out.

Colin Slade was no longer my concern. The syndicate, the new threat to my life, none of it mattered. Brophy was all I could think about. But I couldn't talk to him. I put my phone away, noting a change in my mood. Dark thoughts and a sense of impending failure, of inevitable shitty arguments, of a return to loneliness. Familiar, business-as-usual, dreadful loneliness.

I blinked back tears and finished the garlic bread.

28

IT HAD already gone four, and Brash still hadn't arrived. I decided to leave the International and find something to distract me from the ache in my heart. If the so-called syndicate's latest hired killer was on their way, I had most of the day to walk around in relative safety before they showed.

The air smelled of smoke, distant sirens sounded as I walked along Firebrace Street. A window display of handbags in the shape of different citrus fruit caught my eye. The grapefruit one was open and showed its many zips and interior pockets. A good choice for someone who carried lots of things that needed to be concealed. Taser, Jericho, etc. There was even a place for my speed-dealer sunglasses. The thing was the size of a basketball, however, and somewhat unwieldy. I turned away and went along McLachlan Street, where I faced a public library building.

The long empty afternoon stretched out ahead of me. What to do before it was time to meet Loretta? Obeying an impulse, I went in, acquired yet another library card, and logged onto a computer.

I concocted a complicated search for 'racehorse' and 'owners' and 'syndicate' and 'Pugh' and 'Coleman', not expecting much. After a bit of eyestrain, and pointless scrolling of dead-end hits, I found a media piece on a three-year-old filly named Sister Smug. She was a middle-distance galloper with a mixed record. On this occasion she'd won the Wodonga Cup, and there was a picture of the owners. The caption read: *Marcus Pugh, Allyson Coleman, and the others in the syndicate celebrate Sister Smug's hard-fought win in Wodonga.*

I recognised Pugh. The tall blonde woman in an expensive-looking powder-blue frock with matching hat I assumed was Coleman. Nunzio was there, hiding behind dark sunglasses and a straw boater. And one other man was celebrating with them. He was holding up a champagne flute and seemed overjoyed. He had a freckled complexion and thinning red hair.

Pugh, Nunzio, and Coleman. And a man who matched Colin Slade's description of his contact, the man he called Paul.

Pugh had asked me to find an employee who seemed to be making money on the side. The syndicate was looking for an infiltrator, someone who had made a sloppy attempt at blackmail, someone on the inside who knew about the recording. Velvet Stone had said that someone had called her to set up the initial meeting with Joe Phelan at the market. Joe had needed an insider to make that contact for him.

Nell Tuffnell liked cruises and paid cash for a new car. Not on a prison officer's salary, she didn't. Where was the money coming from?

She wasn't in the photo. Was she in the syndicate? Slade had used her car. Perhaps it was a request from Nunzio, *Lend us your car, we'll pay you*. She may have been an unwitting associate of the syndicate.

What I needed, what would finally convince Bunny to take it further, was those invoices in Nunzio's office. How hard would it be to break into a prison?

I still had time before I was due to meet Loretta, so I did a few idle searches on the live-cattle trade. Export numbers out of Australia were dizzying. Destinations were as far flung as Libya and Vietnam, Kazakhstan and Japan, but the majority were shipped to Indonesia. Most of the ten million head of cattle currently grazing in Queensland would be exported, already slaughtered as pre-packaged meat or alive. Ditto the two-point-two million that roamed the Northern Territory.

There were several organisations that facilitated the smooth delivery of live cattle from farm to overseas abattoir. Some were privately run, some were membership-based not-for-profit organisations. They all claimed to work with stakeholders. They all expressed concern with animal wellbeing. They all offered support with supply-chain efficiency and access to key markets. Some offered technical support, and had a hand in research and development. I picked one at random, jotted down a name and number, and logged off.

I went outside and rang the number.

'Livestock Solutions, this is Amber.'

'Good morning. This is an English Kazak interpreter service. Please hold for your incoming translated message.'

'Oh, okay,' Amber said.

'Translating …' Pause. 'Hello, I am Medina, from Kazakhstan. Can I speak to Mr Julian Fortuna?'

'One moment.'

Electronic 'Greensleeves'.

'Julian Fortuna speaking.'

'Translating …' Pause. 'Hello Mr Julian. I am Medina. My boss has an interest in live cattle importation to Kazakhstan.'

'Certainly, how may I help you?'

Pause. 'Translating …' Pause. 'My boss is a former army man and has great wealth. He wants to start a new business to import live Australian cattle.'

'Your boss sounds like a wise man.'

Pause. 'Translating …' Pause. 'Yes. His question is, can the cattle be mixed up on the ship?'

'We use tamper-proof RFID tags and traceability software we developed in-house. I can assure you the standard of tracking is excellent. From pasture, to loading, to destination port.'

Pause. 'Translating …' Pause. 'No untracked cattle can get on the ship?'

A deep, hearty laugh. 'Not a chance in hell.'

Pause. 'Translating …' Pause. 'My boss has a contact in Australia with excellent cattle for sale. Their eartags are missing. They can still get on the ship?'

A short pause. 'Look, Medina, I'd like to help your boss, but it's just not possible. There's Australian quarantine inspections, Australian standards, international standards. There's just too many regulations, and they are enforced to the letter. If I step out of line, the federal government would take my export licence.'

Pause. 'Translating ...' Pause. 'There is a lot of money involved.'

'I'm sorry, lady. But that's the law. Exporters and service providers must comply with all relevant legislation of state, territory, and local governments.'

Pause. 'Translating ...' Pause. 'That is a shame. I will report this information to my boss.'

'Yeah, you do that. Now, remind me, what's the capital of Kazakhstan?'

'The, um, the capital of glorious nation of Kazakhstan is a very beautiful city.'

'You forgot to say *translating*. Who are you working for? PAWPAC? RSPCA? PETA?'

'I'm sorry, this connection is bad. I can't hear you.'

'You heard.' His voice rose. 'You want to catch me out? Try harder next time, you hippy fuck. That little performance was a joke. I know your kind. Animal-rights terrorists.'

My ear was raw and vibrating. I put down my phone.

With half an hour to go, I wandered into an opportunity shop. Twenty bucks later, wearing a natty black leather jacket, a silk blouse, and a pair of linen pants, I strutted up to the bar of the Baa of the Horsham International Hotel. Loretta was waiting beside her trolley. 'You look nice. Where's your other clothes?'

'In the bin. Where's Nigel?'

'Back at the church.'

'What church?'

She shrugged. 'Can't remember.'

I ordered a lemon squash for Loretta and another beer for me. The first one, with Colin, had helped settle my nerves, or blunted my senses to give an illusion of safety — either way, I'd been happy with the result. As I watched the barman fill my glass, I felt a vibration in my handbag.

A text from Percy Brash: *Been held up, I'll be there soon.*

I replied with a thumbs-up emoji and delivered the drinks to our table. I'd be happy if Brash didn't show up at all, but that was too much to hope for. Loretta raised her head from her phone screen and looked me up and down.

'You okay, Stella?' she asked. 'You seem distracted.'

Could I trust her? She already knew a lot. I recounted some highlights of my day so far.

'Astana,' she said.

'You know your capitals.'

'Geography was my favourite subject in school.'

When I finished the whole story, her reaction was rather subdued. It would seem it took more than conspiracy and murder to shock Loretta.

The mood in the place was lively. It was reassuring to see the CFA volunteers, farmers, council workers, people of all kinds letting off steam on a Friday night. It was so normal, so regular, so reassuring. I drank the beer and realised I hadn't eaten anything since the vanilla slice.

I convinced Loretta to at least *try* a curry. We finished our drinks and walked the trolley down the road to an Indian place. We ordered four different vegetable curries, rice, naan, raita, as well as more lemon squash and more beer. Then I sent Brash a text with our whereabouts.

'Where was I?' I asked Loretta.

'Kazakhstan.'

'Right. So then he accused me of being with PAWPAC or the RSPCA or PETA.'

209

'I've heard of the other two, but what's PAWPAC?'

I shrugged. Loretta looked it up and handed me her phone.

'Promote Animal Welfare, Prevent Animal Cruelty'. There was a page of high-profile 'patrons': a former high court judge, a soap actress, a celebrity V8 Supercar driver, a former fast bowler with the Australian cricket team, a Western Australian billionaire activist. Next, a list of 'ambassadors' who were more actively involved. Verity Savage, journalist with *The Australian Financial Chronicle*, was on the list. I still had the copy of the paper I'd bought at the servo in my bag — the one with her tax avoidance article in it.

If Bunny Slipper wouldn't take up the investigation without so-called proof, maybe another journalist would. One with an interest in animal welfare. Verity's email address was at the end of the article.

'I'll email her,' I said. 'See what she makes of it all.'

My thumbs were too slow for Loretta. She used her own phone and told me to dictate. I recited a message similar to the one I'd sent to Bunny. A bit of background, potential scoops, and my contact details. I watched Loretta's lightning thumbs fly, feeling gratified to have her help. She wasn't a bad person, and on more than one occasion already she'd actually saved the day. Like when she'd given Colin Slade her old phone. It hadn't been by design, but the result was excellent nonetheless, because it meant I still had Joe's phone, and the recording.

We were raising our glasses to a job well done, when a large figure filled the restaurant entrance. Percy Brash stood holding a sixpack, a gust of stale smoke and body odour in his wake. His clothes were smeared with orange mud, and there were smudges of what looked like blood on his hands.

'Here you fucking are,' he bellowed.

He ripped a can out of the pack and snapped his fingers. A young woman brought him a plate and took the rest of the beers and put them in a fridge near the counter.

Loretta looked him over and said, 'What've you been doing? Riding broncos in a rodeo?'

'Yeah, lassoing a runaway calf.'

She laughed. I didn't.

The curries arrived, and Brash filled his plate and waved his empty can at the waitress. Loretta ate a tentative spoonful of rice and announced she was going to the toilet.

When she'd gone, Percy Brash leaned towards me. 'You did good with getting info from that bloke they sent after you.'

'I beg your pardon?'

How did he know? And what did he care? Brash only cared about one thing: the identity of the person who pulled the trigger on the nail gun that ended Joe Phelan's life. Whatever else came to light, the cattle-tag hacking or whatever, that was none of his business.

Brash tipped beer down his throat, swallowing, working the massive muscles in his neck.

'Percy, what are you on about? How do you know what happened?'

He rubbed the knuckles on his right hand with his left. 'He told me.'

Oh God, he'd bashed Slade. 'You didn't need to do that. Slade told me everything without the need for ...' I pointed at his knuckles. 'Is he still alive?'

He shrugged. I felt sick.

'That was a stupid thing to do. He doesn't know who killed Joe. They don't know who it was. It wasn't them. And now you've murdered someone, a British tourist. When they find his body, the cops will ask questions. The whole thing will come to light. We can't afford that kind of attention right now.'

I couldn't believe I was talking to him like that. It must have been the beer. To my amazement, Brash made a grudging sniff of agreement. He moved his jaw and looked at the ceiling, at a dangling cobweb, thinking.

211

'Someone at Athol Goldwater was working with Joe,' I said. 'They found out about this cattle-tag hacking scheme and were planning to blackmail them. But then they somehow got a recording of Pugh, and that changed everything. At first, they tried to blackmail Pugh with it, but then they got scared and tried to call the cops. Joe's last message to Velvet Stone was to call the cops. They must have been shit-scared. I don't know what happened, maybe Joe's partner panicked and killed him to protect themselves. Maybe they had a fight over strategy. I don't know. But that is the person you're looking for.'

He coughed. 'That could be right.'

Loretta returned from the ladies' and looked from Brash to me, trying to gauge the tone of the conversation.

'Try the Mushroom Jalfrezi,' Brash said to her. 'Get it in you. Look like a skeleton.'

She looked at the curry, horrified, and nibbled on a pappadum.

Brash pointed a stubby finger at me. 'He told me one thing you didn't know. Pugh's political mate in Mildura reckons you've been in there, asking questions. It got back to Pugh. He's sure you know about the recording now, and he's not happy.'

Damn Kelton McHugh, the blabbermouth. 'I don't really care if Pugh is happy or not.'

He shovelled curry into his mouth. 'You're a big fat fucking target, Hardy, and I need you still breathing.'

'Fat?'

Brash laughed, showing the contents of his full mouth. I felt ill, like I was drowning in mud, sucked down into a black moral vacuum. What had he done to Slade? Torture? Murder? I'd sort of come to like him. And the taint of it was also on me. 'I need me still breathing, too,' I said, pathetically.

This amused him; his eyes shone. 'Good,' he said. 'Better hurry up. Deadline's tomorrow. Tick tock.'

'Oh for the love of ... Stop with the fucking ticking clock!'

He grinned, and pushed his chair back. 'Night, all.' He went and grabbed the rest of his sixpack out of the fridge.

I followed him outside. 'Percy, wait. Take this.'

In the shadow of the street, I handed him Slade's handgun. 'It was his. It's a Jericho.' I was cognisant of the fact that if Slade had still had his gun, his encounter with Brash might have turned out very differently.

The gangster's eyebrows rose. 'Keep it. You might need it.'

'No.' I hated having it near me.

'Whatever you reckon.' He rubbed his hands on his pants and took the weapon, felt the weight in his hand. 'Nice.'

'Listen, Percy, tomorrow is a bit unrealistic, don't you think?'

He scratched his chin.

'I'm making progress, just give me more time.'

He burped, and I caught a whiff of curry and beer. 'Rightio. Monday then.'

Labour Day? That was hardly any better. But I had to go along with him. 'Fine. And promise me that once I find out who killed Joe, our business together is concluded. We go our separate ways, and I never see or hear from you again.'

He shoved the Jericho into the waistband of his pants. 'Hardy, you've done good. Better than I thought — said that to Mrs Phelan, too. I really thought you'd be dead by now,' he said with a laugh. 'So yeah, once I get that name, you'll never hear from me again.'

He held out a paw, the one he'd probably used to beat up Colin Slade.

The temptation to shove him away was fierce. I wanted to shout in his big stupid face: *I don't want your praise and your condescension. I wish I'd never heard of you. You and I are nothing alike. I want to be as far away from you as possible.* Self-preservation won out. I gripped his hand and squeezed it.

The truth was, I was no closer to finding Joe's killer. But if I could get another look at Enrique Nunzio's files in his office at the Athol Goldwater prison, I might get a proper smoking gun. Maybe even the identity of every member of the syndicate. It was remote, but it was my only idea. And it was feeding a new strategy. Colin Slade was dead because of me, and it made me ill to think of it. How could I give Brash a name and get someone else killed?

Maybe I could avoid giving him a name by going straight to the cops. I'd tell them Brash was blackmailing me. If I gave the police the evidence of the syndicate, including Slade's contact — the man named Paul — and if I exposed the whole cattle-stealing conspiracy, then maybe, *maybe*, I'd receive some leniency. Anyway, it might assuage my guilt about my role in the death of Colin Slade.

I'd give up the gangster money in my storage locker. I'd admit I took it from the scene of the bikie theft, they wouldn't need hairs to compare. And I'd be in a lot of trouble, but at least I wouldn't have to fulfil the appalling deal I'd made with Percy Brash.

29

RAIN APPEARED in a sudden deluge, pleasing the CFA, the farmers, the townies, the greenies, and even me. I watched it fall outside the café, near the hotel where Loretta and I were having an early breakfast. Steam rose from the bitumen. Rarely used umbrellas were opened on the streets of Horsham. Customers in the café laughed with the proprietor. Strangers smiled at each other. Here, people went about their business untroubled by the thought of further trouble from a BlackTack operative. I was on borrowed time, I knew, but somehow I couldn't muster the energy to be scared. I'd had a sleepless night, listening to Loretta whispering on the phone in the bathroom.

We headed back upstairs, and Loretta went into the bathroom as usual. I had nothing to pack, so I sat on the bed with my phone, waiting for her to emerge. A missed call from Brophy had come through while we were at breakfast. Damn. He'd sent a text. *Marigold and I are on our way to Woolburn now! See you soon x*

I should have been elated. But I rolled onto my side and wondered what I'd say to him.

Loretta returned and seemed transformed. She had both hands on her hips, which seemed a strangely officious stance.

'It's time to go,' she said, bossily.

The change in her attitude shocked me, and I stammered like a One Nation candidate, my native language a foreign object in my mouth. 'But ... but ...' I said.

But the truth was, I was too tired to put up much resistance.

'Come on, up you get. We'll drop you back in Woolburn after.'

'After what?'

'Get up, Stella. You need to come with me. *Now.*'

'What's this about?'

'Hurry, Stella. I'll tell you in the truck.'

Outside the hotel, a truck waited. It was an antique, with a fifties-style engine at the front, headlights stuck on like an afterthought, and tyres under curved faded fenders. It waited for us across the street. In the tray at the back, edged by wooden rails, were some boxes of vegetables, a couple of plants in black plastic pots — one common mint, one possibly flat leaf parsley — a toolbox, and a pile of old tarps. All of it was wet and getting wetter. The truck belonged in a paddock somewhere, with grass growing through the floor and a family of quolls living in it. We both climbed onto the bench seat in the front. In the driver's seat was the old bloke from the bottle shop in Ascot Vale.

'This is Grandad,' said Loretta.

He touched his hat. 'Morrie Swindon.'

I touched the nothing on my head. 'Stella.'

He started working an ancient gear stick, the clutch, and a knob on the dash, and the engine responded with increased puttering. Continuing this jiggling of pedals and choke, he kept the car in a sweet spot of revs without labouring the engine, and somehow the vehicle moved off.

Slowly we made our way out of town, heading west into the desert. Windscreen-wipers creaked and made small milky half-circles on the glass. Loretta and her grandfather were silent. I was full of questions, but every time I tried one of them, Loretta just shook her head and told me to wait.

Loretta's grandad turned off the main road, and then turned again. We drove up a dirt track for a while. The rain eased, and Morrie switched off the wipers. We continued for some time, then came to a gate, which Loretta duly opened, and then she waited while he drove through. She closed and chained it again and jumped back in the jalopy, and we drove some distance down the drive. A house came into view, worn down, needing fresh paint and level stumps. A variety of cars in various stages of disassembly stood in an open shed, as well as in the surrounding paddocks.

Nigel the Alaskan Malamute climbed out of a dog basket positioned to catch the sun on the veranda. He watched us drive up, tail wagging. Morrie stopped in front of the house and pulled at a handbrake.

We all piled out. The dog ran to Loretta and licked her hand. A lone magpie sang a warble.

'Well?' I said.

Loretta went to the tray at the back of the old truck and pulled back a tarp.

Benjamin Hardy, my brother, sat up in his prison tracksuit. 'Surprise!'

'Are you insane?' I said to him, which seemed not to be the response he'd been expecting. 'Only two months of your sentence left to serve. The powers that be wrapped around your little finger, with your chicken soup and kreplach, your rabbit pie. And now you've absconded and … and …' What was the point of trying to talk sense into him? It was his life. He was a fully grown adult who was free to mess up his life as he chose, something he chose to do on a regular basis.

Ben said, 'Stella, I'm a target. I'm on their *list*.'

And Loretta said, 'Yes. Because Ben *knows* everything. He knows too much.'

I almost laughed. 'That's never been a problem for Ben.'

Ben, Loretta, and the old man, all three glared at me. I had to remind myself that this moment did not fit within the Hardy family dynamic, in which mocking Ben was normal. This was a Swindon situation, with Morrie as some kind of kingpin, and Loretta as the brains. Theirs was a unique culture, with its own dysfunction. I needed to play along.

'Alright, Ben, how do you know you're a target? That's the first thing.'

He looked lovingly at Loretta. 'She told me. She basically saved my life.'

Loretta stepped towards me. 'You've been telling me all about goings-on at the prison. Joe was killed, then that acrobat, and there was that dangerous man who was after us. And now you reckon they've probably sent someone else after us.'

I raised a hand to stop her. 'After *me*, Loretta. Not you. And not Ben.'

'You don't know that for sure.'

I didn't. She was right. But really. Ben did not know everything. He couldn't. And even if you explained everything to him, he still wouldn't get it. Loretta, on the other hand, was a wily svengali. It seemed to me she probably wanted Ben out of prison for her own reasons.

'Alright. Let's say you're right,' I said to Ben. 'What is it that you know, exactly?'

'The duff.'

I glanced at Loretta, at her belly. 'Uncanny powers of observation, Ben.'

'Not this,' she said, touching her bump. 'He means the massive duffing racket being run out of the prison.'

I squinted in an effort to understand.

'Loretta's right, Stella,' Ben said. 'Athol Goldwater is run by duffers.'

'What on earth are you talking about?'

'Theft of livestock,' Morrie said. 'A duffer steals cattle, sheep. Old as the hills, and still goes on. Changing a farmer's brand is easy. Add a line and the brand goes from N to M or P to R or what have you. Now they change the tags. With these record prices, it brings duffers out. Last week a calf sold for over a grand. Put *fifty* weaners on a truck, you got serious coin. Neighbours steal from neighbours; small-time opportunists make a quick dollar.'

Morrie, like his granddaughter, appeared to be a dark horse. The hayseed guise concealed a whip-smart observer of the world.

'It can go undetected for months. Stations up north with millions

218

of head of cattle, it's hard to keep track,' Loretta said.

'In those instances,' Morrie went on. 'We're talking way more than one truck-load. There's duffing cases upwards of thousands, an industrial scale.'

I didn't know who I was more angry with at this moment: Ben, Loretta, or Morrie. I directed it at Loretta first.

'Why didn't you tell me about the Ben plan before?'

'Couldn't. Not till he was out.'

'You didn't trust me? Well, thanks a lot, Loretta.' I felt betrayed.

Morrie stepped between us. 'It wasn't personal. The fewer people who knew we were planning to get him out the better.'

I backed off and walked a short distance away. I had refrained from contacting Ben for more information because I had assumed there would be tight security and even tighter surveillance of inmates following Joe's death. Many times I'd thought of contacting Ben, but I just couldn't think of how I could do it without revealing what I already knew. If anyone at the prison was listening in, a member of the syndicate would soon hear of it. Nevertheless, it was galling to think that Ben had known so much. I walked back to stand in front of Ben. 'You could have said something.'

'But I did!' Ben said, exasperated. 'That's why I wrote *duff* on the documents you brought for me to sign. Duff. With three exclamation marks. What more do you want me to do?'

Oh, yes. Ben's scrawl on the papers. *DUFF!!!*

'Right,' I said. 'The exclamation marks could only mean a nation-wide plot to steal millions of dollars' worth of cattle by a syndicate of conspirators including the Victorian justice minister and going all the way to Darwin to Allyson Coleman and the mysterious Paul, who is engaging BlackTack operatives to assassinate anyone who finds out about it.'

'Exactly,' said Ben. 'Except for that Darwin stuff, and Allyson whatshername, and Tack Operations, and some bloke called Paul.'

I took that in. It appeared Ben didn't know the details. 'What did

Joe tell you? Was there someone at the prison he was afraid of?'

'He only told me about the cattle scam. He had a plan to make money for himself out of it. I don't know anything else.'

'You don't?' I closed my eyes. 'Then Joe barely told you anything worthwhile. We're no closer to figuring out who killed him. And I doubt very much that you are on any list.'

'You *are* a target, Ben,' said Loretta softly.

'Oh sweetie, keep it up. You're just amazing.'

'Leave her alone,' Ben said. 'Loretta has only ever been decent to you. If you have to be a sarcastic bitch, throw your barbs at me.'

'Very well then, here's three for starters. First, you've blown your parole chances, and Mum will be furious. Second, if you were a target, Ben, you'd be dead by now. And third, I needed you to stay in jail because I was going to break into Enrique Nunzio's office and get some proof of this duffing business. Now how will I get in there?'

Ben blinked. 'You want to break *in* to Athol Goldwater? And you think *I'm* an idiot.'

'I don't get it,' said Loretta. 'What do you care about the cattle stealing? And what is with that horrible creep with the gold chains and the beer gut? He acts like you're working for him.'

'That's none of your business.'

Morrie let out a sigh. He went to the truck, lifted out the box of vegetables, and carried it inside the house. Ben went to follow him. I pulled him up by the arm.

'What did Joe say to you? Exactly.'

Ben gave me a pleading look. I let go of his arm.

'He told me he had a phone, and was in contact with Foxy Meow who was going to help him figure out how they did the hack with the cattle collars.'

'Who?' asked Loretta.

'Velvet Stone,' I said.

'Yeah, her. She's famous for hacking into prisoner ankle bracelets,' said Ben.

'Is that all of it, every word?'

'Later, he said he used the phone to record a conversation. Smoking gun, he reckons.'

'How did Joe Phelan figure out the specifics of Pugh's conversation? It took me ages to work out what was what on that recording.'

Ben shrugged.

'Who was helping him in the prison?'

He shrugged again. 'Never said.'

Morrie came out and took another box of vegetables from the truck into the house.

'What happened about the recording?'

'Nothing,' Ben said. 'He thought he could get a lighter sentence, or money, I don't know. Stuff. Anyway he died before he could put the plan together.'

The old bloke jumped in the driver's seat and drove the truck into a shed.

'Anyone working at Athol Goldwater called Paul?'

He thought for a while, frowned. 'No.'

'What about a redhead? A ranga work there?'

'No.'

A dead end. No way into Nunzio's office. No lead on the shadowy Paul. And I needed to know by Monday. It was hopeless.

'Wait, the contract manager, he's a ginger. Comes to inspect things occasionally.'

At some point in my searching, I'd come across a listing of the Corrections Victoria executive team, including photos. I was certain I'd seen a man with ginger hair and beard. I whipped out my phone. No network. I couldn't verify it yet, and the memory was vague, but it was better than nothing. If I had Paul, I had leverage, and conceivably it was enough to make a new deal with Percy. It was cause for celebration, though perhaps a little premature to open the champagne.

Morrie came out on the veranda. 'Who'd like a cup of tea?'

That would do for now.

30

MORRIE HAD put an ancient cast-iron kettle on the wood stove. Loretta and Ben were last seen wandering off, holding hands, to some secluded place on the farm. Fifty acres, Morrie told me. Not his, he said, he was a caretaker while the owners were having a rare break.

The house used tank rather than town water, and, judging from the candles and lanterns around the place, no mains power. But the little house was clean and tidy. The bare floors were swept. Filtered sunlight shone through large windows on the kitchen table, antique scrubbed pine with a drawer. Morrie had set out floral tea cups. He took a few smaller pieces of split log from a basket on the floor and threw them into the glowing wood stove. The air carried a pleasant tang of wood smoke. It was the perfect off-the-grid hideout. I was tempted to stay.

'How did you pull off the escape?' I asked.

'Talbot farmers' market. I bought some veggies, a few plants, some jars of pickles.' He gestured to the jars on the table. 'Parked the truck round the corner. Told the guard I had a crook back, and I needed Ben's help to carry them to me car.'

He poured some hot water into a teapot, gave it a swirl, tipped it down the sink.

'Ben got in the back, and I drove off. Easy as you like.'

Once he'd made the tea, he went into the pantry and cut a few slices of boiled fruitcake. The tea was strong, and the cake heaven, sending me into a spiral of nostalgia — Sunday visits, distant relations, country football meets — that was not entirely traumatic.

'Any spare vehicles around here that go?' I asked. 'I need to get back to Woolburn.'

He took a set of keys off a nail in the door frame. 'Drive a manual?'

An hour later, the good people of Woolburn celebrated my return with a tickertape parade. Except there were no cheering crowds, and the ticker tape was thousands of pieces of paper, swirling around in what I chose to believe was a celebratory flurry.

I drove to a quiet street behind the pub and parked the white nineteen sixty-four EH Holden — three on the tree, windscreen visor, driver's door visor, and venetian blinds on the back window. As I walked around to the pub, the wind swept up a pile of the loose papers, and one stuck to my leg. I peeled it off. *Kelton McHugh: a steady hand.* I surveyed the main road of Woolburn. McHugh leaflets as far as the eye could see, gathering in damp muddy piles in the gutters. People drove over them and they stuck to their tyres. A man in an apron was sweeping them away from the front of the post office.

'Good bit of rain,' he said.

I nodded. 'How about that McHugh, eh?' I said, holding up a leaflet. 'Claims to care about the environment, and look at this! What a tosser.'

He seemed shocked and turned his back on me.

I walked to the Woolburn Hotel and found Freya's mother in the cupboard used as the accommodation reception.

'Had a few people enquiring after you,' she said.

'Yes, thank you. If it's alright, I'd like to check out and back in under a fake name.'

She didn't blink. 'No worries, I'll put you in a different room, too.' While she adjusted her books, I asked how Freya was.

'Good,' she said.

I took the key and went up to my room. Lime-green walls, orange carpet, mauve bedspread, a good view of the street. I stretched out on the bedspread with my phone. The hotel's wi-fi was up, and I went to the Corrections Victoria website and stared at the photo of Mark Lacy, the executive with ginger hair. If only Colin Slade was still alive to corroborate my hunch that he was Paul.

News of Ben was scant. A low-risk minimum security prisoner who absconded on a day trip to the market was not going to send alarm bells ringing around the state. I put the phone down and stared at the cobwebs above me. *How do I raise the issue of heroin with Brophy?* A part of me clung to the hope that he was genuinely very ill. If I was wrong, I might offend him. If I was right ...

Someone tapped on the door.

'What?'

'Bloke downstairs reckons someone's hit your car,' said a male voice.

The vintage Holden had been in perfect condition when Morrie Swindon handed me the keys. I cursed my luck, grabbed my bag, and slouched down the stairs. I walked out onto the street, wondering who had seen me driving Morrie Swindon's car. Then I pulled up short. There he was, Shane-fucking-Farquhar, leaning on his Commodore, chewing a nail.

'Hardy, you vindictive cow. Where're you going?'

'Farquhar, you brainless slob. I'm checking on my car.'

'That fucked up Mazda of your brother's?'

I ignored him and walked around to the back of the pub. The EH appeared unharmed. I walked around it, all the panels were still in mint condition. Then the penny dropped: someone had wanted me out of my room. I turned to go, but Farquhar blocked my path.

'Thanks to you,' he whined, 'the deal with Kylie's on hold.'

His flipping deal was the least of my worries. 'Thanks for letting me know.'

'Once again, thanks to you, I've lost out.'

I tried to walk around him, he stepped in front of me. Our eyes locked, we stood facing each other in the deserted street, a Wimmera stand-off. If a tumbleweed had rolled by, I would not have been surprised.

'How'd you find out I was back in Woolburn?' I said.

'Bloke in the post office.'

Never mind Facebook, the real threat to privacy was busy-bodies in country towns.

Farquhar folded his arms. 'You deliberately left the farm paper-work at home, didn't you?'

'The truth is, no. I brought the folder with the papers to the farm, when I opened it, someone had taken …' Loretta! I connected that dot to another, and a picture began to form. 'Shane, really, it wasn't deliberate at all.'

He sniffed, moving wet ick in his nasal passages, and spat it at my feet.

I nearly gagged. 'Well, thanks for the chat, but I've got things to do …'

A crowbar he'd been concealing behind his leg clattered to the ground. He picked it up.

'Nice car, this. Shame if something happen to it.'

'It's not mine.'

'Then you have some explaining to do.' He swung the crowbar and smashed the side mirror off.

I froze.

'My message to you, Hardy, is simple. Go back to Melbourne, get the papers, and bring them the fuck back here. Take them straight to Kylie, like, this weekend. Tell her the proposed land-sharing partner-ship between her and your pal Shane is a top idea. Got it?'

I nodded. 'Got it.'

Shane smirked. I reached into my handbag and took three steps towards him. A glorious cloud of confusion came over him. I held the yellow taser in both hands and fired the cartridge at his crotch. The shriek stuck in his throat as his teeth clenched and his body seized up. I held the charge a little longer. Then the current stopped, and he dropped to the ground. He rolled around, clutching his groin, moaning and groaning like a big sook.

I bent to him, used a low voice. 'My message to you, Shane, is simple. Get fucked.'

I gathered up the wires, dropped the taser in a nearby wheelie-bin, and kept walking. There was so much more to say to him, but I didn't. When I reached the corner, I turned to look back. Farquhar was hunched over on all fours, then he staggered upright. Gingerly, legs wide, he picked up the crowbar. Then he stepped, one foot and the next, and got into his car. Without gunning the engine, or a burnout, or any primal roar of man-car hybrid, he made a timid U-turn, replete with indicator.

I hadn't skipped in a long time, not since I was a child. Yet here I was, weaving through the snowdrifts of McHugh leaflets. It was a rare delight. And there was no wiping the grin off my yap. I couldn't wait to tell Phuong: *And then I tasered his ...*

No, I couldn't tell her any of it. There were legal issues, complications. But maybe one day I'd tell her because, damn, I needed to tell someone.

31

MY PHONE rang as I was letting myself into my room.

Bunny Slipper: 'I haven't been able to get any useful dirt on Allyson-with-a-*y* Coleman. What about you?'

'Not so much about Allyson, but I have more pieces of the picture.' I told her everything I had uncovered. And everything Colin Slade had told me, leaving out the bit about Brash killing him. I also told her all the details Ben had given me, but not where I'd heard them. I couldn't trust Bunny not to go to the police about Ben.

'The contract manager?' she repeated when I got to that part. 'That's quite a wild allegation you're making there. If you can't back it up, there's a little thing called defamation law that comes into play. If he sued, it could ruin the ABC, and the lawyers here would never let me run it anyway. Conservative politicians make management paranoid. Imagine their glee if I falsely accuse a senior public servant.'

'But if that public servant was found guilty?'

'They'd all back away, act shocked, and hang him out to dry.'

'And if I can prove Pugh is involved?'

'They'd also take revenge on me, with smears in right-wing press, and on the organisation, with a massive budget cut.'

She wasn't exaggerating. Our once fearless, impartial public broadcaster had been brought low by cowardly ideologues with red pens.

'So, you'll look into it?'

'I'll take a little peek, yes.'

'Bunny, there's another possible angle to try. There's a cop in

Mount Isa, Detective Sergeant Jason Costa of the rural crimes division, or whatever it's called. He won't talk to me, but maybe he'll talk to you. Put on your pink Akubra.'

'ABC wardrobe,' Bunny said dryly. 'It's not mine.'

'Ask him about stock missing from cattle stations up his way. It might be related.'

I ended the call and stood at the window. A couple of teenage boys were sweeping the leaflets into bags and loading them onto a truck. They had some environmental insignia on their shirts. Environmental volunteers, usually planting trees or cleaning the plastic bags out of rivers. Here they were, diverted to fixing McHugh's disaster.

The 'hooker' music tore me away from the window. Phuong.

'Hey,' I sighed, exhaling the word.

'Your brother's broken out from prison.'

Fuck! 'Ben? As if.'

'It's on all the bulletins. It's not roadblocks yet, but they're looking for him.'

'Good. I hope they find him. Menace to society, that bloke.'

'They think he had help, and that he travelled north in an old truck.'

Fuck! 'Oh, right. Okay, I'll look out for him.'

'You in Woolburn at the moment?' she asked me.

'Yes.'

'Good,' Phuong said. 'I'm nearly there, just drove through Horsham. Mount Arapiles can wait till tomorrow.'

Fuck! 'Great. See you soon.'

The phone pinged, a text floated up. Brophy: *20 mins away.* Heart emoji.

A mute TV was on in the public bar, tuned to the local news channel.

I wanted a drink, a beer perhaps, or a bottle of scotch. But I needed to stay alert, so I negotiated with the barmaid for a special lunch of vegetables, which wasn't on the menu, and ordered a lemon squash. I felt like a condemned woman, and this was my last meal. The tension was almost unbearable. I took my soft drink to a table and watched a couple of labourers play pool.

My phone. Number unknown. I smoothed an eyebrow, straightened my spine, swiped, announced myself.

'Verity Savage. I'm calling regarding an email offering information on a rort involving cattle? Am I speaking to that Stella Hardy?'

I turned my back on the room and hunched. 'Yes. I'm that Stella Hardy,' I whispered.

'Right. What's the story? A conspiracy or something?'

'A conspiracy, yes. One involving Allyson Coleman.'

'Go on.'

If I gave her what I had, even a fraction of what I had, she'd take it and go. I'd never get anything out of her. I decided to act paranoid and make her earn my trust. An experienced journalist knew to cultivate a nervous source. And for me, it wasn't hard to act skittish. People genuinely wanted me dead. 'Not so fast. I don't want to say anything on the phone.'

Pause. 'Are you in Melbourne?'

'I can be in Melbourne tomorrow.'

'Let's meet at the Jar Jar Drinks Café in Camberwell. Do you know it?'

Marcus Pugh's favourite eatery. 'Yes. I do.'

'See you there at four.'

There was a story on the TV about the aftermath of the fire. The woman behind the bar turned up the volume. Sheds, fences, and livestock had been lost, but fortunately no one had died. Someone said, 'Fuck the greenies.' And people nodded. There was a general agreement that the greenies had prevented a sensible program of preventative burn-offs.

The next story showed vision of the usually dry salt lakes in the

Mallee now filled with rain to make an expanse of muddy slush. Police in uniform walked around the lake. A screen had been erected at the water's edge. A police officer took photographs.

'A quiet community has been rocked by the discovery of a body in the Murray-Sunset National Park just off the Mallee Highway, near Underbool.'

Cut to the reporter speaking to a couple of hikers. They were positioned in front of a sign that said *Lake Hardy*.

'We'd just completed the walk around the perimeter when we saw this pair of legs,' said the first hiker.

'Yeah, one leg was in a moon boot,' said the other hiker. 'We had to walk all the way around again before we got network coverage. Then we called the police.'

The reporter turned back to the viewer. 'Police are investigating. Jim?'

Back in the studio, the presenter paused for a moment to be concerned, then he read the next story.

'Kelton McHugh has denied that thousands of his electoral materials were found in the streets of Woolburn.'

Cut to shots of the volunteers sweeping up leaflets. Next, the post office man had a microphone in front of him. 'Kelton McHugh is a terrific local member.'

Back to the studio. Next item: a photo of Ben with the caption *Escapee*. The tradies laughed. The woman behind the bar brought out a plate of mashed potato, gravy, and carrot coins and said, 'That's your Benjamin, isn't it?'

The woman was a friend of my mother. If word got back to Delia, we'd never hear the end of it 'No,' I said, rapidly spooning potato into my mouth.

A prisoner had escaped from a prison farm in central Victoria. Voice over: 'While escaped prisoner Benjamin Hardy is not considered dangerous, the public is advised not to approach him, but to call police.'

'It *is* him,' said one of the tradies, a boy of about twenty. 'It's your fuckhead brother.'

I did not recognise him, but sadly my family were well-known around here, and my face was easily recognised as a Hardy. The woman behind the bar glared at me, and then shook her head. Delia to hear of it in three, two, one …

I lowered the spoon and took my drink to a table near the dart-board, secretly hoping a dart might take me out.

The weather was presented by a young woman with a broad smile. What was she so happy about? Hottest autumn on record?

'Spectacular sunsets,' she said. 'Back to you.'

The three tradies, the woman behind the bar, and I all turned our faces to the TV, waiting to see what would come on next. To my surprise, it was a journalist interviewing both Marcus Pugh and Merri Phelan on the subject of youth incarceration.

'Miss Phelan,' Pugh said in his imperious way. 'You know the prison system as well as me. You know very well that the department has excellent oversight of the private contracts, and that they meet all key performance indicators. You can leave the conspiracy theories to the lunatic fringe.'

The interviewer raised her eyebrows. 'Except for in the case of the death of Joe Phelan.'

Cut to a shot of Merri Phelan. 'I'm not interested in conspiracy theories, Marcus. These are the facts.'

'You don't think BS12 is covering something up?' asked the interviewer.

'If the inquiry finds that negligence was involved in the death of my brother, we'll take legal action. But that does not constitute a conspiracy.'

Pugh was nodding. 'Good. Because the people running our state's prisons are executives in a multi-national company. With contracts around the western world worth hundreds of millions of dollars. You don't get to be the biggest and the best by cutting corners.'

The interviewer turned to Merri. 'Sorry, Marcus, but I don't think that business executives are automatically superior, or in any way constitute the moral champions of our age.'

'Boring,' said one of the tradies as he manoeuvred balls into the triangle on the pool table.

The woman behind the counter pulled a beer, took the change, put it in the till. She then reached for the remote.

'Please don't change it,' I said.

The tradie made a sharp jab of the pool cue onto the white ball, it slammed into the coloured balls, dispersing them across the table. 'Boring.'

She raised the remote and changed the channel.

'Leave it!' I screamed.

'Let her watch it. Seems important to her.'

He was indignant. 'Fucking loopy, the whole family are.'

'Language,' she said.

I put my palms together. 'Please change it back.'

She paused, then raised the remote again.

Merri was talking about a teenager who was assaulted in prison by an adult inmate then placed in a suicide unit because of over-crowding in the juvenile wing of an adult prison.

'Miss Phelan, there is no need for your exaggerated histrionics.'

The young man dropped his pool cue, snatched the remote off the bar, and flicked it over. *Infidelity Island* came on. He danced around the room holding the remote above his head, like the conch.

I finished my lemon squash and went out.

The day was clear and bright. I sat on a bench in front of the pub and closed my eyes for a few seconds. When I opened them, Brophy's van shuddered to a halt on the street in front of me.

32

'THE VAN made it,' I said.

Brophy rubbed his neck and moved his head from side to side. 'Yeah.'

'You alright?'

'Yeah.'

Marigold hugged me around the waist the way Loretta did, with an intensity that was a little desperate, almost fearful.

'How are you?'

'Sick of the van,' she said. 'I hate long drives. My stomach feels bad. But Dad's grumpy, and he won't buy me a Coke.'

She'd dropped her usual American manner of speaking, and the bogus swagger that went with it, and appeared to have passed into a new phase, the miserable teenager.

'I bought you chips,' he said. 'And ice cream.'

'Lucky you,' I said.

She effected a long, slow eye roll with only the whites visible. It was quite disturbing.

'Why aren't you at the farm? Dad told me we were going to a farm. And now we're not.'

'We can go there, if you want. It's not far.'

Brophy groaned. 'We both need a break from driving,' he said. 'Let's go for a walk. Stella, show us the Woolburn sights.'

I didn't want to let on to Brophy that I was in any danger. So I led the way and we walked out in the open, down the main street. I was thinking how tired he looked. And at the top of his shirt, his collar bones jutted through the skin, and a couple of ribs showed. His skin was a shade of ashen.

'Your town is weird,' Marigold said.

Brophy looked at his phone. 'No network.'

'Let's go to the pub,' I said. 'I'll get in touch with Kylie. If she's home, maybe we can visit the farm this afternoon.'

Marigold made a scrunched-up face. Pubs, she knew, were boring places for kids.

'I'll buy you both a Coke,' I said, then instantly remembered that Brophy had forbidden it.

Our eyes met. I cringed with remorse. He turned away. Oh boy, did I regret it. It didn't matter that I'd tried to lift Marigold's mood and make her less difficult, not only for my sake, but also for his. I'd stumbled into an area full of landmines: the real parent doing the hard parenting, and the step-parent, or ring-in, or whatever I was, trying to be helpful and liked, and therefore breaking rules and creating all sorts of unintended confusion and conflict.

He was walking ahead of us, towards the pub. No discussion, just cold fury radiating from him. This was one of those watershed moments in our life together, I felt it in my bones. His first visit to my hometown, meeting my family. It was supposed to be our romantic weekend away, the one I had planned and longed for, for so long. This was it. Yet it was this mess, me floundering, his coldness, my heartbreak, this heavy sense of failure.

I trudged behind him, seeing our recent past clearly for the first time. I'd been preoccupied. Those times we were together, we rarely really talked. He'd visit, but rarely stayed over. We'd watch a screen, then go our separate ways.

I didn't need to ask him if he was using. He probably was. Of course he was. And it didn't matter. Because he didn't care anymore. And he couldn't hide it.

Brophy had reached the veranda and was waiting for Marigold and me to catch up to him before going in. Our eyes met again.

It was over.

We both knew it.

We took turns playing pool against each other. When it was Brophy and I, we played in silence. Marigold climbed up on a bar stool, dangling her legs and calling out helpful instructions. Urging us on to the mystery of those odd angles where balls would connect in just the right spot and shoot into a pocket. That was the theory. The reality was a desultory back and forth in which we both either missed or made half-hearted shots that sent the ball rolling slowly across the soiled green felt only to fall far short.

Between shots, Brophy stood with his legs apart, with the cue resting on the ground between them, holding a point in two hands, close to his chest. He had a frozen, inscrutable expression on his grey face. He made some effort to smile from time to time, but the atmosphere was thick with unease. If I asked him straight out if he was using again, it was possible he would give me an honest answer. Did I want it said out loud? What would be the point of that?

I brooded over these thoughts, playing the worst pool of my life, until Phuong walked into the bar.

She wore skinny jeans and a black t-shirt, and her hair was still salon-perfect. The pixie cut accentuated her long neck and the flawless symmetry of her head. A few locals did double takes. It wasn't often someone so extraordinary entered their out-of-the-way establishment. Long legs, high-definition arm-muscles, angular cheekbones. On me, these structures were hidden under layers of cheese pizza. Against the backdrop of the public bar, with the framed photos of sporting history, postcards, foreign currency, and memorabilia on the wall, the contrast of Phuong's presence raised the glamour levels to dizzying, like a celebrity photo shoot in a derelict location. In years to come, strangers would make pilgrimage to this site, take selfies at the spot where she now stood.

She and Brophy greeted each other with a wary nod.

'Just going to have a quick word. We'll be back in a sec,' I said to Brophy. 'Marigold, you take over from me.'

She jumped down from the stool and gripped the cue with ferocious glee.

Phuong and I went up the stairs to my room. I fumbled the key in my haste.

'Stella —'

'Wait till we get inside,' I said, still fumbling.

Phuong turned the handle and swung the door wide. The bedding had been stripped, the mattress lifted up propped against the wall, pillowcases were off the pillows, and the rug was in a heap in the corner. The drawers of the dresser were open.

'You are a woman of trashy habits, Stella Hardy,' Phuong said.

'Habits, mind, all trashy. Give me a hand to get this mattress back on the bed.'

Phuong did most of the lifting, I helped guide it into place. Then we both sat on it.

'Well, Stella. Are you going to tell me what they were looking for?'

This is it, I thought, *I'm going to tell her everything.*

A knock on the door. She gave me a quizzical frown. I shrugged and opened it.

'Fresh towels?' It was Freya.

'No, thanks.'

She glanced in at the room, paused for a moment, looked puzzled. 'Fresh sheets, then?'

'No, I'll fix this up. Don't you worry about it.'

She turned to go.

'Wait a second, Freya,' I said. 'I'll have my phone back now, if that's okay.'

'Oh, sure. I'll go get it now.'

Phuong raised her eyebrows. 'What phone is that?'

'*The* phone. The one the person who turned over my room was looking for. The one that Marcus Pugh and the rest of them are so paranoid about.'

She moved her head a quarter-turn to the window and was quiet for a moment. 'Stella —'

'I know.'

'This is all very —'

'I know.'

She stared out through the milky window at the blue Wimmera sky. 'I've been thinking,' she said, finally, 'I owe you.'

'What? No, you don't.'

'Shut up and let me say this.' She faced me. 'It's precious to me, our long history, and the many times we stretched the limits of legality together.' She smiled. 'Remember when we broke into that meth lab in Diggers Rest together?'

Of course I remembered. We'd found my young neighbour in there, dead. The trauma still haunted my nightmares. Gore didn't affect Phuong, she was a professional. But she had made many concessions for me, and there'd been many lapses of that professionalism over the years. I understood the sentiment. 'Yes, you wore your breaking-in outfit.'

She laughed. 'That black tracksuit? A breaking-in outfit?'

'My God, yes. Very sleek. Very Diana Rigg in *The Avengers*.'

She blinked. Sometimes my pop-culture references were too obscure even for Phuong. 'I've aided and abetted you,' she said with a smile. 'And Stella, you've done the same for me. Every time I needed you, you were there. Even when you had to go against your better judgement.'

'If you mean the time I helped your ex-boyfriend, then don't mention it. It all worked out for the best.' The best being that they broke up. He was an utter bastard.

'So in that light of loyalty and history ...'

'Phuong, what is it? Are you okay?'

'I ... have ... er ... *lost* the DNA evidence from the Sunshine dope-house crime scene.'

'You lost the hair they found?'

She nodded.

In my frantic life, the living in fear, the panic, and the calculating, I sometimes forgot that there are good things in this world. That a friend was a wonderful force for good. All it took for friendship to work its power was a simple phone call, or a hand on your shoulder, or the destruction of incriminating evidence.

I was lost for words. We embraced. There were tears.

Phuong got up and walked to the window. 'Homicide is investigating a body found in the Murray-Sunset National Park. He'd been tortured before being killed. And the word is that the deceased is a match for Velvet Stone's murderer. You were right about the Navara showing up on CCTV footage.'

She glanced over at me, scrutinising my reaction. I shrugged. It was old news. I knew Brash had murdered Slade. And Slade had admitted to me that he'd killed Velvet Stone.

'They don't have an ID yet, but they're working on it.'

'It's Colin Slade. British national. He worked for BlackTack, a private intelligence agency. He was on assignment for a syndicate — his contact was a client who called himself Paul.'

'Are you serious? There's a private Blu-tack?'

'BlackTack.' I told her about my encounter with Slade: the accident with the mob of kangaroos outside Sea Lake, the fire, and his confession that he'd killed Velvet Stone, but that he didn't know who killed Joe Phelan.

She stared at me with her mouth open. 'Go back to the beginning.'

So I told her about Joe Phelan's death, and my meeting with Pugh and his bogus prison inspection team. I said some things about Mrs Phelan and the awful Brash and his threats, but I left out what he had over me. I told her how I'd found Joe's phone, and that I'd met with Velvet Stone. How Velvet had drugged me, and how Loretta,

238

who was pregnant by Ben and staying with me, had done the phone switcheroo on Colin Slade. The phone, I said, contained a recording of Marcus Pugh, talking about his daughter and losing out on a bull at auction. And then I told her that the bull, Van Go Daddy, had since been stolen. I gave her my theory about the cattle tags and BS12 and Allyson Coleman.

'They claim to be developing their own version of the new GPS-based cattle tracking system called iDrover, but in reality, I think Enrique Nunzio, their agricultural tech expert is working on hacking *into* that system. That is what the syndicate is planning: stealing cattle by hacking.'

'But the logistics of something like that are impossible. How can they pull it off?'

'Another member of the syndicate is this bloke "Paul", who I think is actually Mark Lacy, the contract manager for Corrections Victoria. BS12 provides a diverse range of industrial solutions, including transport services. Lacy signs off on contracts for cattle haulage, all on the Corrections budget. BS12 makes a profit on the haulage, and BS12 company management don't ask questions.'

'Oh, come on,' Phuong said. 'Isn't there *some* oversight? In the government or in the company?'

I told her what Father Baig had said — that BS12 had a history of corruption. And their contracts were lightly managed. There was minimal oversight.

'The cost of mounting this heist,' I said, 'has been paid for by the Victorian taxpayer.'

She considered that last remark for a moment, then frowned. I got the impression she found it credible. 'So, the syndicate is comprised of some rogue BS12 people, plus the minister and a Corrections Victoria loose cannon, and this Allyson Coleman. Do I have that right?'

'I think so, there may be more.'

'So who is Allyson Coleman?'

239

'She's been described as a disastrously unsuccessful nut farmer.'

Phuong looked askance. 'That's not a crime.'

'She's a scam artist who recently bought a couple of properties in the Northern Territory. Plenty of space for stolen cattle to roam around on until they're herded onto ships.'

'And they've all joined forces to steal cattle and export it?'

'If they can get them out of the country quickly enough, they stand to make millions. Like, over fifty million.'

'And why did the syndicate, or whoever, want to kill Joe Phelan?'

I stood up and paced around, telling her what Ben had told me yesterday. All about how Joe Phelan and some unnamed accomplice had found out about the planned hack at Athol Goldwater. And about his cack-handed attempts to blackmail Pugh.

Phuong frowned again in concentration. 'So, Joe Phelan had a recording of Pugh talking about the scheme — not in relation to the larger plot to make millions on the theft of thousands of cattle, but regarding a smaller and, it would seem, quite stupid plot to steal a single bull for his precious little girl because she'd set her heart on it at an auction and missed out?'

'Yes.'

'Pugh. The Victorian minister for justice?'

'Yes. Marcus Pugh is involved in this massive cattle duffing racket. He owns a horse with Allyson Coleman. Presumably he smooths the way for Lacy. It was all going swimmingly, but Pugh's privilege got the better of him, and he had a careless conversation that implied he had a way to obtain a bull that was no longer for sale. It was enough for a prisoner to blackmail him.'

'So they brought in some British contractor to murder anyone who found out about it?'

'Yes, but Colin Slade said he did not kill Joe. I believe him. My problem is, I don't know who did, and Brash is getting impatient.'

'And your brother fears he might be next, and that's why he absconded.'

'No, well, yes. I don't know if he was in any danger, but Loretta convinced him to escape. She and the grandfather have taken Ben to some off-the-grid place. I'm not sure what she's up to. Something is up — she's a schemer. Claimed she'd been sleeping rough, but who knows where she's been and what she's been doing. I think, possibly, she wants to take over the farm.'

'Your family farm?'

'The Hardy family farm. Yes.'

I sat down on the bed. That was it. I'd told her everything.

Phuong frowned. 'I'm sorry, Stella. I can't quite believe it.'

Before I could respond, there was a knock at the door. Phuong stood by the door, ready to do some sort of karate chop, I assumed, and I cautiously opened it. It was Freya returning with her Tardis pencil case. She unzipped it and pulled out Joe Phelan's phone. I thanked her and waited until she left.

'Exhibit A,' I said and played the recording. 'Skye is Skye Redbridge, Pugh's daughter. Al is Allyson Coleman. Vincent is the bull called Van Go Daddy.'

Her eyes narrowed as she listened. I played it a couple more times.

'It's *Pugh*,' she said, incredulously.

'That is what they were looking for in here. He's desperate to prevent it from becoming public. Slade believes they've hired another BlackTack operative to find it.'

'Why not go public?'

'I can't yet. I need to find Joe's killer.'

'My God, Stella. You're not serious.'

'Believe me. I have no choice.'

She shook her head. 'Let me help you.'

She had a mountain to climb, death to defy, gravity to disrespect. I had to work things out with Brophy.

'Yes, please. But not today. Go do your thing, climb the rock, I've got stuff to do here.'

'It's not safe for you here.'

241

'I know. I'm getting out of Woolburn. After that, I'm not sure.' I handed Phuong the phone. 'You take it,' I said to her. 'Keep it safe.'

Phuong put the phone in her back pocket. 'Call me.'

We embraced again. Phuong was a complicated person. Maybe I was, too — probably not as much as her. Over the years we had let each other down, and also supported each other fiercely. Each time, in each case, we understood each other a little better. And it was true that some things were worth so much more than money or status. This mad loyalty was one of them.

33

BACK IN the front bar, I'd started to ring Kylie to arrange a visit to the farm, but Brophy took the phone out of my hand and placed it on the pool table.

'I didn't drive all this way to have cake with your sister. I came to see you.'

It was one of the nicest things he'd ever said to me. Warmth radiated from my chest. Hope survived, love would triumph. We would be okay. I put the phone in my bag and beamed.

'Besides,' he said, 'families are weird. I don't understand the compulsion to meet them.' He had a point, but it was blunt. And only two weeks ago he'd been saying himself he wanted to meet Delia.

'So, what's the plan? I have to get out of Woolburn, so maybe we could drive somewhere, find a nice bed and breakfast, tell Marigold to take a long walk.'

'Can't stay in Woolburn, eh? You're on one of your missions, aren't you?'

'I ... Wow, how did you guess?'

'I can tell. Your energy levels go up, you're focussed. You're happier.'

He knew me well. This person was a sensitive, empathic human being, capable of deep insight. What if, instead of separation, there was a chance for restoration?

There was the problem of Morrie Swindon's Holden. We decided I'd drive it back, with Brophy and Marigold following me in the van. My memory was hazy, but by sheer luck, I found the way to the farm where Morrie and Loretta were hiding Ben.

When we came to the gate and grid, Brophy jumped out and opened the gate.

Morrie was sitting outside the house, with Nigel the Alaskan Malamute lying down beside him. He had a cigarette in his mouth, held a steaming mug in one hand, and was gently pulling on one of Nigel's ears with the other. Near where the dog's head rested on his knee, he had a long dark object balanced across his lap. As the van drew up near the house, he whistled, and the dog jumped down from the veranda. Morrie moved the object, a double-barrelled shotgun, and rested it against the house, and came down the steps to take the keys from me.

'What happened to the mirror?' Ben asked, coming outside with Loretta.

'Shane-fucking-Farquhar. He broke it off with a crowbar. What's left is in the glovebox with a couple of fifties. Should cover the repair costs.'

'Farquhar shoulda paid for it,' Ben said.

'You ask him. I never want to ever speak to him again.'

'But why'd he do it?'

'To intimidate me. He told me to find those papers you signed. He wanted me to tell Kylie that I support the idea of a cattle partnership with him. To sell it to her as a great idea.'

Morrie lit a cigarette with a plastic lighter, blew smoke, amusement shining in his eyes.

'What does that mean?' Ben looked confused. 'Has Kylie changed her mind again?'

Loretta grabbed Ben by the shoulders. 'This changes nothing,' she said to him.

'What's all this?' I asked.

Loretta pointed her finger at me. 'What did you say to him? To Farquhar?'

'I ... I said *no*, of course.'

Ben looked at Loretta. She nodded. 'I have the papers,' Loretta said. 'I took them with me when I left your flat that night.'

'And why would you do that?' I asked, though I was fairly certain why.

She ran inside the house, and left Ben to weather my glare.

He looked at his feet, coughed. 'Because ... because I've changed my mind.'

Loretta returned and held up a wad of papers. She took Morrie's lighter. 'Ben's going to sue Kylie for control of the Hardy family trust. We'll take control of the farm.'

Even Brophy and Marigold laughed.

'Ben's not on a solid legal footing to be suing anyone, being an escaped criminal,' I said.

'We've had advice from a lawyer. We have a very good case.'

'We? Loretta, that's a bit presumptuous, don't you think? You don't have any claim to the farm.'

Ben put his arm around her. 'She's Mrs Hardy now.'

Morrie chuckled and puffed his cigarette.

'Congratulations,' said Marigold.

'It was a beautiful ceremony,' Ben said. 'Morrie did the service, since he's a registered celebrant And Loretta's dress — wow — you should have seen her.'

I had my doubts about Morrie's bona fides. Loretta's, too. 'Well.' It was all I could say.

Loretta flicked the lighter and held the flame under the papers, waving the flaming sheets in the wind. Pieces of smoking paper broke off and drifted away. When it was fully alight, she dropped the flaming mass on the dirt.

Morrie dropped his cigarette at his feet and stepped on it.

34

THE NEXT big town south of Woolburn was Warracknabeal. Brophy drove us there in the van, the three of us squashed in together on the front seat. Random items rolled around in the back. The engine roared, everything rattled, vibrations numbed our arses, and mysterious fumes sedated and nauseated us. Marigold wore headphones and bopped her head and sometimes sang a few off-key words. Brophy squinted at the highway for want of speed-dealer sunglasses. I offered him mine, but he wasn't interested. For my part, I was in the throes of miserable indecision. Was he right for me? Should we continue?

We passed a sign that said: *Caution, soft shoulder*

We passed a sign that said: *Open your eyes*

We passed a sign that said: *Seek alt route*

We had dinner in a crowded pub on the main road, near the creek. People talked and laughed around us, while I studied Brophy for signs of withdrawal — both emotional, and the other kind. All I could say was that he was distracted, and that was a kind of withdrawal. That lapse into hope I had suffered earlier passed. The pendulum swung to despair, and I found myself wondering what items of mine I'd left at his place.

Later, in the motel, the three of us sat on one of the beds and played Uno. When Marigold went to fetch another glass of water, I shifted closer to him and held his hand. He squeezed mine back. I smiled at him; he gave me a sad half-smile.

My phone buzzed, I did a Loretta and took the call in the bathroom.

Bunny: 'That Mount Isa cop, Jason Costa, he agreed to let me do a story on him. In the middle of our face-to-face interview, he gets a call about missing cattle. He goes, *Not another theft*. Says he's been getting calls on a daily basis, a thousand head of cattle vanished from one station, next day, two thousand gone from another station. So far, he reckons he's upwards of forty thousand missing, from all across western Queensland.'

I was stunned. It confirmed all my suspicions, and yet I couldn't quite believe it.

'It's huge, Stella. One old bloke called it the biggest duff of all time. The cops are pulling over every cattle truck on every highway west of Longreach.'

'They might like to inspect the cattle stations owned by Allyson Coleman.' I tried to remember the names. 'Costa will know them. They're huge. There's two near the port at the Gulf of Carpentaria and the third is Fly Hole Station. It's a finishing property — whatever that means — near Mount Isa.'

'I suggested that to him. He's doubtful. The Coleman name is pretty big up here. Need a pretty good reason to go marching up onto her land and demand to check the cattle tags.'

It was extremely frustrating to me that some people were considered above scrutiny.

'I better go,' Bunny said. 'I've sent you my story on Costa.'

I heard the ping as Bunny's video file finished downloading. I clicked on the file, and the video opened on a mob of Brahman cattle. Her voice over the image.

'I'm speaking to a cop whose beat covers almost a quarter of Queensland. From the Gulf of Carpentaria to the South Australian border.'

Cut to a man in a Queensland Police uniform walking into a police station.

'I spoke to Detective Sergeant Jason Costa about his role in the stock squad, dealing with all manner of rural crimes, from trespass on mine sites to the theft of stock.'

Costa: 'The trouble with investigating stock thefts is they're often not reported until months after they happened.'

Cut to Bunny walking alone in a paddock, cattle grazing behind her. Voice over: 'The detective sergeant, with over twenty years in the Queensland Police Service, remembers one incident in 2010 in which five hundred head of cattle were stolen.'

Costa: 'Never found the thief, nor the cattle for that matter.'

I shut the video, turned my phone off, and went to look in on Marigold and Brophy. They were in the middle of another game of Uno. I made a mug of tasteless tea. I took it outside to the landing and thought about all those cattle, snatched even with their ridiculous iDrover collars on. They had to be somewhere.

BS12 managed prison farms all over the country — maybe they were being held on one of those. Amazing how it was going on right under the nose of Ranik at Athol Goldwater. But he was a simpleton, coasting to retirement.

I thought about Marcus Pugh. His prison inspection team was a cover. 'My office is concerned that some off-the-books enterprise has been going on under the radar,' he'd said to me that day in the café. What a liar! It wasn't his office, it was him. And he was being blackmailed. He was using me to find out who was working with Joe. He'd just wanted me to ask Ben. 'Just ask him if he knows of any prison employee taking extravagant holidays, or turning up with a new car.'

And I did ask Ben. God help me, I was in league with Pugh and his corrupt cronies.

Ben hadn't known any guards who were living large, but he'd helped me get Joe's phone. And that was even better for Pugh. I'd set up and delivered. Almost.

It dawned on me then. That phone call Colin Slade had made after Velvet Stone had drugged me, I presumed, was to Pugh. Slade might have killed me that night, but Pugh had wanted to wait.

That was Pugh's mistake. Phuong had the phone now. And the

evidence was mounting. I tipped the dregs of my tea into a dead pot plant and went inside.

The town was shrouded in drizzle in the morning. We ate cold toast in the motel room. After we packed up and checked the room for phone chargers, we filed into the van once more.

Brophy sat behind the wheel. I looked out at the grazing cattle on the green hills. Marigold put her earphones in. Brophy tried calling her name, and when she didn't answer, he looked at me. 'We need to talk,' he said in a whisper. 'When we get back to Melbourne.'

'Right,' I said. 'Good.'

I then spent the next hour and a half wondering what Brophy was planning to say. Maybe he planned to drop me pre-emptively. 'You're dropped.' Did people say that anymore? All this angst was exhausting. My ears were ringing from the endless roar of the motor. When we stopped at a service station for a toilet break, I went into the cubicle and cried my heart out. I couldn't say why, exactly. Everything, everything, everything, everything.

Then it was back in the van. So what if the syndicate had hired another BlackTack operative to wait outside my building, I had bigger fish to fry. I spent the rest of the journey wondering if Brophy and I could work this out. If not, life would go on. Autumn would turn to winter, fog and frost and cold wind. I'd go to work, as usual, and come home in the dark. The pain would subside, winter would turn to spring.

Two hours later, a bit after midday, Brophy pulled up outside my flat. He and I looked at each other.

'Meet me later this arvo?' he said.

'Yes. This arvo would be good.'

He gave me directions to a new café/bar in Footscray. I said I'd let him know when I finished my meeting with Verity Savage.

Marigold took her head phones off and shouted after me. 'Bye, Stella!'

'Bye!' I waved back. That girl would leave a gaping hole in my life, too, if it came to that.

Once they'd left, I made a careful sweep of my street looking for replacement BlackTack operatives. I probably wouldn't know one if I saw one, but it made me feel in control. Once upstairs, I searched my flat and found it operative-free. Being vigilant was exhausting. I had a therapeutic fifteen-minute shower and dressed in preparation for my meeting with Verity Savage.

The reading matter for customers in Jar Jar Drinks was a mix of light-weight and impenetrable. I picked up a magazine and glanced at an article on how the handbags-that-resemble-fruit trend was stupid. Handbags that resembled vegetables, however, were bang on trend. I left the magazines, picked up a copy of *Australian Financial Chronicle*, and took it to a booth at the back of the café.

A woman entered the café in a rush. Early fifties, tall, slim, with grey hair in a ponytail. She wore a tan trench over a print dress, and slung over her shoulder was a large bag the shape and colour of a watermelon. She scanned the room, settled her gaze on me. I waved and she waved back.

'Verity Savage.' She hung her watermelon handbag over the seat and took off her coat.

'Stella Hardy.'

She beckoned the waiter and asked for chai.

'Two,' I said.

'So, Allyson Coleman, what's your interest in her?'

'Call it a hobby,' I said. 'An *obsessive* hobby.'

Verity nodded and gave me a gentle, non-threatening smile. 'Fair enough.'

'You've profiled her various previous business ventures, what's up with this cattle-grazing project?'

'Well, all I can say is, she's done it again,' Verity said, appearing baffled. 'It takes a lot of front to convince new investors, but she's got some Asian backers to buy into her Taurus Beef Trust. From what I've read of the deal, they provide the money, and she holds the titles, despite making no investment herself. The investors get a huge slice of Australia while fooling the Foreign Investment Review Board.'

'Why does she need to fool them?'

'There's limits on foreign ownership of Australian agricultural land.'

I nodded, like I understood. 'Why would these investors do business with her, given her reputation as a scam artist?'

Verity frowned. 'The news of her past doesn't seem to have travelled. She trades on the appearance of wealth and her family name. It sucks them in, but it's all a sham. The Karmann Ghia is a rental.'

'The family name — it implies old money and a solid business?'

'Probably. She sold it to them as a win-win, but the investors are exposed to take the hit, while she's in complete control. The properties are in her name. But that's how she operates: on a grand scale. Coleman says this deal makes her Australia's biggest cattle baroness.'

'She has the cattle station, but where are the cattle?'

'I don't know about the cattle,' she said.

Two glass jars of chai arrived. Verity stirred honey into hers. 'Your email implied you think she has found a potential market,' she said, as we both wrapped our serviettes around the jars in order to grip them.

'If by "market" you mean a conspiracy to steal millions of dollars' worth of Australian cattle for immediate live export, then yes, she has.'

Verity nodded, not convinced, not surprised, not outright derisive. She took a spiral-bound notebook and a pen from the watermelon. She placed them on the table with manicured hands, a silver ring with large stone on the left index finger.

'Do you believe me?' I asked.

'As a journalist, I couldn't say without more evidence. But with my PAWPAC hat on ...'

I brought the jar of steaming hot tea to my lips. 'PAWPAC, the animal rights outfit?'

'Yes. From that point of view, I believe it is possible because it's happened before.'

My jar of chai hovered in mid-air. 'What did you say?'

'That's right. Everyone will tell you — the industry, the various governments — that there are checks, and that accountability is built into all steps along the export chain, but standards are not enforced. We know that the bureaucrats are in cahoots with the exporters. The ships are appalling, and vets are complicit. There's so much profit to be made that everyone lets bad practices slide.'

'What about tags? They say they keep track *from paddock to plate*.'

She gave an audible snort. 'You can game the system quite easily. There was a famous case of a bloke who — this was discovered quite late in the process — had fitted false National Livestock Identification System devices to the cattle, made false declarations on waybills, and transported the cattle for sale. That's deliberate deception, but there's also the sheer incompetence side of things. On one ship, over fifty per cent of the cattle tags were lost. No accountability, no traceability.'

She sipped her chai. I put mine down. This was a stunning disclosure to me, but she seemed so matter-of-fact.

'Some big cattle stations are using extra tags,' I said, 'more like bulky collars. Satellite GPS tracking technology. The collars force the cattle to move in certain directions using audio signals.'

'That's new.' She clicked the pen and started writing in the notebook.

'It's all public information. But I believe that someone inside the BS12 organisation, who is also someone involved with Coleman's group and who is familiar with the technology, has found a way to hack it.'

'Whiz-bang system turns out to be vulnerable to hacking,' she muttered as she wrote. 'Who would have thought? Got a name?'

'No. Well, it might be an employee at the Athol Goldwater prison.'

'Who else? You said it was a conspiracy.'

I paused, not sure how she would react. Laugh in my face and walk out? 'Marcus Pugh.'

She noted the name. 'Go on,' she said without looking up.

'A man in Pugh's department who handles prison contracts, Mark Lacy.'

She looked up. 'A senior public servant?'

'Yes. Where I work, if you accept a bag of lemons, that's corruption, but awarding contracts and ordering services without oversight ...'

She jotted down the name, while issuing a world-weary sigh. 'What's the smoking gun?'

'I have a metric fuck-ton of smoking guns.'

She leaned back in her chair and clicked the pen back into itself. 'Like what?'

'A recording of Pugh talking about getting Allyson to help him "acquire" someone else's bull for his daughter.'

She frowned. 'Can I hear it?'

'Actually, I gave it to someone. But I've heard it. It's legit.'

'Who made it? How did you get it?

'A prisoner at Athol Goldwater had it, he tried to blackmail Pugh. That prisoner later died in a freak nail-gun accident at the prison. BS12 cronies have been trying to get hold of it ever since.'

Two hands undid and redid the ponytail, pulled it tight. 'Good Lord.'

'A cop in Queensland reckons large numbers of cattle are unaccounted for across multiple Queensland cattle stations.'

'You think Coleman plans to stock her properties with stolen cattle?'

'She'll claim they're hers and take them directly to port. Use her Taurus Beef Trust ID on the fake tags.'

'Makes sense, I suppose,' Verity said. 'Once sold to the live trade, it's all profit. She gives the investors a tiny cut, claiming massive overheads, and keeps the rest.' She picked up her jar of chai and drank the rest in one go.

'Seems like a lot of trouble to get the cattle on a ship,' I said. 'Even if the system is easy to game. Why not just slaughter the cattle and sell them as meat?'

She sighed, like she was sick of arguing the obvious. 'Live exports get a much higher price than packaged and frozen meat. The industry is worth over a billion dollars. That's why no government has the guts to shut it down. Public opinion is clearly against it.'

That said, she stared into the distance for a moment.

'What?' I asked.

'Just thinking about what I'll say if I have to front another Senate inquiry.'

She shook herself and gathered her coat and watermelon. 'Metric fuck-ton of smoking guns.' She almost laughed. 'You had me there for a while, Stella Hardy. You're entirely in the dark, aren't you?'

I neither confirmed nor denied. 'What would convince people?'

'Find the cattle, obviously. And also, if you can present the tags and any signs of tampering or changing them. If you can provide the GPS collars. That's a smoking gun. Payments for the stolen cattle, bank accounts, money laundering through off-shore accounts. That's a smoking gun.'

'Find the cattle. No worries.'

She shrugged. 'If they catch Allyson Coleman with a stolen cow in the boot of her Karmann Ghia, let me know.'

'Where is Allyson now?'

'Somewhere in Asia, I think,' Verity said, getting out her wallet. 'I'll get this, shall I? You're probably broke as well.'

I finished my chai. I wasn't short of a quid, but I was kind of broke.

35

I WAS starving hungry as I walked down Barkly Street, Footscray, looking for the place Brophy had chosen for us to meet. It was a café by day and bar by night called, appropriately enough, the Bad Love Club. It served cocktails until late on a Sunday night. When I walked in, Brophy was sipping something in a long glass with lots of ice. When he saw me, he raised the glass without smiling. My heart sank. I ordered a mango daiquiri at the bar and brought it over to join him.

We danced around the topic with small talk for a while. I finished my drink and went to buy another. Brophy said he was content with water.

I returned to find him looking resolute. He took a breath and plunged in. 'It started with some painkillers,' he said.

I tipped some daiquiri down my throat. I had no inclination to hear the details. I wanted no account of the times he'd scored when I'd assumed he was working or painting.

'Okay,' I said. 'You're using again. Sometimes it takes a few attempts to kick an addiction before it sticks.'

'You're not angry?'

Anger was in there, yes. But it wasn't helpful to go into that right now. I gave a noncommittal shrug.

'But you said it was a deal-breaker.'

'It is … and it isn't. I mean. I understand addiction, it's a community worker's fate to see its impact on a family. But this is complicated.' I put my hand across the table, and he grabbed it with both of his. 'Because I love you,' I said.

'I love you, too.'

I swallowed a huge gulp of daiquiri. 'You can kick it again!' I declared.

He nodded and stared into his drink. 'I have to. For Marigold's sake as well as for ours.'

'Yes,' I said. 'Exactly! For lots of people.' I was tired and emotional. Just like always. But the alcohol had hit my empty stomach, and I was getting over-excited.

'There's a monkey on your back, as they say. But what if — hear me out — what if you rip the monkey away?'

He looked up at me, a searching hope in his eyes.

I felt warm and slightly feverish. 'Yes. Tell that monkey to fuck off! Get it off you and get back in control. Instead of the monkey on you, you get on the monkey!'

'What?'

'Get a monkey *saddle* and get on the monkey's back. Get back in charge, and get on the monkey's back ... and conquer this thing.'

He frowned. 'Stella, I don't think that's how this works ...'

'You've done it once. It just takes a couple of goes. Just keep thinking of Marigold.'

'And you?'

'If you manage to kick it, then yes.' I raised my drink. 'To the monkey saddle.'

We clinked glasses and drank.

We went out together and stood on the street, in the middle of a crush of people going about their evening. He put out his arms. I melted into them. We kissed. We were both crying. And all the while, the mad, glorious, no-fucks-to-give life of Footscray went on around us.

When we stepped apart there was genuine hope in my heart. 'Get in touch as soon as you're clean, I'll be waiting for you.'

At home, I did my cursory search of the flat, and then dead-locked and chained the door. I drank litres of water, and took another shower. When I came out, there was a text on my phone from Bunny: *My interview with MP is on now ...* I pulled a green can from its plastic packaging in the fridge and turned on the television.

A picture of Pugh, with his usual smug expression. Bunny's voice over announced we were in for a treat. 'With the Victorian state election later this year, both major parties are well into electioneering mode. Tonight, I sit down with Minister for Justice Marcus Pugh to discuss the state's new law-and-order policies.'

Cut to Bunny in the studio: black, sheer blouse, pink blazer. She sat at a curved desk facing Pugh. 'Victoria's prison system is in crisis. I asked the minister about the use of ankle bracelets for home detention.'

'Minister, are you aware that tracking technology entered the justice system in 1983, when a judge in America read about ankle-bracelet tracking in a Spider-Man comic?'

Marcus had an amused twinkle in his eye. 'You make it sound fun,' he laughed. 'The delinquents in youth detention will all want one.'

'He ordered it be used to keep tabs on prisoners released on probation, but nowadays it's a commonplace method of monitoring prisoners without the expense of incarceration.'

'We are always looking for ways to save taxpayer money, Bunny.'

'But the technology has been compromised. Just last year a hacker who goes by the name of Foxy Meow, or Velvet Stone, demonstrated how it could be misused.'

A tiny flicker of alarm appeared in Pugh's eyes. 'No. The technology is sound.'

'That person, Velvet Stone, was recently murdered. The alleged murderer was a UK national, Colin Slade, who was working for BlackTack, a private intelligence organisation.'

He glanced away, eye contact terminated. 'If you say so.'

'Slade's body was found in the Murray-Sunset National Park this week. Police believe he had been beaten to death.'

A dead bat from Pugh. 'The matter is being investigated by the police.'

'Moving on, Minister, what do you say to accusations that the privately run prisons in this state are mismanaged and that the company that runs them, BS12, is corrupt?'

'Australia is consistently ranked as one of the least corrupt countries in the world.'

'A whistle-blower in the UK said that BS12 operates in a "vacuum of accountability". What do you say to that?'

'The oversight of the BS12 contracts are thorough and meticulous. I can assure you, Bunny, they are very much accountable.'

'There is a pattern of indifference to prisoner welfare on the part of BS12, and they have failed to deliver on prisoner safety time and time again.'

Big sigh. 'I reject that, Bunny, the oversight is intensive.'

'BS12 donates thousands of dollars to your party.'

'They donate to both parties. It's not against the law.'

'Western Australia recently cancelled all contracts with BS12 after a series of avoidable deaths in custody in their prisons.'

'That is a matter for Western Australia.'

'Running a prison for profit, some would argue, is a flawed business model that leads to taxpayer dollars going to profits while not improving conditions in jails and prisons or pursuing alternatives to incarceration.'

'You're overstating the situation, Bunny. The BS12 service is a short-term solution to our current overcrowding, a situation exacerbated by the previous government.'

'So you're promising to address the root causes of incarceration?'

Three gentle raps on my door. I checked the peephole. Phuong smiled and waved. I turned the deadlock and pulled back the chain.

'I can't believe what I'm seeing.' I turned up the volume. 'Sit down and feast your eyes.'

Phuong perched on the edge of the sofa. I pulled another can free and handed it to her.

'Only my government is tough on crime,' Pugh was saying.

'Minister, thank you for your time.'

'He's toast.' Phuong nodded at the screen. 'I checked out the Redbridge farm on the way home from Mount Arapiles tonight.'

I hit the remote. 'You did what?'

'I went to Dougal Park, or whatever Skye and Alistair Redbridge call their farm. Just to have a look. I didn't go on the property.'

'And?'

'Nothing much. I used my camera lens to zoom in, but I couldn't see anything. Didn't really know what to look for. I mean, what does a stolen bull look like?' She laughed.

I sensed she was warming up to something, so I waited.

'Nearest town is a little place called Cavendish, like the banana.'

'The banana?'

'A variety of banana. Never mind. I got talking to the lady in the shop. Her son works at the Dougal Park sometimes.'

'Oh my God, Phuong! Get to the bloody point.'

'He told his mum that Skye Redbridge has a magnificent new bull. Bought it direct from a farm in Queensland, not the usual cattle auction.'

'Bullshit, she did.'

'Exactly. I'll call the local cops tomorrow. But I thought you'd want to hear it first.'

I raised my can; she touched hers to mine. 'Thank you,' I said.

'Steal three hundred grand in cash, there's uproar,' Phuong said. 'Redbridge will get a barrister and a suspended sentence.'

'She'll have to name her accomplices, won't she? Her father and Allyson Coleman.'

'Maybe.' Phuong put the can down. 'I'd better go, I'm exhausted.'

We hugged. I stayed at the door while she went down the stairs. As she rounded the landing, she looked up. Her beautiful face was full of foreboding, and I had a strange feeling of dread, like this was goodbye, as I waved back at her.

36

MONDAY, THE Labour Day holiday. And where was I? In bed, entwined with Brophy? No, I was up early and ready for work. Inspired by Verity Savage, with her smooth pony tail, I'd pinned and sprayed my hair into submission.

I bought coffee from Buffy's, as usual — Lucas never closed. Took the tram to work, as usual, though there was no crush of city workers, no cloud of overpowering cologne and perfume. Just me and a couple of random strangers. They stared at their phones, while I read the actual paper newspaper. What a dinosaur I was.

A text message jangled my phone. Percy Brash: *HURRY UP.*

I replied: *new phone, who dis?*

Brash: *Lol! But seriously. A name thank you. Or your mush and bone.*

I replied: **You're**

I'd give him a bloody name. A lot of names. If it hadn't been for Pugh and the rest of the syndicate, Joe Phelan would still be alive. Why not give him all of them?

Because I couldn't live with myself. Even Pugh, whom I loathed. I couldn't be a party to his murder. I had to find a way to get out of this thing with Brash with my life intact.

At the WORMS offices, I used my key, something I had rarely done before, since I was rarely first to arrive. I had the place to myself, and it felt good; I would get a lot of work done. Being on time, looking professional, these were unfamiliar experiences for me, and I liked the feeling of control it gave me. I might be genuinely productive today. Maybe even work on that presentation for Fatima.

My mobile rang as I was logging on.

Phuong: 'Stella, I'm sorry. I couldn't stop them.'

'Stop what? Slow down.'

'A task force has been formed to trace drug money, starting with the missing motorcycle gang money.'

'But you destroyed the hair.'

'They have multiple samples from the scene. I had no idea. As someone known to have been at the house, it's only a matter of time before they pay you a visit.'

'But a hair, what does that prove? That I was there.'

'That you were in the hidden space under the floor where the money was hidden. It's sufficient to get a warrant, search your flat, look into your banking records.'

A hollow feeling stretched out inside me. Even if the cash wasn't in my flat, my transaction history would lead them to the locker. Fate had finally caught up with me.

'What will you do?' Phuong was saying.

I didn't know. Tears blurred my vision. I reached for a tissue, and then I saw Fatima. I wondered how long she'd been standing there with her arms folded, wearing that frown.

'Talk to you later,' I said to Phuong and dropped the phone back in my uninteresting, conventional black handbag.

Fatima pulled up a spare chair and sat.

'Is anything wrong?' I asked.

'Stella, do you have medical certificates for Thursday and Friday?'

'Um.'

'I'm sorry, Stella. But I have to let you go.'

'Let me go? What does that mean?'

'It means I want you to clear out your desk.'

'But ... but ... what did I do?'

She exhaled, and there was an aura of exhaustion about her. It struck me that, lately, she was in an almost permanent state of deep disappointment. I understood I was not the only one under pressure. My indifferent attitude to work probably hadn't helped. In fact, it was highly possible that I was solely responsible for the dark circles under her eyes.

'In accordance with WORMS dismissal policy, you've had several written warnings.'

Had I? I remember getting one or two. But several? 'What for?'

'For underperformance, for failure to follow directions, for arriving late, for failing to turn up to work and not providing adequate certificates. You treat your role here like a hobby rather than a job.'

That did sound like me.

'I need you to leave, Stella. Pack up your things and go.'

'Oh. Right. I see.'

She got up, went to her office, and shut the door.

In a daze, I opened the drawers at my desk. One USB, one nail file, one Twisties packet with one stale Twistie remaining. Next drawer down, a highlighter and a pen that didn't work. Next drawer down, the purple folder I'd put together ten million years ago. The *Pugh/Prisons* folder. I'd printed the organisational structure of Corrections Victoria, as well as the results of my searches on Pugh, Enrique Nunzio, and Mark Lacy, the read-haired contract manager for Corrections Victoria and the man I believed to be Colin Slade's contact, 'Paul'.

I stuffed it all into my handbag. Then I took my lanyard with its ID pass and my WORMS key and left them on the table in the staff room. I couldn't bear to hand them directly to Fatima, to face her and see the disillusionment in her eyes again.

I took the tram home, went upstairs, sat on my sofa, and stared at the wall.

I'd had a good run. Not an Allyson Coleman run, not boom and bust, not scam and new scam. But a good run. Now, however, it felt like I was finally being called to account for every wrong thing I'd done. And there were some doozies.

What was I going to do? Single and unemployed. I was probably going to jail for stealing the gangster money. And I was out of time with Brash.

This was the time to go to the cops and tell them the whole story. Admit everything. It was better than being killed by Brash or some faceless BlackTack operative.

If I fessed up, I could expect no special treatment. Hardy name did not carry any weight. Not like the name Coleman, which, much to my vexation, counted for a lot, even in Australia, even now. Old money and dynasties of land-grabbing rent-seekers were respected above all by certain quarters in Melbourne and Sydney. School ties and shared holidays on a mate's yacht.

I was a Hardy. No international wheeler-dealers would do major property-purchasing deals with me. No one would lend me a few million dollars to buy a couple of ships. Fucking *ships*.

Ships that leave from a port. A convenient port that she'd drive to in her Karmann Ghia.

I'd bet my bikie loot all those newly stolen cattle were being transported to pre-export holding lots near the port of Darwin right now. Verity Savage's words echoed in my head, *Find the cattle ... provide the GPS collars. That's a smoking gun.*

I sprang to my feet and reached for my phone. I hit Bunny's number, got her voicemail, and left a long message. Minutes later, I was in a taxi, driving to the self-storage facility in West Footscray. While the taxi waited, I removed the bag with the money and handed the key in at the desk. Then I asked the driver to take me back to Ascot Vale via a series of detours. I kept looking through the back window for any suspicious-looking cars, but could see none.

The taxi dropped me in front of a travel agent on Union Road. I paid cash for a one-way direct flight to Darwin, leaving around eight in the evening, arriving in the Top End around midnight, Australian Central Standard Time. Then I walked all the way Puckle Street and started looking in the windows, trying to use the reflection to spot anyone watching me. I saw no one. It would be pretty obvious if someone *was* watching me, I thought, because there weren't many people about and some shops were closed for the public holiday. At a sandwich place, I bought a salad roll. I bought a red-and-white striped wheeled suitcase with copious compartments at a luggage shop and took a cab back to Ascot Vale. I asked the driver to wait, and carried the bag upstairs.

Into the new suitcase's various sections, I arranged shoes and toiletries. All my summer clothes, I threw on the bed. I divided all the cash into small bundles and wrapped each bundle in an item of clothing. Then I spread the clothes throughout the suitcase, filling the various pockets and sections.

The airport was full of Australian Federal Police, armed Border Force Neanderthals, and a gazillion security guards. Surely, I'd be safe there. No one would try anything untoward with that much heat in screaming distance. My plan was to spend the day hiding out in an airport bar until I boarded my flight and left my troubles behind.

I emptied the fridge and the pantry and took everything downstairs to the foyer with a note that said *free food*.

Percy Brash sent a text: *Time's up I'm coming over*

I blocked his number.

Adrenalin kicked in. In a fit of self-preservation, I flung open drawers in a frantic search for my passport. Escape, flight, running away: words to live by. I dropped it in my handbag, pulled the door shut, and carried the red-and-white striped suitcase down three flights of stairs. Rushing onto the street, I looked about me everywhere for the bloody taxi.

The taxi had left.

I stopped dead in my tracks.

In its place was Nell Tuffnell's silver Nissan Navara ST-X. Slouched against it, eating an onion, was Tuffnell herself. A warm midday light washed over her, and she was all angles: cheeks, nose, teeth, even the lapels on her blazer.

I started to walk off down the street, pulling the suitcase behind me.

'Stella Hardy! Where are you off to?'

I kept walking.

'Let me give you a lift.'

I broke into a run, the stupid suitcase rocking and bouncing around behind me.

'Don't be like that.'

There was fifty metres to go to the corner. Once I made it to Union Road, I'd flag a passing taxi, pay cash, leave no trace, and disappear. A man appeared out of nowhere, grey sweatshirt and track pants. He stood in my way, arms akimbo. I stepped to the side, he stepped, too. Then he put out two hands and pushed me hard on the shoulders. I floated upward, saw clear blue sky, and fell on my back.

Get up, I roared at myself. *Go, just go.* I rolled, trying to scramble to my feet, but was meeting some kind of resistance.

His boot was on my chest. Nell Tuffnell pulled up beside us in the Navara. The man grabbed one arm and Tuffnell gripped the other and they wrenched me upright.

'No,' I said. 'I can't go with you. I'm expected somewhere else.'

'Not anymore,' she said. They hauled me into the back seat. The floor was littered with McDonald's litter.

'What about my case?'

'This ugly thing?' The man kicked my fancy new suitcase. 'Leave it for the garbage collector, man,' he said in a Spanish accent. I took a better look at him. Enrique Nunzio. But this time up close.

'Put it in the back,' Tuffnell said. 'We'll dispose of it later.'

He threw it in the rear tray and climbed in beside me. Tuffnell drove, the top of her blonde do visible above the headrest.

'Door on your side's locked, Hardy,' she said. 'In case you were planning to escape.'

Nunzio laughed. He took a handgun out from under his sweatshirt, checked the clip, and snapped it back in place. He raised his eyebrows as he pointed it at my stomach.

'What's an IT hacker doing with a Jericho?' I asked. 'Hacking's not serious, but murder? You're looking at twenty years, then they'll deport you.'

'Shut up.'

Tuffnell turned onto the Western Highway and headed out of the city.

This was it. I was a steer on a cattle truck bound for an abattoir. And I'd made it so easy for them. The police would look at my flat and conclude I'd gone away voluntarily, and not investigate my disappearance as an abduction and murder.

Tuffnell turned off the highway near Bacchus Marsh and followed a narrow back road cut through green pastoral country. Contented cows grazed on gentle slopes. The dams were full. Birds flew in synchronised flocks. The road morphed into an unsealed track, potted with holes and corrugation. The car lurched in and out of craters in the road. I was nauseous and put my head in my hands as I rocked violently around next to Nunzio in the back seat. Objects in the cabin bounced around. Something hit my foot. I opened my fingers slightly and looked down. Colin Slade's Swiss Army pocketknife, the one he'd used to cut me free of Velvet Stone's tape.

I glanced left. Enrique was looking out the window. Slowly, I lowered my right hand and scooped it up. It was thick with functions. Keeping the pocketknife hidden between my right leg and the door, I tried to pull out a blade and managed to open the corkscrew. No good. The car slowed. I looked up. We'd rounded a rise and were coming to a house, concealed from the road by hills on three sides.

I checked Enrique, he seemed bored, still staring out the window to his left. I glanced down, pulled out another slice of metal. Scissors. Quickly, I tried again. Screwdriver. Damn. I knew they could do damage, but I wanted the blade.

Tuffnell turned the car and drove it down a narrow driveway towards the house.

I tried another function. A five-centimetre blade locked into position.

She stopped the car and turned off the engine. 'Everyone out.'

I gripped the knife in my fist, keeping it low. Nunzio opened the door, and then leaned over to grab me. I jabbed the blade into his ribs.

'Hey!' he called out, more surprised than hurt.

He brought the gun up. I dropped the knife and made a grab for it. I knocked it just before it went off, shattering the rear window. Tuffnell was frantically trying to undo her seatbelt.

Nunzio and I both had a hand on the gun, pulling it so it waved wildly around, pointing in all directions. His other hand was pushing at my face. My other hand clawed around the headrest in front of me and caught a hank of Tuffnell's hair.

'Shoot her!' Tuffnell shouted.

I let go of the gun and the hair, twisted and heaved my bodyweight against Nunzio, pushing him off balance. He let go of my face and fumbled the gun. I spotted the knife on the seat next to me. I grabbed it, two hands on the handle, shoved it hard into Nunzio's abdomen, and jerked it sideways. He screamed and clutched his belly. Blood leaked in spurts from between his fingers.

I picked up the Jericho. Tuffnell watched me warily. I pulled back the slide, put both hands around it, straightened my arms, finger on the trigger. It was aimed directly at Shanelle Tuffnell's face. 'You move, you're dead.'

I kept the gun on her face and said to Nunzio, 'Get out.'

He looked ashen and weakly backed out of the car and slumped to his knees, holding his stomach. I slid over and got out behind him. 'Now you,' I said to Tuffnell, keeping the gun aimed at her. 'Out.' She did as I said. 'Call an ambulance.'

She baulked. 'No way.'

I lifted the pistol and fired into the air, then levelled it at her again and pulled back the slide. She took her phone out of her back pocket and hit the screen. A man had been stabbed. Urgent medical attention required. She gave the address.

'Throw the phone on the ground.'

She dropped it near Nunzio, who was whimpering as he applied pressure with both hands on his bleeding wound. Keeping the gun aimed at Tuffnell's head, I got into the front passenger seat.

'Get in now and drive.'

She glanced at Nunzio, then got back into the car.

'Where to?'

'Turn the car around.'

She did a laborious three-point turn and headed out. Soon, we came to the highway.

'Right,' I said.

'Back to the city?'

'The airport.'

As we turned on to the highway, an ambulance passed us at a roaring clip, sirens screaming, lights flashing.

Tuffnell drove on, heading back towards the city. She kept glancing across at me and the gun, and seemed to be calculating her chances of disarming me while driving at a hundred kilometres an hour on the Western Highway. Evidently she gave up on that idea and tried making conversation instead.

'I didn't think you had it in you, Hardy. Your brother's such a fuck-up. But you're not like him, are you?'

I said nothing, though I was secretly rather pleased.

'Slick move with the knife. Where'd you learn that?'

'Girl Guides,' I said.

My childhood growing up on a sheep farm was none of her business. And I wasn't about to tell her that Colin Slade, one of their hired goons, had shown me how to use the handgun.

After that, Tuffnell drove in silence. My arms were beginning to ache, but I kept the Jericho pointed at her. Mainly, I was trying to figure out what her role was, and where she fitted into the syndicate. I was struggling to believe that someone like Pugh saw her as an equal. Slade had used her car, so she was a party to the scheme somehow. Was Tuffnell really one of them, with her tacky nails and chicken nuggets?

'That rubbish in the back from your takeaway meals or was it Colin Slade?'

She scowled. 'Slade's. I haven't had a chance to clean it out. Man was a pig.'

'Why lend him your car?'

She pursed her lips. 'No choice. They said he just needed it to get from A to B, get around in the city. Then the bloke used it when he killed Velvet Stone. They didn't care.'

'Who didn't care?'

'Lacy and them. They throw people like me under the bus. Cop rang me about it. Lucky I wasn't charged.'

'Why are you still working for them?' I asked. 'I presume you and Nunzio picked me up on their orders.'

'Yeah,' she said. 'They pay me for odd jobs.' She shrugged. 'Girl's gotta pay the bills. Pugh and Lacy were getting more.'

I heard the bitterness in her voice. 'You worked for them sometimes. So you knew what they were doing?'

'Some of it.'

'But not all. So you told Joe Phelan, for some reason. Why? What was *he* to you? ... Oh my God ... were you lovers?'

She laughed. 'Gawd no. We fucked a few times in AGP Shed 6. That's not lovers.'

'You and Joe were curious about what Nunzio was working on. You knew it had to do with hacking. So you got Velvet Stone to meet with Joe at the market and figure out the hack.'

'*Curious*. That's a cute word.'

'Well, you wanted to blackmail the syndicate.'

'Of course we did. You have any idea how much money they stand to make?'

I knew. 'You must be some kind of cold if you shot a nail into Joe Phelan's skull.'

She sniffed, a little bit pleased with herself.

'But why kill Joe?'

'He was a fool. I was the one who made the Pugh recording on his fucking phone. The idiot didn't understand a word of it. All he knew was that Marcus Pugh would pay us. He didn't know who Al Coleman was, or Pugh's daughter. It was me who knew Pugh was making visits to Nunzio. Then Pugh asks me for an empty office to make a private phone call. I was in the next cubicle recording it. Of course, I had to have an intermediary to make the demands.'

'Of course, so you involved Joe.'

'And he got greedy and careless. He gave me no choice.'

Tuffnell kept her eyes on the road. I watched her, but said no more. She had no idea that a massive creep, a ruthless, murdering member of a criminal gang, would gladly send her out the way she had sent out Joe. Percy Brash would execute Nell Tuffnell without a second thought, if I told him what she'd just told me.

But I wasn't going to tell him.

We drove the rest of the way to the airport in silence.

37

I WAS onto my second bowl of chips and my fourth gin and tonic in a bar at Melbourne Airport, my feet up on the red-and-white striped suitcase, watching planes take off and land as the day's last gleams of sunlight disappeared over the runway. A wall-mounted screen flashed departure information, boarding calls, and arrivals. It was next to a mute wall-mounted television, tuned to back-to-back reruns of *Infidelity Island*. At last, after half a day of loitering around, my flight's status flicked over on the screen to *now boarding*.

When we'd reached the airport, I'd told Tuffnell to go into the carpark near Terminal Four. I ordered her to hand me her jacket, since I was covered in Nunzio's blood. I'd stepped out of the car, and she'd sped off. The last I saw of her was the red Navara tail-lights as she changed lanes to exit the airport. I'd zipped up the jacket and dropped the Jericho in a rubbish bin. Then I'd entered the main terminal for domestic departures and wheeled the suitcase to the ladies bathroom. In a cubicle, I'd dumped my old clothes behind the loo and emerged in a clean tropical-print dress, in preparation for Darwin's heat. I'd scrubbed my hands and face in the sink, and then headed for the nearest bar.

At every step, I'd expected to be stopped, but I had not been. Even as I now stowed the suitcase in the overhead locker, I feared a tap on the shoulder. It followed that Pugh would not come after me in an official capacity since he didn't want any negative publicity, and I would certainly be negative, I would openly, widely, and freely go public. But he may have sent an unofficial somebody. Would Tuffnell

271

report back on the failed mission — that she and Nunzio hadn't managed to kill me? And would she provide them with my current whereabouts? I doubted it. I hadn't felt the need to point out to her that if she told Pugh and co about me, I'd tell Pugh and co about her.

Cabin crew closed the doors. The engine roar intensified, and the jet hurtled down the runway and launched itself improbably into thin air.

Alright. So far so good.

I put on my standard-issue headphones and played with the screen in front of me. Sitcoms or a full movie, it was hard to decide. Darwin was a five-hour flight, or a five-episode binge of something. I flipped through the options, but was too agitated to make a decision. In the end, I selected a touristy bit of guff about the Top End. Crocodiles, Kakadu, waterfalls. It sounded quite good. When that ended, I hit a packaged news service, only a couple of hours old. It began with a shot of Enrique Nunzio in a wheelchair outside a hospital giving a sheepish thumbs up to the camera. A young journalist holding a microphone under her chin told viewers that the opposition had called for a Royal Commission into Victoria's prison system, following a series of incidents at Athol Goldwater Prison. She read out a list of security breaches, including the death of Joe Phelan, cost blowouts, an injured worker (Nunzio), a missing guard (Tuffnell), and an escaped prisoner (Ben).

Mrs Phelan appeared on screen with the title *Dead Prisoner's Mother*. She sprayed the journalist with sharp invective about the jacks, the government, the mismanagement, and the lies. Much of it had to be bleeped to comply with television standards. She was flanked by Merri, who said she supported the call for a Royal Commission and hoped she'd have the opportunity to give testimony. I noted her relish at the thought.

'The escaped prisoner, Benjamin Hardy, alerted a local Wimmera television station that he intended to walk into Horsham Police Station this afternoon with his lawyer,' the journalist said. There was Ben, flanked by Morrie, very pregnant Loretta, and a woman

272

in a dark pants suit. Back to the journalist, reading out Ben's written statement, in which he said his life was in danger at the prison. He had information.

I looked at Loretta's face, flushed with triumphal glee. Casting Ben as an innocent victim, helping authorities, and appearing to uncover the syndicate's corruption was a brilliant tactic. And it was all Loretta's doing — with help from Morrie. Soon, she'd orchestrate her successful takeover of the Hardy farm. Ben's claim on the farm would probably end in the courts, and Kylie would lose.

Loretta must have been planning this move for months. Probably as soon as Ben told her about the farm. The fake street urchin act had had me completely fooled. Sure, she and Morrie probably *had* moved around a lot, working on farms around the country. But she was no semi-illiterate itinerate lackey. *Au contraire.*

I switched off the screen. Ben's gambit may well come off. I hoped it did. I loved my family — of course I did. I might complain constantly, but it was everyone's prerogative to complain about family, while having feelings of deepest loyalty. If anyone said a word about the Hardys, I'd be the first to defend them. But as for the coming wrangle for control of the farm, on account of Loretta, I did not want to pick a side, I didn't want to know about it. There was a baby coming — that was way more interesting.

I ordered another gin and tonic and flicked through the inflight magazine. There was a special feature with pictures of crossbody handbags in the latest designs: persimmon, dragon fruit, pink lady. 'Oh dear,' I said out loud, 'it's just so last year.'

At two a.m. that same night, I was an hour south of Darwin, standing at the entrance to the Depot for Export Animals in Transit and Holding. It sat in the middle of an expanse of swampy lowlands, the only structure in the vicinity, a long way off the main road. As visitors drove through the entrance gates, I could see rows of hi-vis vests on hooks. To one side, a parking area, to the other, a broad turning area for trucks towing multiple trailers.

The complex itself, though large, was basically a couple of covered sheds, lit with rows of florescent lights, and a series of open yards with multiple water tanks and troughs for feed and water. Every yard was fully stocked with cattle. Their soft moos and snuffles were the only complaints at being herded into such a confined space. A slightly swampy smell — the Adelaide River was nearby — mingled with the dank odour of manure and feed. It was still a few months until the dry season and the warmth and humidity in the air was intense.

When a couple of workers arrived in a rusty Nissan Patrol, I slipped into the shadows. Before that, I'd been waiting there for about fifteen minutes, plenty of time to read the sign at the entrance.

DEATH is a proud subsidiary of BS12.
We help our clients to achieve their objectives. Years of local and international experience mean we design, fund, construct, operate, and maintain major projects and manage infrastructure assets across diverse industries such as:
Transport | Roads | Telecommunication | Water | Power | Defence | Local Government | Maritime | Justice | Oil and Gas | Mining
Providing services as diverse as:
Correctional Management | Waste Management | Corporate Real Estate | Public Private Partnerships | Logistics

What a diverse range of services BS12 offered. The Australian government used BS12 for off-shore detention services in a blatant bid to ruin the lives of asylum seekers. They didn't mention *that* on the sign. Most Australians seemed to be comfortable with off-shore detention. It seemed to fit with our past, our need to see harsh punishments dished out. I found it perverse, and I struggled to comprehend it.

As for BS12, if they were operating prisons *and* transport *and* maritime services, it would allow an insider to control every stage of the cattle theft. As the Queensland cop Jason Costa had said to Bunny, there was often a time lag before station owners realised any cattle were missing. It was possible that the syndicate had more time than we knew in which to transport the stolen cattle, and that nothing was here.

I was deep in these thoughts when I heard someone say 'Pssst.'

I clutched at my chest.

A radiant tropical moon emerged from behind a cloud, illuminating Bunny Slipper's face.

'You scared the shit out of me!'

She didn't explain, she didn't say anything. Instead, she just stared at me.

'What's happened?'

'Jason Costa is dead.'

He'd gone out on patrol. When he didn't return, or make contact again, a constable on patrol was diverted to look for him. He was found by the side of the road near his squad car. Cause of death was a single bullet to the back of the head.

There was nothing to say; it was horrific. Their fifty-million-dollar swindle was worth more than any life. It was risk, a cost, but that was part of their business model. Not a far cry from the cost associated with desecrating rivers, poisoning the air, or crushing workers with insufferable working conditions. All acceptable losses against staggering profit.

'How long have you been here?' I asked

'Came straight here as soon as I got your message. I've had a look inside,' Bunny said.

'What? How?'

'I don't think the people running this facility have any idea where these cattle have come from. I asked for an on-camera interview with the DEATH manager late this afternoon, and they were all for it.'

'Free publicity.'

'Exactly. So this place is currently holding four thousand head.

275

Which is the capacity of most G-class vessels.'

'What capacity are Coleman's ships?'

'Funny you should ask,' Bunny said. 'While I was recording, guess who showed up?'

'Allyson Coleman.'

Bunny nodded.

'What's she like?'

'She breezed into the manager's office without knocking, like she had the run of the place. She introduced herself and insisted I restart the interview. The manager didn't offer much resistance, so I did. After that, it was all her. The manager barely got a word in. She kept saying "we", which I thought was interesting. "We have an arrangement with DEATH" and "we are working together to create jobs" and "we are bringing wealth into the country". It was a lot of rot, like listening to someone reading out one of the DEATH brochures.'

'Did she mention her ships?'

'Not specifically, she kept it vague. But when she finally left — some story about having another meeting to go to — I got to ask the manager about this lot. He told me they're due to go out tonight. He said they've had their busiest period in years. After the good times, the drought is beginning to bite, and some graziers want the income now.'

'How do the cattle get from here to the port?'

'Trucks. They're constantly getting on and off trucks. Every step of the way, they're supposed to be inspected, to make sure they meet the Australian guidelines at every stage.'

'Are they enforced, the guidelines?'

She gave me a look as if I'd asked about an honest politician, or the existence of the bunyip. 'There's other depots like this one — pre-export quarantine with ready access to the port. They have an arrangement with a veterinary service. Vets go in, give the cattle the all-clear, send them out.'

'Tick and flick.'

'Flick and out. They're in most South-East Asian destinations within six days.'

'Are we too late?'

We looked through the fence at the restless mob. Creamy Brahman with loose neck skin, humps and tags in their floppy ears. A steer put his head up above the herd and bellowed.

We followed the razor-wire-topped fence along its river-side boundary. Half way down, I saw another company sign, lit from above with a spotlight.

DEATH is committed to animal welfare.

We went on our way, checking the compound for side entrances. Contemplating the river, I realised the fence was not to keep out thieves, but to keep the cattle safe from a saltwater crocodile dashing out of the water. They'd been known to latch on to even quite large animals and drag them to the river. Bunny must have had the same idea, because we both suddenly turned and rushed back to the entrance. Headlights flared down the road, followed by the sound of gears changing and a large truck's guttural deceleration. It stopped at the gate: three trailers, and the words ROAD TRAIN on the front. A man in hi-vis jumped down from the cabin. Another man came out of the compound and spoke to him.

Bunny and I ran to the back of the rear trailer and when they opened the gates, we snuck through on the dark side of the truck. She pointed to the row of hi-vis vests hanging on outdoor hooks and we hustled them on. Now we looked like we belonged. We could be vets, or government inspectors, or concerned cattle-owners, making sure our investment was being well-treated.

'Walk slow,' Bunny said.

I tried. At one point, we stopped to lean on a yard fence, each with a foot on the lower rail. Someone muttered *g'day* as they passed by. We nodded.

A forklift, revolving safety lights on top of it, barrelled down a nearby pathway with a packing crate on the forks. Bunny and I locked eyes, then moved.

We followed it to an open area at the rear boundary of the facility that was both a parking area, with a couple of company-branded vehicles and an old flat-bed truck, and a dumping ground for the depot's junk. Piles of broken crates, old boxes, and big black plastic bags of rubbish were stacked, ready for collection. The forklift stopped, and a youth jumped out. He walked around the crates, throwing black plastic bags onto the back of the flat-bed truck. Then he started taking bags out of the crate on his forklift and flinging those up there, too.

Bunny moved towards him, hands in her back pockets. Easygoing. 'What're you doing?'

'Garbage pick-up's late. Boss reckons I have to take all this to the tip myself.'

She walked around the piles of crates. 'What about this other rubbish?'

'That can wait. This lot has to go tonight.'

Bunny held up her wallet, showed her union card. 'I'm going to get you to stand over there while I have a look.'

The youth hesitated, frowning. 'Can't wait too long.'

'That's alright,' I said, stepping forward. 'We're just going to have a quick look.'

Bunny had already pulled a garbage bag off the truck and ripped it open. Cattle tags cascaded onto the dirt.

She was on the phone to Darwin Police while I opened another bag. Pieces of iDrover GPS collars, with the small solar panels and aerials still intact. They hadn't been unlocked; they'd been cut through with some kind of power tool. Smoking guns.

It was all very well to hack the system and use it to direct the cattle towards your waiting get-away truck, but what do you do once the cattle are yours? You need to get those old incriminating collars and tags off, before you can say *silly duffer*.

38

IN A harbour-side Darwin pub, I bought a few drinks and made a few friends. I bonded with locals buzzing with gossip about how Allyson Coleman had been dragged out of her Karmann Ghia and arrested. And I learned who to approach. I paid cash for a berth on a thirty-metre yacht, heading for South America. The rest of the money is now clean. I spent a long afternoon offering a twenty to various backpackers, who changed unremarkable amounts of Australian currency into US dollars at different locations around Darwin.

On deck, as a breath of warm air moved across my skin and the port of Darwin disappeared into the distance, I felt like Scrooge on Christmas morning, giddy and overjoyed. In a few weeks, a mere jaunt across the Pacific with some stops at tropical islands along the way, I'll be in Concepción. I could stay there, or I could make my way to Buenos Aires. Acting on a whim is bang on trend. Fear is so last week. Everything is in flux. This crazy freedom is the fulfilment of a dream. In most versions of the escape fantasy, Brophy has been by my side. I have no doubt that, at some point in the future, once he gets clean, he will be.

Countries without an extradition treaty with Australia have become a new interest of mine. I like to picture Victoria Police sending Phuong to, say, Rio de Janeiro, to find me, and the two of us drinking mojitos at a beachfront bar. If that's too fantasy-land, I'll tell her about the rock climbing to be had in South America. The reality is, my best friend will probably only manage to swing over once a year, and that won't be so bad.

My pocket vibrates. I swipe and put the phone to my ear.

Kylie launches into a rambling tirade. 'Stella, what the hell is happening? The fucking farm is being pulled out from under me. I *knew* this would happen! It's your fault. If you'd done things right in the first place, I wouldn't be in this predicament.'

She draws breath, and I'm about to respond, but she keeps going.

'You need to get in touch with Ben. You need to tell that idiot to stop the lawsuit. We can't afford to fight it. Tyler's talking about going back to shearing. I won't hear of it.'

My hand moves almost of its own volition, taking the squawking voice magically away from my ear. I hold the phone over the water, relishing the exact moment I release my grip, and, a second later, savouring the satisfying plop as it falls into the sea.

My ears prick up as I hear a familiar name on the little staticky transistor radio propped against a deck chair. 'And, in breaking news, beleaguered Victorian Justice Minister Marcus Pugh has announced he will not contest the upcoming election. In a short statement, the minister strenuously denied involvement in corruption of any kind and said recent accusations were a pack of disgraceful lies. He looks forward to spending more time with his family.'

I walk to the bow of the yacht and stand by the railing to watch the sun set over the sea. I did not deliver Tuffnell to Percy Brash, and I am pleased. I let her go, and I am sorry. But Tuffnell, wherever she is, will get caught, sooner or later. And that will be some consolation for Mrs Phelan and Merri. And for Joe. My feelings are decidedly mixed. If there is to be a Royal Commission into the goings-on at Athol Goldwater, everything will come out. And the truth is a kind of justice.

But none of that is up to me. The over-accommodating Stella Hardy no longer exists. I'm finished with all that.

ACKNOWLEDGEMENTS

FIRSTLY, A huge shout-out to Linda Smith, for her work on early sections of the manuscript. Also, a big grateful hug to my sister Maryanne Sweeney for her invaluable help with the final draft. Thank you also to Catherine Quin of Red Cliffs library for her assistance with research. I'm grateful to Tania Chandler, SJ Finn, and Kate Richards for their fantastic advice. And my thanks, as ever, go to Henry Rosenbloom and everyone at Scribe, especially Lesley Halm for her considered comments, my gimlet-eyed editor, Anna Thwaites, who was a pleasure to work with.

My deep, deep gratitude to Clinton Green, for his love and support.